Thicker Than Blood

Holly Ash

For my sister, Kelly, who as a teenager promised to read my story when it was published and followed through fifteen years later when Crystal and Flint came out. You are the most amazing mom, teacher, sister, and friend. I am in awe of you.

Chapter 1

The engine room buzzed with activity. Crystal had pulled every available engineer on her team to conduct a thorough inspection of all the machinery. There were only three days left in *Journey's* first tour. After that, the ship would be going into to dry dock for six weeks to make repairs and upgrades before the next tour. Since Crystal wasn't going to be overseeing the dry dock herself, she wanted to make sure she provided them with a complete list of all the work that needed to be done. It wasn't that she didn't trust the repair team— they just didn't know the ship the way she did.

Chief Wong walked over to Crystal, wiping his hands on a cloth. "There's some minor wear on the turbines, but that's to be expected; otherwise everything appears to be in great condition."

"Fantastic." Crystal tapped the tablet in her hand to make note of the wear. "I think we can let the turbines go for another tour, but I'm going to increase the inspection schedule for them."

"You're the boss."

"Lieutenant Commander Wolf, please report to the Ward Room."

Crystal looked up at the intercom as if it had personally insulted her. She didn't have time for this. The ship was slowly making its way back to Kincaron through LAWON waters. They shouldn't have run into anything that would warrant an unscheduled meeting. "It looks like you're the boss, Wong." Crystal handed him the tablet. "Check in with Stiner once your team is done in here."

"Yes ma'am." Wong took the tablet and walked away.

Crystal made her way through the ship. There was a restlessness in the air that only came with the end of tour. Everyone was ready to get home and enjoy a little rest and relaxation before the next tour started. Most of the crew had already signed on for the next sailing, including the entire command staff. Well, everyone except Flint. Crystal had tried to get an answer out of her, but Flint avoided the topic every time it was brought up. Despite their rocky beginning, Crystal really hoped she would decide to stay. *Journey* wouldn't be the same without her.

Crystal pushed open the door to the Ward Room to find Grady, Tyler, Justin, and Flint already there. They looked as confused as she felt. That wasn't a good sign.

"What took you so long?" Flint straightened up in her chair. "They must have called you at least three times on your communicator before broadcasting the request over the ship-wide intercom."

"I was down in the engine room," Crystal reminded her. "You can't hear anything down there." Crystal took a seat next to Justin, who gently squeezed her knee under the table. Something that would have sent a shiver through her six months ago. They had come a long way since then. They both had a few hours of down time later that evening, and she was looking forward to spending it with him. They had been sharing every free moment they had over the last week. The end of the tour would also mean six weeks without Justin, who was headed back to Earth to visit his family. "I'm still waiting on those software upgrades for the battery control room, by the way," Crystal said, turning to Tyler.

"I uploaded them ten minutes ago and sent the repair team the installation instructions," Tyler responded with a grin. "Once we're in dry dock all you'll have to do is hit start."

"Actually, I won't be there for the dry dock." Crystal avoided his eye. She hadn't told anyone her plans for leave. She wasn't sure why. Part of her felt guilty about taking the time off.

"Why not?" Grady leaned forward; the concern apparent in his voice. He knew she had only taken a handful of days off in her five years of service. She could only imagine where his mind went. This wasn't like their counter-terrorism days when the only time she took a break was when she was recovering from a gunshot wound.

"I'm just spending the leave at Homestead Colony," she assured him. "The family that's been renting my grandparents' house moved out, and I need to figure out what I want to do with it."

"Are you thinking of selling it?" Tyler asked. Crystal wondered if he had some kind of emotional connection to the place, she wasn't aware of. That was where they had first met and learned they had the same father. Maybe she should offer it to him.

"Maybe." Crystal shrugged. "It's not like I'm ever there."

"When was the last time you were there?" Justin asked.

"It was shortly after my grandfather died, so maybe eight years ago." She decided it was best to leave out that Ryan had been there with her to help her pack up her grandparents' belongings.

Crystal turned at the sound of the door opening. Captain Reed walked in, his silver hair shining in the bright lights of the room. Crystal tried to read his face, but it was expressionless. Never a good sign. "Thank you all for coming. I know you're looking forward to some much-deserved leave, but I'm afraid LAWON has one more mission for you." Reed hit a button on the control panel built into the table, and Admiral Craft's face filled the screen at the front of the room.

Crystal looked at the screen. This mission had to be something pretty serious for the orders to come directly from Craft. "As I'm sure you are aware," Craft began, without preamble, "we are nearing the end of the trial period of the officer exchange program with the U.S. military."

Crystal felt Justin tense next to her. Even though he had already signed on for the next tour, they both knew there was the possibility that he would be recalled to Earth. A fact they both had been avoiding talking about. She placed her hand on his and gently rubbed it until she felt him starting to relax.

"LAWON would very much like to see the program extended," Craft went on. "However, the U.S. military isn't convinced that the program should be continued. They are holding a hearing to determine if the exchange program should be extended." Craft shifted in his seat.

"What exactly does this have to do with us, Sir?" Flint asked. Crystal noticed her foot tapping under the table. It wasn't like Flint to let her nerves get the better of her.

"We would like the five of you to go to Earth and represent LAWON at the hearings."

If Crystal had had the rest of her life to guess what the mission was, she never would have guessed that Craft was sending them to Earth. She looked around the table at her teammates. Grady and Tyler looked as shocked as she felt, but the looks Flint and Justin were exchanging were different. They were laced with concern. Earth was their home planet; if they were worried, Crystal knew there must be a good reason for it.

Crystal turned back toward the monitor. "With all due respect, why send us?" As far as she knew there were at least two dozen U.S. military officers currently serving on Neophia as part of the exchange program. There had to be a more qualified team to speak at the hearing. None of them were diplomats or politicians. In fact, Crystal was known for her ability to avoid talking to politicians whenever possible.

"This team has accomplished great things over the past six months, and a large part of that is due to having Flint and Anderson as members of our crew." Reed nodded to each of them as he spoke. "LAWON recognizes that. We feel that the five of you are in the best position to show the U.S. military the benefits of the program and convince them to extend it."

Crystal should have been taking notes. Reed was choosing his words very carefully. What was he not telling them? She looked back at Craft to see his eyes linger on Flint. What Reed said about them being the most accomplished team in the program might have been true, but Crystal suspected the real reason they had been chosen was because of Flint and her strong reputation within the U.S. military.

"Do we have any idea which way the U.S. military is leaning?" Tyler asked, looking back and forth between Reed and Craft.

"I can tell you that." Flint leaned back in her chair and folded her arms across her chest. "They see it as a drain on their resources that doesn't add any value to them." She shook her head in disgust.

"Which is why we need you to change their minds." Craft glanced down at his watch. "Your space shuttle leaves first thing in the morning from the launch pad at LAWON Headquarters. We've arranged for you to stay at the LAWON embassy. You'll have a day on Earth to prepare before the hearings start."

"Yes sir," they said in unison, though Crystal noticed that it lacked the normal conviction she felt from her team before a mission. Craft nodded and closed the connection.

Reed sighed and sat down at the table. "This mission will take you through the end of the tour. Wolf, Price, and Grady, you'll receive your leave orders once you return to Neophia. Flint and Anderson, once the hearing is over, you will be able to remain on Earth for your leave. Anderson—and Flint if you decide to join us for a second tour—you'll receive your return orders at the end of the leave." They all nodded. "A launch is being prepared to take you to the mainland in two hours. I suggest you all go pack."

They stood up and slowly started to make their way out of the room. Crystal noticed that Grady hung back to talk to Reed. "Sir, I'm sure you're aware that I have another commitment after *Journey's* tour."

"Don't worry Lieutenant, you'll be back in time."

Reed stood up and put his hand on Grady's shoulder, leading him to the door where Crystal lingered. Reed smiled at her and then took off down the hall.

Grady tried to follow him, but Crystal reached out and grabbed his shirt. "Not so fast." Grady turned to look at her with a guilty look at his face. "What kind of commitment do you have?"

"I'm not supposed to talk about it," Grady mumbled.

"You took a special ops mission, didn't you?" She put her hands on her hips.

"Maybe."

"I swear if you miss the next tour, I'm going to hunt you down and drag you back here myself."

Grady draped his arm around her shoulder and started to lead her down the hall toward their quarters. "Relax, it's only supposed to be a two-week mission. A quick in and out."

"Your last two-week mission lasted over a year," she reminded him.

"That was different. Our intelligence was sorely lacking on that organization. It wouldn't have been right to pull out after two weeks once I had befriended their leader." Grady shrugged his shoulders like this was a completely logical response, and Crystal hated that she agreed with him.

"And who's to say the same thing won't happen this time?"

"It won't. It's just a simple recovery mission," he promised. "No undercover work involved."

"It better be." Crystal gently elbowed him in the stomach, just to get her point across. The possibility of losing Justin and Flint was too much already. She didn't want to entertain the idea of the ship without Grady too.

Desi paced in her quarters. Something about this mission didn't feel right. She was sure she wasn't the only one to pick up on it. She had seen Justin's eyes fill with fear when Craft told them about the hearing. He knew as well as she did that the U.S. military wasn't going to waste their time weighing the pros and cons of the exchange program. It had been a miracle they had agreed to it in the first place. If the government was having second thoughts about the value of the program, they wouldn't hesitate to cut it. There had to be something else at play here, something the military couldn't control. She just wasn't sure what.

Desi whipped around at the sound of the door opening. "Where have you been?"

Wolf held her hands up in surrender as she walked in. "I was talking to Grady."

"Oh." Desi resumed her pacing.

"What's got you on edge?" Wolf pulled her duffle bag out and laid it on her bed. How could she be so casual right now? Didn't she realize what they were walking into? But of course Wolf didn't understand. Craft had told them that the hearings were to determine if the exchange program should be continued, so that's what Wolf believed. And why shouldn't she? LAWON was always upfront with the objective of the mission they sent their people on.

"We need to discuss this mission." Desi stopped pacing again and turned to look at Wolf who was carefully putting her uniforms into her duffle bag. "Could you stop packing?" Desi's words were laced with more panic than she intended.

Startled, Wolf dropped her clothes on the bed and turned toward Desi. "I'm sorry. What's going on?"

Desi took a deep breath. "We need to be ready for the possibility that these hearings are about more than the exchange program."

"You think Craft isn't telling us everything?" Wolf pulled a chair out from the table that divided the room in half and sat down. Desi wished she could tell what was running through Wolf's mind, but her commander was so skilled at hiding her emotions, it was impossible.

"No, I think the U.S. military isn't telling LAWON everything." Desi plopped down in the chair across from Wolf.

"Why wouldn't the U.S. military be up front about the hearings?"

Desi had to choose her words carefully or Wolf would think she had cracked. "There's a lot of mistrust on Earth toward Neophians."

"That's not really a secret," Crystal said calmly. "I mean that's why the exchange program was created in the first place. To help ease that distrust by better understanding one another."

"That might have been LAWON's objective, but I doubt the U.S. military had the same goals for the program." Desi got up and started to pace again. She was too nervous to sit still. "You have to understand, the U.S. military doesn't do anything unless they think it can further their own objectives. And they never had a mission to increase understanding with Neophia. I mean what could they gain from that?"

Wolf shifted in her seat. "Then what do they care about?"

"They only care about recruitment numbers and gaining new resources."

"You mean Neophian resources."

Desi stopped pacing and turned to face Wolf. She

wasn't prepared for the intensity in Wolf's eyes. "It's possible. There's a theory on Earth that Neophia is hoarding an abundance of natural resources, and that if the U.S. could get their hands on it, then none of the other countries on Earth would dare to challenge us."

"Are you trying to tell me that you were sent here to spy on us for your military?" Wolf cocked an eyebrow at her. Desi wasn't sure if she was trying to humor her, or if Wolf was trying to assess if she was a threat.

"No, of course not," Desi huffed. "But I wouldn't be at all surprised if Justin and I both get asked a lot of questions about what we've seen while we were here."

"Why are you telling me all of this?"

"I want you to be prepared in case things go south. This mission may be framed as a simple political visit, but it won't be that way once we get to Earth. Who knows what we're going to face once we get there?" Desi locked her fingers behind her head.

"I'll keep my guard up, I promise. I'm not sure what else we can do." Wolf stood up. "Let's finish packing. We need to be in the launch bay in an hour."

"You're right. It's too late to do anything now. I've got to go grab some things from the laundry." Desi pointed behind her back toward the door and took a few steps backward. "I'll be back."

She couldn't help but feel defeated as the door closed behind her. It wasn't that Wolf had dismissed her, but she certainly didn't seem as concerned as Desi thought she should be. Could Desi be wrong? Was it possible that the hearings were just that? She knew in her heart that nothing with the U.S. military was ever that straightforward. She thought back to her last time on Earth, when she had been told she was getting the Medal of Honor and was to be paraded around the media like some kind of mascot. It was the reason she had signed up for the exchange program in the first place. She was no one's mouthpiece. Desi was sure she would pay for that decision once they were back on Earth.

Chapter 2

Crystal dropped her bag in the back of the launch before making her way up to the cockpit. They were set to leave in half an hour, which meant that Justin would be up there doing the preflight checks. She wanted to talk to him before the others arrived. If anyone could put her mind at ease it would be him.

Justin stood in the back of the cockpit checking the fuel gages. "Hi." She gave him a quick kiss on the cheek before sitting down in the copilot's chair.

"Did you come to help?" Justin didn't turn to look at her. Crystal appreciated how focused he was. He took his job seriously. It was one of the main reasons their relationship worked.

"I can help if you need me to," Crystal said.

Justin turned away from the gages. "But that's not why you're here." He cocked an eyebrow at her.

"No." Crystal folded one of her legs under her.

"Then what can I do for you Commander?" Justin set

his tablet down on the empty chair next to her. He grabbed the armrests of her chair, leaned down, and slowly kissed her.

She gently pushed him away with a chuckle. "I didn't come here for that either." Justin went back in for another kiss anyway. Crystal couldn't help but kiss him back before pulling away. "We don't have time for that." It was impossible to hide her smile.

"The others won't be here for another twenty minutes, probably twenty-five for Desi." Justin was still leaning over her.

"Yes, but you're only on step two of forty-five of your preflight checklist." Crystal grabbed the tablet and held it out to him.

Justin breathed out slowly before kissing her forehead and grabbing the tablet. "So what's on your mind?" Justin sat down in the pilot's chairs and started a calibration check on the ship's level gages.

"Desi. She was pretty on edge when we got back to our quarters. She seems to think that the hearing is a cover for the U.S. military to gain intelligence on LAWON." Crystal watched him carefully as she spoke, noticing how he had tensed up when she mentioned the U.S. military before going back to work on the controls.

"I've honestly been wondering that myself."

Crystal sat up and turned his chair so that Justin was facing her. "Do you really think that anyone participating in the program could be spying on LAWON for the U.S. military?"

"Not intentionally, but the military doesn't know much about Neophia other than there are a lot more natural resources here than on Earth. The whole political arena here is a complete mystery to most people. Throw LAWON in on top of all that, there's no doubt the U.S.

government will try to get whatever information they can from their soldiers in the program."

Justin nodded toward the controls in front of Crystal. She turned and grabbed them, testing to make sure they responded properly. It was a good distraction as she tried to get her mind in order. The whole point of the exchange program was for the governments to get a better understanding of one another. It made sense that the U.S. military would want to know what their people learned while serving on Neophia. Crystal was sure LAWON would do the same thing when their officers returned from Earth. Flint was just making a big deal out of nothing. It wasn't like the lieutenant hadn't jumped to conclusions before. "What do you think your government will do with the information?"

Justin sat back and crossed his arms. "It's hard to say. They might try to use it to pressure Neophia to provide more resources to Earth. I'm not sure how successful they'll be, given Neophia's export regulations. Beyond that I'm not sure what else they could do with it."

"So you don't think they'd use it plan an attack on Neophia?" It was Crystal biggest fear. Even if LAWON and Teria joined forces, they couldn't match the fire power of Earth.

Justin shook his head. "It would cost a fortune to get their army here. It wouldn't be worth it."

"Good." Crystal breathed a small sigh of relief. "The way Flint was talking, I figured we would be attacked the second the shuttle landed on Earth. I've never seen her that on edge before."

"I'll talk to her." Justin gently placed his hands on Crystal's knees

"Thank you."

"Now, would you get out of here so I can finish my

checks." Justin playfully spun her chair so she was facing the back of the launch. Crystal made her way out of the cockpit, shaking her head. She glanced back over her shoulder to see Justin working at the helm. Six months wasn't a lot time, but she couldn't bear the thought of losing him if they failed their mission and the exchange program was canceled.

Desi wasn't surprised to find the rest of the team waiting for her in the shuttle. She wasn't late, technically, but she had cut it as close as she could. After six months on Neophia, she still hadn't adjusted to the fact that everyone always showed up at least ten minutes before their actual report time. Desi needed every last minute to try to get her nerves under control. She had thought talking things through with Wolf would put her mind at ease, but she was wrong. If anything, it only opened up new theories for her mind to explore while she tried to finish packing.

Desi stowed her bag and took a seat next to Wolf at the back of the shuttle. Justin was still doing his preflight checks. Desi knew that the system Wolf had put in place meant that the shuttles were always in top notch condition, but those checks were extensive and took up a lot of time.

"All right boys and girls," Justin said as he emerged from the shuttle's cockpit. "Let's get this show on the road. Hey Desi, how about you be my copilot?"

"You don't need a copilot. You got this under control." Desi leaned back in her seat and propped her feet up on the bench across from her. She planned to use the three-hour ride back to Kincaron to try to relax.

"Come on Flint." Justin kicked her feet off the seat.

"If you insist." Reluctantly, she got up and followed Justin to the front of the shuttle. Desi could have sworn she saw Wolf mouth "thank you" to Justin. This was a set up. She should have known.

Desi settled herself into the copilot chair next to Justin. She watched as he started the launch and pulled away from *Journey*. She felt a pang of longing once the ship was out of view. That might be the last time she ever saw *Journey*. She had been so worried about the hearing that she hadn't taken the time to say her goodbyes. She shook her head slightly; now was not the time for regrets. She was on her way home. A home she had missed while on Neophia.

"How about you transfer control over to me and I can see what this baby can do?" Desi gripped the wheel in front of her and looked at Justin with a wicked grin.

"Oh, not a chance." Justin set the auto pilot and turned to face her. "How about we talk instead?"

"Wolf asked you to do this, didn't she?" Desi turned to face Justin with her arms crossed in front of her. She shot him a look she knew would make him feel guilty about ambushing her.

Justin hunched his shoulders, a light blush crossing his cheeks. "She's worried about you. She thinks you might be overreacting about the hearing."

"And you think I'm being crazy." Desi glared at him. She knew Wolf wouldn't fully understand the situation on Earth, but she had been sure Justin would. He couldn't have forgotten everything in the six months they'd been gone.

"I didn't say that. I actually agree with you, though I'm not convinced it's as drastic as you think it is." Justin glanced back at the monitors to make sure they were still on course.

"You know they're going to grill us on what we've seen here. I wouldn't be surprised if they try to use the exchange program against us." Desi was tempted to tell him about the medal of honor she had turn down by signing up for the exchange program, but she couldn't put that on him. Besides, the only thing that might save her from some serious retaliation was the fact that no one knew just how badly she had undermined the government.

"We both knew there were risks taking the assignment in the first place," Justin said with a shrug. "But since I don't plan on going back, I'm not sure what they can do to me. You wouldn't be so worried either if you'd signed up for *Journey's* next tour."

"Are you looking forward to seeing your parents?" Desi plastered an over-the-top smile on her face. She wouldn't take the bait.

"Very smooth," Justin said with a chuckle.

"I'm sure your mom has been going crazy with you being on another planet," Desi said, refusing to let Justin change the topic back. Justin's whole body relaxed, and Desi knew she had won the battle. It was reassuring to know that Justin didn't think she was completely insane, even though that meant he didn't trust the U.S. military either. She wasn't sure that made her feel better.

"I'm pretty sure if we were going to be gone any longer, she would have come to Neophia to drag me home herself. She about lost it when I called to tell her we would be home a few days early, and that Crystal would be with me," Justin said with an excited grin.

"You're going to introduce Crystal to your parents?" Desi sat up straighter in her chair. She knew the two of them were serious, but meeting the parents was a big step.

"Well yeah, when else will they have a chance to meet her? It's not like we can pop down to Earth for dinner."

"No, I know, it's just—have you talked to Crystal about it? You know she gets a little more closed off than normal whenever family stuff comes up. And I don't think she's really over everything that happened at Stapleton Farms with Ben. Seeing another big happy family might be tough for her." Desi didn't want to be a downer, but someone needed to be the voice of reason. She knew he didn't mean to be insensitive, but he didn't always think things through when he got excited.

Justin's smile faltered. "I hadn't thought of that. I'll call the whole thing off."

"I'm not saying that either," Desi said quickly. "You just need to talk to her about it first. You can't spring something like that on her."

"You're right. I'll talk to her." Justin turned back to the controls.

"Good. Now are you going to let me drive this thing or not?" Desi reached for the controls again.

"Nice try. Why don't you get some shut-eye, and I'll make sure we make it to shore without getting anyone sick." The carefree smile was back on his face.

Crystal kept glancing toward the cockpit every few seconds. She wished she could hear what Justin and Flint were talking about up there. She wanted to make sure that Flint went into the hearing with a clear head. Justin had known her since they were kids; he would know what to say to her.

"What do you think Earth will be like?" Grady had spread out on the bench in the back corner. The launch was built to comfortably seat twenty people. If felt huge with just the three of them back there.

Tyler looked up from the computer on his lap. "I don't know. It can't possibly be as bad as everyone makes it out to be, can it?"

"It might be. Would so many people be trying to come to Neophia if Earth was a great place to live?" Crystal had been spending a lot of time researching Neophian immigration laws with Justin. He was determined to find a way to bring his family to Neophia, and Crystal wanted to help him any way she could. She'd never realized how long the waiting lists were. It could take years to be granted citizenship, and that was only after the nearly impossible task of getting your name on the waitlist in the first place.

"Maybe it's a grass is greener kind of thing, you know," Tyler said with a shrug of his shoulders.

"Whatever the conditions are, I think we need to keep our guard up while we're there." Crystal looked pointedly between Grady and Tyler, but neither of them was really paying attention to her. "I'm being serious."

"We're going to Earth as representatives of LAWON to speak in some meetings. It's not like anyone's going to be shooting at us," Grady said.

"I don't think it's going to be that simple." Crystal tried to find the right level of urgency to convey her words. She didn't want to come across as paranoid as Desi had, but she needed them to understand what they might be going into.

"Why not?" Tyler asked.

"Flint seems to think these hearings are a cover for the U.S. military to gain intelligence on Neophia. Intelligence they could use against us if they ever decided to attack us." Crystal chose her words very carefully.

"We all know that Flint tends to over exaggerate

things," Tyler said. "How do we know she's not doing that now?" He closed the laptop and set it on the seat next to him.

"Because Justin agrees with her." Crystal decided to leave out the fact that he'd said it was unlikely Earth would ever try to attack Neophia. She had just gotten their attention, and she wasn't about to let it slip away.

"What are we supposed to do? Craft wants us to convince them to keep the exchange program going. We're going to have to give them at least some information about Neophia in order to do that," Tyler said.

"There has to be a reason Craft is sending us and not people that know how to navigate this stuff," Grady put in. "Let's be honest, if you were going to send a team that works well with politicians would you chose us?" Grady gestured from himself to Crystal with a proud smile.

She knew he was right. She'd had more than her fair share of bad run-ins with politicians over the course of her career. The way they constantly skated around giving any kind of real answer drove her crazy, and she had called them out on it more than once. She had gotten better about it since her counter-terrorism days, though that was mainly due to the fact that she tried to avoid politicians at all costs.

"I wish I knew what he was thinking, sending us," Crystal admitted, "but there's nothing we can do about it now. We just need to be careful about what we say and who we say it to. The last thing we want is to start an interplanetary war or something." Crystal leveled her gaze at Grady.

Grady threw his hands up in surrender. "I promise I'll let you do all the talking."

"Believe me that's not what I want," Crystal said wryly. "I want them to have picked a different team to send, but since it's too late for that, we need to be prepared." She was already counting down the minutes until this mission was over.

Chapter 3

The armrest dug into Crystal's side. She didn't know how long she had been asleep, but it wasn't long enough. They were still in space. She would never admit it, but space travel terrified her. At least if something went wrong on *Journey*, she could fix it. She had no control here. If the spaceship they were on broke down, they could spend the rest of their lives floating aimlessly through space, never to be seen again.

Besides the pilots, the five of them had the ship to themselves. It seemed a bit excessive. It certainly would have been cheaper for LAWON to book them on a public shuttle to Earth. She wondered whose budget request would go unfulfilled due to the expense of this trip. Justin and Crystal were the only ones who had decided to share a row of seats. The rest of the team was sprawled out, trying to find a position comfortable enough to get some shut eye.

Gentle fingers brushed through her hair. She kept her

eyes closed as she soaked in the feeling of Justin's touch. The ship started to shake violently. Crystal bolted up, throwing Justin's hand off her in the process. She clenched the arm rests while she searched for the cause of the turbulence. It stopped a moment later. No one else seemed to notice.

Justin's hand covered hers. "It's ok. We just entered Earth's atmosphere. We'll be on the ground soon.

"Ok, good." Crystal forced her fingers to relax their grip on the armrest. "Did you get any sleep?" she asked, hoping to keep herself distracted.

"A little, but I was about to go on duty when we left so I was pretty well rested before this all started," Justin said, rubbing his thumb across the back of her hand.

Crystal glanced down at her watch. She wasn't sure how long it would take to land now that they had entered the atmosphere. She thought she could feel the shuttle starting to slow down, but it was hard to tell. Did the vibrations indicate the same things they did in a submarine?

"Are you excited to see Earth?" Justin asked. She knew he was trying to distract her, and she adored him for it.

"If it means we're out of the air, then yes."

"You're not afraid of flying, are you?" The smile on Justin's face made her heart skip a beat.

"Of course not." She tried to keep her voice steady, but she was sure Justin had heard the tiny crack that had escaped. The shuttle shook, causing Crystal's hands to clench the armrests again.

Justin pried one of her hands lose and brought it to his lips. "There was something I wanted to talk to you about before we land."

"Sure." She probably should have been nervous about

what Justin wanted to tell her, but she was just grateful for the distraction.

"I was hoping to introduce you to my family before you went back to Neophia."

Crystal shifted in her seat so that she could look at Justin. He was visibly tense. He couldn't be nervous about the landing; he had been so relaxed the whole trip. No, he was nervous about what she would say. It was enough to make Crystal forget what that they were hurtling toward Earth at a high speed. "You want me to meet your parents?"

"I know it's a big step, but I think we're ready for it. I've told them all about you and they're really excited to meet you. Besides, who knows if we'll ever get this chance again?" Justin's words flew out of his mouth, at a speed Crystal had never heard from him before. It was sweet.

"Of course, I would love to meet your parents." Crystal was surprised to find she actually meant it.

"Thank you." Justin leaned over and kissed her on the cheek. "By the way, we're on the ground now," he whispered in her ear.

She didn't believe him. She leaned over him to look out the window, and sure enough they were parked in the middle of a concrete pad. She had made easy docks underwater that were rougher than that. Flint was the first one out of her seat. Crystal wondered if she was excited to be home or if she also hated space travel.

Crystal followed Justin off the shuttle. Her first sight of Earth froze her to the platform. She hadn't expected it to be this bad. There wasn't a hint of color anywhere, not unless you counted black and grey. She checked her watch. Justin had helped her set it to the right time. It should have been early afternoon, but there wasn't any natural light. The only lights came from thousands of electronic billboards that papered the horizon. She would have to ask Justin if this was normal. There had to be sunlight at some point. Maybe Earth was on a different cycle than Neophia?

The noise threw her the most. The billboards blared marketing campaigns into the air. A steady line of cars off in the distance peppered the air with the sound of horns blowing and tires squealing. The air generators that provided the planet with breathable air added a constant buzz to underline it all. How could anyone even hear themselves think? There was so much sound that it blended together in an annoying hum Crystal was sure would give her a migraine within an hour.

"Am I supposed to be able to taste the air?" Grady asked from behind her. He was right. Crystal took a deep breath and instantly regretted it. A chemical taste filled her lungs. It had to be coming from the air purifiers scattered around the city.

"You guys are seeing this, too, aren't you? I mean I'm not imagining this, am I?" Tyler asked.

"No, this is real." Crystal scanned the horizon again, hoping to spot a tree or something natural, but found nothing.

"I was hoping I was still sleeping." Tyler rubbed his eyes for good measure.

"Look guys," Crystal turned to face them, "we can't let them know how bad we think Earth is. We need to pretend like this is normal so we don't offend anyone. This is Justin and Flint's home after all."

"I'm not sure I'm that good of a liar," Grady said.

Crystal poked Grady in the chest. "Try." She gave their surroundings one last scan, hoping to find some redeeming quality. She let out a sigh when she couldn't find one. "I guess we should get down there."

Justin and Flint were standing off to the side, talking to a man wearing a suit, who looked happy to see them. Behind him were two black cars bearing LAWON flags. Crystal made her way over. It wasn't much of a welcoming committee, but Crystal was grateful they wouldn't have to find their way to the LAWON embassy on their own.

"You must be Lieutenant Commander Wolf." The suit held his hand out to Crystal. "I'm Jax Donnelly, the LAWON ambassador to the United States of America."

"It's a pleasure to meet you Mr. Donnelly." Crystal shook his hand. "Allow me to introduce you to the rest of the team, Ensign Price and Lieutenant Grady."

Jax enthusiastically shook each of their hands. "The pleasure is all mine. There haven't been a lot of visits to the embassy lately and no one nearly as prestigious as you."

Crystal chose to believe he was referring to the whole team from *Journey* and not the fact that she was still considered the daughter of the nation's greatest war heroes, even if that fact was only partly true. It seemed to be a title she would never shed.

"I've got cars to take you to the embassy, where we have rooms made up for all of you," Jax continued. "However, I thought Lieutenant Flint and Ensign Price might be staying with their families, so I have a second car just in case."

"Do you want us to go to the embassy first and start strategizing for the hearing?" Justin asked.

Crystal knew it wasn't a sincere offer. It was clear that he wanted to go home. "We have all day tomorrow to prepare for the hearing," she answered. "You two should go be with your families. I'm sure they're excited to have you home."

"If you'd like to take the first car, my driver will take you wherever you need to go. I'll make sure he's there in the morning to bring you to the embassy." Jax waved to the first of the two cars parked on the landing pad. The driver got out, came and took their bags, and then returned to the car to wait for them.

"What do you want to do about tomorrow?" Flint asked.

"How about you come to the embassy tomorrow at 0700," Crystal said.

Grady leaned over and coughed "0800."

Crystal rolled her eyes. "Fine 0800." There wasn't any harm in sleeping in a little.

"Works for me." Flint took off toward the car.

"See you tomorrow." Justin gave her a quick kiss on the cheek. "If you need anything, just call. I'll have my communicator on me at all times."

Out of the corner of her eye Crystal saw the ambassador giving her a strange look which she chose to ignore. Her relationship with Justin wasn't any of his business. "I'll be fine. Go be with your family."

Crystal watched as Justin got in the car behind Flint and it pulled out of sight. A knot grew in her stomach as they drove away, as if having a human escort from Earth had offered them some level of protection. Though protection from what she wasn't sure.

Desi stared out the window of the car as they drove to their neighborhood. Each familiar sight caused her heart to skip a beat. She was home. She hadn't realized how much she had missed Earth. This was where she belonged. She knew that now. Part of her had always known it. It was the part that had kept her from signing on for *Journey's* next tour when everyone else on the ship had done so the day the second tour was announced. Now all she needed to do was find the right time to tell the others she wouldn't be returning.

"It's great to be home, isn't it?" She turned to Justin, sure that she would see her smile mirrored on his face. It wasn't.

"Yeah, sure." Justin glanced out the window only to return his gaze back inside the car immediately.

"What's wrong? Aren't you excited to see your family?" Desi felt betrayed by his lack of enthusiasm.

"Of course, I am. I just forgot how bad it really is here."

"What do you mean?" Desi didn't see anything that looked that bad to her. In fact, it looked like a lot of the graffiti had been cleaned up around the neighborhood. If anything, things looked better than when they left. It might not be as pretty as Neophia, but beauty was in the eye of the beholder.

"There's no life here," Justin said with downcast eyes.

Desi gestured toward the window. The sidewalks were full of people coming home from work and kids playing in the alley. "Look around, there are people everywhere. What more do you want?"

"Sure there's people, but where are the plants? Where are the bugs and animals? They aren't out there, because there's not any left. The only environment we have is a man made one full of concrete and steel. Even the air feels dead." Justin gestured out the window without looking out.

"It's the same as when we left," Desi said.

"I don't know," Justin responded. "It doesn't feel like home anymore. I miss the fresh air, the colors, and the sunshine we had on Neophia."

Desi tried and failed to hold back a laugh. "You spent the last six months on a submarine. Underwater. There was no sunshine or fresh air there either." She shook her head. After all these years, she should be used to Justin's idealistic nonsense, but there were still times when it took her by surprise.

"It was just nice knowing that it would be there when we surfaced. I don't expect you to understand." Justin looked down and started picking at the stitching in the seat cushions.

Desi looked out the window. They were pulling up in front of their apartment building. Justin's parents and two youngest sisters were outside, holding up a huge welcome home banner. Desi's mom was standing off to the side. She was smiling, but Desi could tell from her posture that she was nervous about something. She turned back to Justin. "You'd better wipe that melancholy look off your face. You don't want your parents to think you aren't happy to see them."

Desi jumped out of the car as soon as it stopped. She ran over to her mom and gave her a big hug. "Hi Mom."

Desi felt her mom pulling her away from the curb as they hugged. Desi released her mom and looked her in the eyes. They were darting from the flags on the car to the people passing by. "It's so good to have you home and away from those Neophians," her mom said.

Desi gave her mom a strange look. "What are you talking about?" Desi had no idea where this was coming from. Her mom had never been anti-Neophian. Sure, she hadn't been pleased when Desi signed up for the exchange program, but Desi thought that had more to do with her being on another planet. Had her mom been hiding some anti-Neophian feelings all this time?

"Did you have to take that car home?" her mom demanded. "Couldn't you take one from the U.S. military? People need to know whose side you're on."

"The U.S. military didn't send a car." Now that she thought about it, it was odd that there wasn't at least someone from the U.S. military to greet them when they landed. They had been the ones to call for the hearing; the least they could do was send someone to greet the LAWON representatives. Though if they had, Desi was positive they wouldn't have offered her and Justin a ride home.

"Well I guess there's nothing we can do about it now. Let's just get inside." Desi's mom kept looking around the street to see who was passing by.

"Mom, what's going on?"

"It's nothing."

"Then I'm going to go say hi to the Andersons." Desi didn't wait for an answer before walking over to Justin's family. Mrs. Anderson released Justin as soon as she saw Desi. A second later, her arms were draped around Desi's neck.

"Thank you for looking out for our boy," Mrs. Anderson said.

"He doesn't need me to look out for him anymore." Desi hugged Mrs. Anderson a little tighter.

"I know. Still, I slept a little better knowing the two of you were together." Mrs. Anderson gently ran her hand down Desi's cheek. She had been like a second mother to Desi for much of her life. Desi would spend the evenings in the Andersons' apartment on nights when her mom had to work late. It was nice to be part of a big family, even if it was only pretend. Desi loved her mom, but it was lonely just the two of them. The Andersons' house with their four kids was always full of life. Desi knew they were taxed heavily for having more than two children, but it never seemed like a burden.

"All right everyone, let's get inside. Dedria and I made all of your favorites," Mrs. Anderson said, finally releasing Desi.

She turned and looked at her mom in surprise. Her mom rarely cooked, usually brining home leftovers from the restaurant she worked at. "Now we're talking." Desi had never warmed to the food on Neophia. While similar to food on Earth in a lot of ways, it wasn't the same. She would have done almost anything for a normal meal. Coming home to a homecooked feast was a dream come true. Her mouth started to water just thinking about it.

"Maybe tomorrow I'll cook you a Neophian meal," Justin said. "I wonder how hard it would be to get the ingredients here."

"Don't you dare ruin this for me." Desi grabbed his arm and dragged him up the steps and into their apartment building.

Crystal wasn't sure what she expected the LAWON embassy to look like, but it certainly wasn't the gated mansion they pulled up to. It was like something out of a storybook. The inside was even more elaborate. Jax showed them through the main level, explaining that the mansion was several hundred years old, and while most of the house had been outfitted with modern technology, the bones and decor had been kept as close to the original as possible. Ornate furniture was perfectly placed in each room. Large rugs with elaborate patterns covered warm wood floors. Crystal could have spent hours examining the paintings that hung throughout the house. It was like finding an unexpected pocket of beauty on an otherwise bleak planet.

They were shown to rooms on the third floor, each with a private bathroom. It was so much more than they needed. Crystal would have been happy staying in a military barrack for the few days they were here. They were left alone to unpack, but not before Jax had invited them all down for dinner. Crystal wanted to refuse but didn't. The last thing she wanted to do was insult their host on their first night, especially when he had gone out of his way to make sure they were well taken care of.

Crystal hung up her uniforms, then took a shower. She headed down to dinner a few minutes early. She ran into Tyler as soon as she stepped into the hall. "So, is this normal for a mission like this?" he asked.

"I have no idea. LAWON doesn't usually let me talk to anyone important unless it's about something safe, like ship design," Crystal said with a smile.

"They're probably justified." Tyler nudged her gently with his shoulder as they walked down the stairs.

"Which makes me wonder why they asked me to come here."

"Maybe they don't think it's important to have the finesses of a seasoned politician for the hearing. I mean the U.S. military has a very different culture than ours. Maybe your blunt honesty is what's needed here." Tyler stopped at the bottom of the stairs, looking in both directions.

Crystal pointed to the right. "Now there's a terrifying thought."

Crystal followed Tyler into the dining room. Gardy was already sitting at the table when they arrived. He had a glass of wine in his hand and was chatting casually with the man sitting across the table from him. Jax was off to the side, talking with a man in a suit who Crystal assumed would be serving them. This was all way over the top.

The ambassador excused himself as soon as he saw Crystal and Tyler. "Please let me introduce you to my partner, Marcel. He's a surgeon at the local hospital and thankfully was able to take the evening off to join us for dinner."

Marcel stood up and shook both their hands. "It's an honor to meet you both."

Crystal and Tyler took the seats on either side of Grady. Crystal noticed that there was still an empty chair across the table where Jax and Marcel were sitting. "Is someone else joining us?" she asked.

"Our daughter, Natasha," Marcel said. "She's studying at the local university and should be here soon."

As if on cue a young woman walked into the room. "I hope you weren't waiting for me." She walked over and gave her fathers a kiss on the cheek before taking a seat.

"You're right on time," Jax told her. "Let me introduce you to our guests." Jax quickly introduced them. Crystal had to kick Grady under the table when Jax got to him. He seemed to be entranced by Natasha's long sleek hair and brown eyes. This was the last thing Crystal needed. She had enough to worry about without Grady lusting after the ambassador's daughter.

The first course was served quickly, a salad with some kind of white sauce drizzled on top. "It's ranch dressing, a staple in American cuisine," Jax said. "I hope you don't mind, but I ordered a meal that would highlight all the best food Earth has to offer." Crystal's cheeks hurt just looking at the size of the smile on his face.

"It's perfect." Crystal took a small bite. The taste was

overpowering, but she didn't mind it. "It's a great opportunity to learn about American culture while we're here. It's nice to get an unfiltered view. You know the rumors back home can get pretty jaded about Earth." She was trying her best to sound like a politician. It would be good practice for the hearing.

"Unfortunately, I think there's more truth to the rumors than we want to admit," Marcel said.

"It's really not that bad, once you get used to it," Jax said quickly.

"How long have you been the ambassador here?" Tyler asked. Crystal noticed that he had pushed his plate away slightly after taking a few bites of the salad.

"It's been almost twelve years." The smile faltered on Jax's face.

"That seems like a long time for an appointment like this," Grady said in between bites. That man could eat anything.

"It is. LAWON has had a hard time getting anyone to agree to take over for us, especially in the current climate. Though it's not so bad. The extended appointment has allowed me to form real bonds with my counterparts here and be an advocate for Neophians on Earth." Jax was a politician through and through. Crystal should be taking notes.

"What do you mean by current climate?" Grady asked.

Jax and Marcell exchanged another look that clearly housed some deeper meaning to them. Crystal had always been impressed when her grandparents could have whole conversations with just an exchange of glances. It was something couples in long-term relationships could boast over the rest of the population. Crystal wondered if she would have that deep a connection with Justin one day.

"You might as well tell them." Marcel casually took a bite from his salad.

"Tell us what?" Crystal's insides were screaming at her. Whatever Jax was hesitating to tell them had to have some bearing on the hearing. Jax kept looking from Marcel to Natasha. Crystal watched his eyes bounce back and forth like a tennis match. "Mr. Donnelly, if there's something going on, something you know that will help us do our jobs, then you have to tell us." Crystal set her fork down so she could give him her undivided attention.

"It's nothing to do with the hearing directly," Jax started.

"But it's something you think is important for us to know?" Tyler asked. Jax picked up his glass of wine and took a sip.

"If you're worried about confidentiality, we all have the highest levels of security clearance." The more the ambassador put off telling them, the more Crystal needed to know what he was keeping from them.

"It's not classified, it's just—" Jax started but stopped as the servers came in to clear their plates and bring out the main course. Crystal was given the biggest piece of meat she had ever seen. There was no way she would be able to finish it. No wonder there were always food shortages on Earth. She was pretty sure the food on her plate alone would be enough to feed everyone at the table.

"As you were saying," Grady said as he poked his slab of meat with his knife.

"The political climate on Earth is changing more drastically than anything I've ever seen before. There has always been a small segment of the population that harbored a deep seeded mistrust of anyone from Neophia. Up until four months ago, that segment of the population pretty much kept it to themselves. You would hear about the occasional hate crime, but they were pretty isolated incidents."

"Then the Neophian Integration Alliance started to surface," Marcell said.

"The Neophain Integration Alliance?" Crystal was surprised she had never heard of them. It had been a few years since she worked counterterrorism, but she still tried to keep up to date with the major players. She looked to Grady, but he shook his head.

"They're a terrorist group who claim they want to make Earth respect Neophia and everything we have done to help the humans," Jax said with a sigh.

"But all they're really doing is fanning the flames of hatred and mistrust toward Neophians," said Natasha.

"What kind of things are they doing?" Grady shot Crystal a look. She knew where his mind was heading. Her's was going in the same direction.

Jax took off his glasses and squeezed the bridge of his nose. "It started off as nothing more than threats. Hacked billboards and computer viruses that flashed messages of Neophian superiority on whatever got infected. Then about a month ago they got violent."

"Violent how?" Crystal asked.

"The first attack was on a Wednesday morning," Jax said. There was a faraway quality to his voice. "The subways were full of commuters and kids heading to school. When the first train crashed into the platform full of people, everyone thought it was some kind of terrible accident, but then the other two trains hit a few minutes later. There was no denying it was intentional."

Marcel set down his fork and folded his hands in front

of his face. "I was working in the ER that morning. We were overwhelmed in minutes, but since we're the closest hospital, they kept bringing people there. We saved as many as we could."

"The NIA took credit for the attack fifteen minutes after it happened. They said it was a warning, and that more people would die if Neophians didn't start receiving the respect and gratitude they deserved for saving Earth from destroying itself." Jax shook his head and started to cut up his steak, though nothing made it to his mouth.

"How did they get their statement out without being caught?" Tyler asked

"They hacked into the emergency broadcast frequency," Marcel explained. "It played on every screen in the country every twenty minutes. It took the government seventeen hours to regain control."

Natasha picked up her wine and took a sip while smiling across the table at Grady. Thankfully, he was too caught in the terrorist group to noticed.

"Impressive," Tyler muttered while looking down at his plate.

"In the end, 117 people were dead and countless more sustained life altering injuries," Marcel said.

"The media and politicians ran with the story. They fed into the fears people already had. Overnight the number of crimes against Neophians skyrocketed. Everyone from Neophia is now viewed as a potential threat," Jax said. "Our people are starting to leave Earth at an alarming rate."

"Can you blame them? If it wasn't for your position, I'm not sure I'd stay either. People just want to protect their families." Marcel glanced over at Natasha.

"Did they ever catch the NIA?" Crystal asked.

"No, and the government has refused to give into their demands, which of course they have to," Jax admitted, "but they're taking it a step further and antagonizing the NIA. It's only a matter of time before they strike again. And in the meantime, innocent Neophians are living in fear of retaliation every day."

Crystal picked up her knife and fork and started to absentmindedly cut the meat on her plate. This would certainly make things more complicated at the hearing. How were they going to convince the U.S. military to keep the exchange program going when they were openly condemning Neophia and its people?

Chapter 4

Crystal lay awake in her bed. She had been trying to fall asleep for several hours. She couldn't shut her mind down. Thoughts of the NIA and the hearing kept competing for her attention. She finally gave up and got out of bed. There was no point lying there when she knew sleep wasn't going to come. She grabbed her tablet out of her bag and headed downstairs.

She wandered around the main level of the house until she found an out of the way room. She didn't want to bother anyone. She flipped a switch near the door and the room filled with light. The walls were covered in antique paper books. Crystal ran her hand along one of the shelves, taking in the beauty of the room. She spotted a drink cart in the corner and poured herself a glass of amber liquid she hoped was whisky before taking a seat on one of the couches.

She took a sip of the drink while she waited for her tablet to turn on. It was whiskey, though it was slightly different than back home. Hopefully it would help to calm her mind. She tried to get a connection to Neophia. She wanted to check in with Stiner to make sure they had finished the repair list for the dry dock. *Journey* should be getting to the base soon, and Crystal knew things tended to get forgotten when everyone had leave plans on their minds. The connection lagged, and she couldn't get her video call to go through. It was probably for the best; she didn't actually have any idea what time it was back on Neophia. Crystal quickly typed out a message to Stiner. She took another sip of her drink while she waited for the message to send. She wasn't excepting a quick response, so she closed her connection with Neophia.

She set her tablet down on the table and looked around the room. She needed to find something else to distract her. She considered picking up one of the books, but knew it wouldn't hold her attention. "Screw it." She put down her glass and picked up her tablet again.

She opened the internet browser and searched for the Neophian Integration Alliance. Article after article appeared. Jackpot. As Crystal started to read them, she realized Jax hadn't told them everything. The NIA had taken credit for several more attacks since the train crashes. Several hotels were bombed next, and only a week ago, a sniper had targeted a sporting event and taken out half the players on the field within minutes. Crystal got up and started to pace. She needed to piece this all together. She went over to the desk in the back of the room and started to search through the drawers, looking for something to write on.

"What are you doing?"

Crystal nearly jumped out of her skin. Grady was standing behind the couch she'd been sitting on, watching her with a smirk. "I couldn't sleep," she answered. She closed the desk drawer and went back over the couch, picked up her drink, and sat down.

"So you thought you'd just go through the ambassador's things? Bold move." Grady walked over to the drink cart and poured himself a drink before sitting down on the couch across from Crystal.

"I was looking for something to take notes on."

"Strategizing for the hearing already?"

"Not exactly." She nodded toward the tablet on the table between them. Grady picked it up and looked it over.

"I should have guessed." He shook his head, but didn't put the tablet back down. Crystal could see his eyes scanning the story.

"Don't act like you haven't been thinking about the same thing." She took a sip while she waited for Grady to finish reading the article.

"Old habits are hard to break." He set the tablet back on the table and picked up his drink. "Have you pieced anything together yet?" he asked leaning back into the couch.

"Just that there's been a lot more attacks than the Donnellys told us about. I was about to get started on a timeline." Crystal raised her glass to him. "You in?"

Grady tipped his glass in response. "Just like the good old days." They both took a sip, got up, and started to search the room again. Grady opened a closet door. "Jackpot." He rolled out three large touch screens.

"Nice." Crystal grabbed her tablet and connected it to the first screen. She selected the information she wanted, and it appeared on the touchscreen. "Can you start putting together a map while I start on this?"

"You got it." Grady pulled the second screen over to

hers. He took her tablet, pulled up a map, and transferred it to his screen.

Crystal removed the stylus attached to the bottom of her screen and used it to draw a line across her board, sectioning it off for a six-month period. She then started to arrange the news stories in chronological order. The NIA were escalating quickly. It looked like there was an attack about every three weeks, each causing more death and destruction than the last. It had been two and half weeks since the last attack. "Hey, Jim, look at this."

Grady turned away from his screen. "The next attack could be any day now."

"Looks that way." Crystal took a step back and surveyed her work to make sure she hadn't missed anything.

"Think they'll wait till we're off the planet?"

Crystal hit him in the stomach. "Maybe the hearing is a way to try to appease the NIA without directly giving into their demands. I mean, at least the government is considering Neophian's contributions to the military."

"I think it's more likely they're going to use the hearings to try to humiliate us," Grady said.

Crystal knew in her gut that he was right, but she couldn't bring herself to face it. Instead she turned to the map he had been working on. The attacks were spread out across the entire county. Either the NIA was a huge organization or they were highly mobile. Neither was a great option. "I wonder if LAWON has any information about them?"

"It couldn't hurt to check. Why don't you check the intelligence databases back home, and I'll reach out to some of my connections and see if they know anything," Grady said.

"You don't have any connections on Earth do you?"

Crystal was always amazed by the people that Grady knew, so it wasn't outside the realm of possibility.

"No, but it's possible someone I know does."

"Meet back here in five?" Crystal cocked an eyebrow at him with a half-smile. This was going to be fun. They both left to go gather what they would need to start doing a deep dive into the NIA. Crystal returned first with her laptop and the single booster LAWON had given her before they left. It was meant to be used for real time communication with Craft to provide updates on the hearing, but no one had told her she couldn't use it for other purposes.

Grady walked in a few minutes later with his laptop and tablet tucked under one arm while he carried a large tray loaded with food. "I raided the kitchen. Hope no one minds."

Crystal eyed the metal pitcher on the tray. "Kiki?"

"Coffee. It's the best I could do." Grady set the tray down in the middle of the large table between the two couches.

They both set to work. With the booster set up, Crystal was able to get a much more reliable connection to Neophia. She searched through every intelligence database she could access for anything to do with the Neophian Integration Alliance. There didn't seem to be a single mention of them, which Crystal found odd. Usually LAWON had a pretty up to date listing of all known terrorist organizations, even if there was little intelligence on them. Crystal decided to send an encrypted message to Wilder, the current leader of her former anti-terrorism team, to see if he had heard of them. She had no idea what the team was working on at the moment, so it was a long shot that he would see it. Across the table Grady didn't appeared to be having better luck. He had gotten a few calls through to his contacts, but none of them had heard of the NIA.

They needed a different tactic. Crystal got up with her tablet and walked over to the touch screen she had been working on earlier. She had already added all the major attacks to her timeline, but she knew there were likely a few smaller scale incidents that took place before they entered the spotlight. She searched through old news stories focusing on local papers in the areas where the major attacks happened, scribbling notes on the board as she went.

She wasn't sure how long she had been working. She turned around to see Grady lying down on one of the couches with his tablet in front of his face. "You know," Crystal said as she glanced back at the screen. "I don't think the NIA is actually connected to Neophia in any way."

Grady pushed himself up. "What do you mean?"

"If this group had originated on Neophia, or even had some ties there, someone would know about it. But we haven't been able to find anything from any of our normal contacts."

"So you think they're from Earth?"

"I do." Crystal squeezed the bridge of her nose to help her focus. "There was no mention of Neophia in any of the early incidents that are linked to them."

"What incidents?"

"A few small-scale robberies and hacking jobs, all originating on Earth. These people have probably never even set foot on Neophia."

"Then why demand the government acknowledge Neophia's superiority over Earth?"

Crystal paced in front of the touch screen with the tip of the stylus in her mouth. "Because they know the U.S.

government would never do it. Maybe they were trying to increase the hatred between the two planets."

"It sounds like a long shot." Grady stretched out on the couch again.

"I bet you two months of combat gear quality check inspections that I'm right." Crystal put her hands on her hips as she stared him down.

"You're on."

Crystal's computer started to chime, alerting them to a new message. They both looked at it. Grady shot up and grabbed it first. "That Wilder's a good man."

"What did he find?" She rushed over to the couch and sat down next to Grady so she could read the message with him.

"Not a lot. They are just starting to hear about the NIA, but they can't find any connection to any known terrorist group on Neophia."

"Told you," Crystal said with a smirk.

"That doesn't mean anything." Grady kept reading. "He was able to get his hands on a fragment of the coding they used to hack into the emergency broadcast system."

"Put it on the screen." Crystal turned to the third screen where moments later the code appeared. Crystal had no idea what she was looking at. It was just a jumble of letters and numbers.

"Have you guys been up all night?" Tyler stood in the doorway of the room looking at them with concern in his eyes. Was it really morning already?

"Just the man we need. Come take a look at this." Grady jumped up, grabbed Tyler's shoulders, and led him over to the screen with the code on it. "What can you tell us about this?

Tyler rubbed his eyes and studied the code. "This part

here is some kind of timed repeater." He pointed at a piece of the code. "I've never seen anything like the rest of it before. What is it?"

"It's a piece of the code the NIA used to hijack the emergency broadcast system," Crystal said.

"And here I was thinking that you two had been working on a strategy for the hearing." Tyler turned away from the screen to face them. "Anderson and Flint should be here soon. You two should go get dressed, and I'll see what I can get out of the code." He waved them out of the room before turning back to the screen. Crystal left without protest. It wasn't like she could help with the code. Besides a shower would help to recharge her. They still had to prepare for the hearing, though Crystal wasn't sure it would make any difference to the outcome at this point.

The car from the LAWON embassy was waiting outside of their apartment the next morning. Desi was grateful that her mom was still asleep and didn't see her getting in. Desi noticed she had skirted around any conversation involving Neophia, which was pretty impressive since Justin's parents had been full of questions last night.

Justin was already waiting in the car when Desi got in. He was quieter than normal and didn't even bother to look up from the tablet in his hand when she got in.

"Good morning to you, too." Desi closed the door and put on her seat belt. The car pulled away a moment later.

"Sorry. Hi," Justin said without looking at her.

"What's going on with you?"

Justin finally looked up from the tablet. Desi wasn't

sure she had ever seen him look so serious before. "Have you looked at the news at all?"

"When would I have had time for that?" They had spent the entire evening in his parents' living room. It wasn't like she could have watched the news without him knowing.

"Things have gotten bad since we've left."

"What do you mean?" Their access to American news stories had been limited while they were on Neophia, not that Desi ever really followed the news anyway. Still, she was certain that if something major had happened she would have heard about it.

"What did your mom say after you went home last night?" Justin asked.

"It was weird actually. She kept making comments about how dangerous Neophia is and how happy she was that I wasn't going back." The last part just slipped out. She hadn't told anyone her decision yet. She wanted to break the news gently when the time was right.

Justin gave her a strange look, but thankfully let her slip up go. "I'm not surprised. My parents told me that discrimination toward Neophians is on the rise. People here are scared of them."

"That doesn't make any sense. Neophians as a whole are relatively passive."

"I guess not anymore."

"What changed? I mean we've only been gone for six months." Desi looked out the window as if she would be able to see the answers on the street.

"It's better if you see for yourself." Justin handed her his tablet.

Desi reached for it carefully, as if it would bite her if she moved too fast. Justin already had a video cued up. All Desi had to do was hit play. An old news broadcast started. She recognized the anchor; he was the one they pulled out when something really bad happened.

"Five hundred sixty-three people are confirmed dead in the latest attack by the Neophian Integration Alliance. The bombings of sixteen hotels across the eastern seaboard is only the latest attack by the group that claims they won't stop until the United States formally acknowledges the debt that is owned to the planet of Neophia for all that they have provided to Earth over the last three hundred years. We take you now to the president of the United States, who has a message for the terrorist group."

The screen switched to an image of the oval office. The president sat behind his desk with a solemn look. "It is my sad duty to come to you today. This is the second attack by the NIA in only three weeks. Make no mistake that my office is doing everything in its power to catch those responsible for the tragic deaths of our people. But until we do, I want to make something very clear: The United States of America will never bow down to this group or the planet of Neophia. We were the ones that brought civilization to a planet full of people barely capable of creating homes, let alone the advanced technology we brought to them. We owe the planet of Neophia nothing. Until the terrorists are caught, I caution all citizens to have your guard up when dealing with anyone from Neophia. If they speak any kind of support for the NIA, please call one of the tip lines that have been set up. Stay strong my fellow Americans. We will get through this as we always do: together."

Desi could feel her insides grow colder with every passing word. She had never heard of the Neophian Integration Alliance. It concerned her that they had become a major threat in such a short period of time.

Had the U.S. intelligence community missed the signs that they were forming, or did they think Neophia was so weak that the NIA wasn't worth their time until it was too late? What really shocked Desi was the president's reaction to the attack. He had basically condoned violence again Neophians. What good could possibly come from that? At least now her mom's behavior made sense.

Desi handed the tablet back to Justin without looking him. "Well, retention numbers should start to improve now." There was always a surge of support for the military when something like this happened.

"Do you think it will affect the hearing?" Justin tucked the tablet back in his bag.

Poor naive Justin. "Are you kidding? Of course it will. We're walking into a room full of people who already think we're guilty. In fact, I wouldn't be surprised is the U.S. military called these hearing as a direct response to the NIA."

Justin sighed. "I wish I didn't agree with you."

"I hope Wolf can come up with some kind of plan to flip the tables, because I got nothing." Desi looked out the window. All those people out there didn't trust her, just because of the flags on the car and the uniform she wore.

Crystal quickly showered and changed. She was anxious to see what Tyler could tell them about the code. It was the biggest lead they had come up with. She ran into Jax on her way back downstairs.

"Good morning, Commander," Jax said in an overly cheery way. "I hope you slept well."

"I didn't get much sleep," Crystal said awkwardly.

She saw Jax's face fall. "I haven't adjusted to the time changes, that's all."

"That's understandable. I'm having breakfast laid out in the dining room if you care to join me." Jax gestured toward the dining room.

Crystal didn't want to be rude, but she really wanted to get back. "Actually, Lieutenant Grady and I kind of took over your library last night to do some work, and I need to get back. I hope you don't mind."

"Of course not. My house is your house while you're here. I'll have breakfast brought to you." Jax's overly large smile returned. "I've already sent the car to pick up Lieutenant Flint and Ensign Anderson. Shall I show them in there when they arrive?"

"That would be great, thank you." Crystal excused herself and quickly made her way back to the library. Grady was already back. He was standing with Tyler next to the board with the code.

"What have you figured out?" Crystal went over and joined them. Tyler had broken up the code into pieces and scribbled notes for each section.

"It's honestly a pretty straight forward code once you break it down. It looks like they added a lot of extra text and randomized the sequence to make it look more complicated than it is." Tyler crossed his arms and admired the code as if it were a painting.

Crystal looked over his notes carefully, not that she could understand a lot of it. "Anything in there tell us where to find these guys?"

"No. Maybe if I had the whole code, I could get a general location it was sent from, but there's no way to tell with just this piece."

"We should see if we can match the coding style up with any known hackers," Gardy said.

"Good idea. Get started on that." Crystal pointed at Grady.

Before Grady could move the door to the library opened. Crystal turned to see Flint, Jax, and Justin walk in. "You decided to get started without us?" Justin walked over and gave Crystal a kiss on the check

"Not exactly," Crystal said.

Desi was examining the detailed timeline Crystal had put together. "I guess we don't need to tell you about the NIA."

"You did all of this in one night?" Jax was looking from one board to the other.

"We were just killing time," Grady shrugged and slumped down on one of the couches. Natasha came in pushing a tray of food. Grady quickly straightened up.

Crystal rolled her eyes and turned back to the boards. "I'm sure the U.S. intelligence community is a lot further along than we are."

"They might be, but I'm sure they didn't get there as fast as you did." Jax walked from board to board taking in all the information they had pieced together.

"Commander Wolf and I use to run an anti-terrorist team on Neophia, so we have a lot of practice." Grady got up and went to where Natasha was setting up the food. He took a plate from her with a huge smile and started to load it with scrambled eggs, muffins, and fruit, while making small talk with Natasha.

Crystal went over to him and nudged him with her shoulder, "Hey moron," she whispered, "you're allergic to strawberries." He blushed and put his plate back down.

"As interesting as all of this is, I think we need to focus on the hearing tomorrow." Flint turned away from the boards and put her hands on her hips.

"You're right." Crystal went over to the boards and wiped them clean, but not before saving all the information to her tablet. She'd need something to work on if she had another sleepless night. "Craft said he would be sending some files about the Neophian officers currently participating in the program. How about we start there?" Crystal went over to the couch and grabbed her laptop. She hadn't actually looked to see if Craft had sent the files or not. As she waited for her messages to load, she caught Justin's eye and nodded toward Jax who was still hanging out in the room.

"Mr. Ambassador, I think we have everything we need right now." Justin ushered Jax and Natasha toward the door and shut it behind them.

"Thank you," Crystal said. Justin came over and sat down next her, putting his arm around her on the couch as he did. Crystal leaned back and gave him a quick kiss on the lips — something she wasn't comfortable doing in front of the ambassador and his daughter.

When Crystal turned back to her laptop, she saw that Craft had in fact sent her several files the night before. If she hadn't been so caught up in the NIA, she probably would have noticed them. Pushing the guilt aside, she opened the first one. It contained summaries of the service records for the thirty LAWON officers that had been sent to Earth. "All right let's see whose been acting as the face of LAWON here." Crystal clicked a button and sent the files to one of the boards so everyone could see.

"Shit," Flint said from the back of the room.

Crystal looked at the screen to make sure she had sent the right file. The only thing showing was a cover page with CONFIDENTIAL across it in big bold letters. She turned to look at Flint who wasn't looking at the board, but at the tablet in her hand.

"Justin check your messages," Flint said.

"What is it?" Tyler looked from Flint to Justin and back again.

"I've been ordered to report to the Pentagon for debriefing immediately." Flint put her tablet away.

"Me too." Justin stood up. "You think the ambassador will let us use the car again?"

"I'm sure he will." Crystal wasn't sure what else to say. She studied Justin's face. He looked more concerned than she had ever seen him. They all knew this was a possibility, even if she was hoping it wouldn't happen. She looked to Flint who was shifting her weight from one foot to the other as if she could run from the room at any minute.

Flint nodded. "We need to go. We don't want to give them a reason to think we aren't following order."

"Come back here when you're done, ok?" Crystal squeezed Justin's hand. She wished there was more she could do for him. Justin nodded and left with Flint.

Chapter 5

Desi and Justin were separated as soon as they set foot in the Pentagon. It was like the military thought Justin and Desi would gang up on them if they weren't separated. They were all U.S. soldiers. Did the LAWON patch on her uniform really make that much of a difference? These were people she had fought alongside for years before her six-month tour on Neophia.

Beyond the grunted "Follow me," Desi's escort didn't speak to her. He barely even looked in her direction as they moved through the halls. It was a very different experience than the last time she was at the Pentagon when they had been considering her for the Medal of Honor and a job as the military's spokesperson. A job that had driven her to Neophia in the first place.

She was shown into a small conference room. Every other time she had to give a debriefing, there was always someone waiting for her, but not this time. She knew it was a tactic to put her on edge, but she wouldn't let it. Waiting made her antsy, but she could hide that. She sat down at the table and forced herself to assume a relaxed posture.

Ten minutes later, the door open. Commander Gensen walked in with an over large smile on his face. Desi has served under him a few years ago, and while he wasn't the toughest commander she'd ever had, he wasn't good-natured either. Something was off. Desi rose to her feet and saluted.

"As you were." Gensen waved her back down into her seat, his smile never wavering. "Welcome home Lieutenant Flint." Gensen took a seat across from her.

"Thank you, sir." Desi eyed him carefully. She wished she knew what game he was playing. If he had come in here hot, demanding answers, Desi would have known how to handle it, but this false pleasantry was throwing her for a loop. She decided to go on the offensive. "Why am I here? We both know you didn't bring me in just to welcome me home. Why don't we cut through all the crap and get down to business?"

The smile on Gensen's face faltered, but he recovered quickly. "The U.S. military is anxious to hear the details of your deployment on Neophia. So little is known about the military strength of Neophia — and who better to provide us those details than our own people?"

Desi tried hard not to roll her eyes. Had she really been this clueless about Neophia before she went there? "You make it sound like Neophia is a single entity instead a planet with hundreds of countries and independent colonies."

Gensen folded his hands under his chin and leaned forward. "Why don't you educate me then?"

Damn it, Desi had fallen right into his trap. "I haven't memorized every nation on the planet."

"Then start with LAWON."

"The Lands and Waters of Neophia organization is a partnership between several nations on the planet. They pool their resources and work to keep peace and prosperity on the planet," Desi said, as if reciting from the LAWON handbook.

"How about the size of their military?"

"I'm assuming it's pretty big, though I only ever saw my ship." Desi leaned back in her chair. This was going better than she thought. At least she hadn't given up any sensitive information, and she hadn't even had to lie.

Gensen didn't seemed to be concerned about her lack

of answers so far, but Desi knew she wouldn't be able to get away with it forever. "Yes, let's talk about your ship. You served aboard the mega submarine *Journey,* which LAWON claims is the most technologically advanced sub on any planet. What can you tell me about it?"

"The officer quarters are twice the size and a thousand times nicer than anything we have on our ships." Desi wasn't afraid to play games too.

"I meant, what can you tell me about the ship's technology? How does it compare to our ships? What are its weaknesses?" Gensen asked.

This was what Desi had been waiting for. She was grateful that she only ever half listened to Wolf when she would drone on about *Journey's* details. "Look, I'm a fighter, not an engineer. Is the ship impressive? Yes. Does that mean that it's more advanced than ours? I have no idea."

"You're telling me that after six months on the ship, you can't remember a single detail about its design?" There was an edge in Gensen's voice now. Desi knew she was on thin ice.

Desi sighed. She had to tell him something. He was her superior, and if she pushed him too far, there would be hell to pay. "The ship runs on batteries that are recharged via the ships bio-skin. I don't know the specifics of how it works."

"Good. I was starting to wonder where your loyalties lay. After you ran away from the Medal of Honor, people started to wonder if you were going rouge."

"I just wanted to keep fighting instead of becoming the military's mouthpiece," Desi countered. "Why is that so hard to understand?" She threw her hands up. The very idea that anyone could think she would turn on the U.S. after everything she'd sacrificed was insane.

"I understand," Gensen said, sounding like he did — or that he wanted her to believe they were on the same side. Which, Desi reminded herself, they were supposed to be. "We're fighters: it's what gives our lives purpose, and you were always one hell of a solider. Which is why you're getting a second chance to prove yourself to the U.S. military." Gensen pulled out a tablet and slid it across the table to her. Desi looked at it cautiously, but didn't pick it up. "New orders." He nodded to the tablet.

Desi wanted to stand her ground, but her curiosity got the better of her. She picked up the tablet and scanned it quickly. She couldn't have read that right. This wasn't just new orders, it was a promotion. "Is this for real?" Desi read through it again, slower this time to make sure she was reading it right.

"Yes, and it's completely your decision if you want to take it or not. We are aware that Ensign Anderson has signed on for a second tour on *Journey,* which will be granted if the exchange program continues. We are also aware that you haven't made a decision on whether to continue on in the exchange program or return to Earth. This should make the decision easier for you." Gensen leaned back in his chair. It was clear he thought he had won the battle.

Desi looked down at it again. They were offering her command over the SEAL team covering South America. It was everything she had always wanted. She was tempted to jump on the offer right then and there, but something was holding her back. She had enjoyed her time on Neophia, more than she ever thought she would. Was she willing to give that up? The chances of ever going back were slim if she took this position. "I'm going to need to think about it." Desi set the tablet back down on the table. It couldn't be this simple. Were they trying to butter her up before the hearing to make sure she swung things the way they wanted? Did they think this promotion would loosen her tongue and she'd give up classified information about LAWON?

"Of course. You have a week to make up your mind. If we don't hear from you in that time, we'll assume you have declined the promotion. You're too important to the U.S. military to lose." Gensen got up and walked out of the room.

Justin was waiting outside when Desi finally made her way out of the Pentagon. He didn't say anything to her as they got in the car and rode back to the embassy. Desi didn't press him; she wasn't in the mood to talk either. All she could think about was the promotion they offered her and wondered what strings were attached. She knew there had to be some kind of catch. The military didn't reward rebellious behavior, and there was nothing more rebellious than refusing the Medal of Honor and leaving the planet. But it was her dream position, what she had been working toward her whole career. She couldn't pass that up, even with the strings attached.

They pulled up in front of the embassy. It felt like days had passed since they had left. Desi wasn't surprised to find the team still camped out in the library. She was relieved to see that there was no new information about the NIA plastered around the room. They needed to focus on the hearing. The debriefing had only increased Desi's concern that the U.S. military's interest in the Neophia wasn't entirely innocent.

"You're back." Wolf looked up from her laptop with a grim expression. Desi was afraid to ask what she was reading. "How did it go?"

Justin plopped down on the couch next to Wolf, who looked at him with concern. "Pretty terrible."

"What kind of stuff did they ask you?" Grady got up and went to the drink cart in the corner of the room. He poured two drinks and handed them to Desi and Justin.

"They wanted to know about the political landscape on Neophia," Desi answered, "but since I never really paid much attention to that I couldn't tell them much." She took a sip of her drink.

"Unfortunately, I know a lot more about that than you do." Justin drained his cup. The debriefing must have really shaken him.

"What did you tell them?" Wolf asked. Desi noticed she was working to keep the edge out of her voice. Wolf couldn't really be mad at Justin, could she?

"Some of the major countries that are members of LAWON. They were really interested in Teria and their recent actions to acquire new territories." Justin didn't look at Wolf as he talked. Desi didn't like the faraway look in his eyes. She had seen others wear it when they got home from the front, but Justin never had.

"They would have been able to piece all that together for themselves if they bothered to look it up. There's nothing classified there." Price patted Justin's shoulder from behind the couch.

"They also wanted to know about *Journey* and its technology. I don't think they liked that LAWON claims that it's the most advanced ship on either planet," Desi said.

"Did you tell them anything?" Wolf stood up and turned to face her.

Desi crossed her arms over her chest. "Just that it's battery powered, and that the ship's bioskin recharges them somehow."

"That is classified," Wolf said angrily.

"I had to answer the questions the best I could. I'm a U.S. solider, even if I've been serving with LAWON." What did Wolf expect? Desi couldn't lie to a superior officer.

"So that's all we were — a way to prove some kind of point to the U.S. military? Show them how valuable you are, and then sell us down the river?" Wolf's voice was a decibel or two louder than normal, though Desi wouldn't say she was yelling. Not yet.

Desi put her hands on her hips. It had been awhile since she had squared off with Wolf, but she was up for the challenge. "That wasn't my intention, but it worked."

"What do you mean it worked?" Price asked. Desi felt her smug smile fade as she looked at him.

"I was offered command of my own SEAL team. It's the most elite group in the Navy."

"Really?" Justin turned around on the couch to look at her.

"Yeah." Desi couldn't meet his eye.

"So that's it. You aren't coming back," Wolf said. "I guess we know whose side you're on."

"That's not fair," Desi said.

But Wolf didn't acknowledge her point. "Tell me, at the hearing were you even going to try to help us keep the program going?"

"Of course!" Desi protested. "I might be staying on Earth, but that doesn't mean I don't think good can come from the exchange program. I just have to do what's right for me, and this is the opportunity of a lifetime. Like it or not, I'm a U.S. solider first."

"Does it even matter to you that your military killed fourteen of our officers?" Wolf waved a hand toward her computer that lay forgotten on the coffee table.

That couldn't be right. Desi was rattled, but she couldn't let it show. "Maybe they shouldn't have signed up then."

Grady jumped in-between them. "That's enough. Everyone take a few minutes to cool off."

"Who put you in charge?" Desi challenged. Of course, Grady would jump in to protect Wolf. He always did.

"He's right." Wolf let out a deep breath. "We're still a team until the end of this mission. Let's call it for the day. I'm not sure how much we can prepare for the hearing anyway." Wolf turned and walked to the other side of the room.

Justin got up and went over to her. "Let's take a walk." He held his hand out to Wolf, who nodded and took it.

Desi stepped in front of the doorway to stop them. "I didn't mean what I said about your people. I'm sorry so many were lost while serving here."

"I know," Wolf sighed, "and I know that you're loyal to us even if you're not coming back at the end of this. I do trust you."

Desi nodded and stepped away from the door. There was nothing else to say. Somehow, she doubted it would be the last time she and Wolf would butt heads before the hearing was over. It was hard trying to be loyal to everyone. At some point Desi knew she would be forced to pick a side once and for all.

It was weird walking the streets on Earth. Crystal kept looking for trees or flowers, but there were none. She didn't understand how they could live this way. She held Justin's hand as they walked. For once, she wasn't worried about her communicator going off and pulling one of them away. It was a nice change, even if the landscape left a lot to be desired.

Justin stopped and turned to her. "Don't be too mad at Desi. It wasn't like they gave us much of a choice. They just kept asking questions until we told them something."

"Were you questioned together?"

Justin shook his head. "No, but I assume she was treated the same way that I was."

Crystal could feel the guilt radiating from him. She knew he had given them details about the ship or Neophia, but she was determined not to ask him about it. He felt bad enough already. The worst part was that while Flint might not have actually paid attention to the finer details for the how things ran, Justin did. He was a bigger threat to them than Flint was.

"So, you were offered a big promotion to return to Earth too?" Crystal shot him a teasing look she hoped would break the tension.

Justin chuckled. "Ok so not exactly the same. I'm clearly not as important to the military as she is." He took her hand and they started off down the sidewalk again.

"Where are we going?" Crystal asked.

"I figured I'd show you around a little. There's a river not too far from here."

"That sounds nice." She had only been away from *Journey* for a few days, and already she was missing the ocean. It would be nice to be near water again. Crystal wondered if she would be able to take a quick swim. That always helped to clear her head.

"My parents first met when they were both working in that warehouse over there." Justin pointed to a building with boarded up windows and a hole in the roof.

"Looks romantic," Crystal said not even bothering to hide the sarcasm in her voice. Still, there was something heartwarming about finding love in such a depressing place.

"It was different back then. This whole block use to be full of businesses."

"Used to be?"

Justin shrugged. "They all moved to another city with better tax breaks."

"What happened to the workers?"

"Those that could afford it moved too. Those of them that couldn't rejoined the military, which is what the government wanted anyway." Justin looked away, lost in thought again.

Crystal couldn't shake the feeling that they were being watched. None of the people they passed would make eye contact with her, and she was certain they picked up their pace to get past her faster. The people on the other side of the road openly stared as if she couldn't see them. A few even pointed at them while whispering to their companions. "This is a friendly place," Crystal whispered to Justin.

"What?" He must have been really lost in thought. She bet he didn't even realize how oddly people were behaving. Or maybe it wasn't odd behavior for Earth, and that's why he didn't think anything of it?

"Have you noticed that people are going out of their way to avoid us?" Crystal nodded toward a woman up ahead who was quickly crossing the street, dragging a small child by the hand. The woman hadn't even looked for oncoming traffic before stepping into the street.

Justin watched the woman and child dart down an

alley and out of sight. "Maybe she was in a hurry or something."

"They're afraid of us, of our uniforms, and where we're from. They think we're dangerous because we're from Neophia." Crystal was surprised by how much it hurt to admit it.

Justin squeezed her hand tighter and kept walking. They reached the river a few minutes later. Crystal had never seen water that color before. It was a deep brown with streaks of green running through it. The sight of it broke her heart. How could they destroy their water? Crystal was glad she hadn't brought up wanting to go for a swim. There was no way she would get in that. She turned away and leaned against the brick wall that lined the river's banks.

"We aren't going to win this time, are we?" Crystal turned to look at Justin, who was still facing the water with his hands folded on the top of the wall.

"What do you mean?" Justin didn't look at her as he stared across the water.

"The hearing. We're not going to be able to get the program renewed."

This time he did turn to look at her. There was a hint of panic in his eyes. "Don't say that."

Crystal sighed. "I'm just trying to be realistic. I honestly believe that your government is only holding the hearing as a way to humiliate the NIA and Neophia."

"That might be the case, but that doesn't mean we can't change their minds," Justin argued. "The program hasn't been canceled yet. Trust me, if the U.S. military didn't want it to continue, they wouldn't bother holding a hearing in the first place. There's still hope."

"But should there be?" Crystal diverted her eyes and looked down the street toward the abandoned warehouses they had passed. Part of her wished she could have seen this area in its prime. Maybe Earth was better back then.

"Crystal, what are you saying?"

She turned to face him. She knew what she was going to say was going to break his heart, but she had to be honest with him. "I'm not entirely sure that the program should be renewed."

"Why not?" She expected to hear despair, pain, or even anger in his voice. Instead it was flat.

"Almost half of the LAWON officers that came to Earth are now dead. I'm still waiting to get details on how they died, but regardless, the survival rate of the program is too low. How can I fight to keep the program going knowing that whoever will be sent to Earth will likely be killed? Is that the right thing to do for my people?" Crystal could see the spark of anger in Justin's eyes as her words sank in. She just wasn't sure if he was angry with her, the U.S. military, or both.

"I'm sure Craft is aware of the deaths, and he still sent us here to try to keep the program going," Justin pointed out. "Everyone knows that serving on Earth means going to war, and death is unfortunately part of that."

"Maybe," Crystal acknowledged, "but that doesn't mean we should be sending our people to fight someone else's war."

"So, what are you going to do tomorrow? Sit back and let the U.S. military humiliate LAWON? Because that's what they'll try to do." Justin waved his hands as he talked.

"You know me better than that. I'll follow Craft's orders." Crystal took both of his hands in hers. "But I think we need to be prepared for the possibility that we fail, and the program gets canceled, and…"

"And I don't get to go back to Neophia," Justin finished for her. The muscles in his body slacked, and he leaned back against the stone wall for support.

"This could be the end for us, and I want us both to be ready to face that if it comes to it." Crystal felt a pain shoot through her chest as she spoke the words they both had been avoiding for weeks.

Justin sighed and squeezed her hands. "Even if the exchange program is canceled, it doesn't mean that our relationship is over."

"Of course, it does. You'll be on Earth and I'll be on Neophia. We'll never see each other again."

"Crystal, I intend to make a life for myself on Neophia," Justin reminded her. "If the exchange program is canceled, then I'll find another way to get to Neophia. Maybe LAWON would let me enlist directly in their military since I've already been part of it, or I'll find a civilian job that gets me there. I'm not ready to give up on us, and I hope you're not either."

"I don't want to give up on us, but I think we need to be realistic so that we don't get hurt," Crystal said.

Justin's hands felt warm over hers, and she didn't want to let that go. "Let's just wait and see what happens," Justin said quietly. "There's no sense worrying about something that might never happen, right?"

Crystal nodded. "Right. Maybe the hearing isn't a ploy to try to humiliate LAWON, and they are really interested in knowing the full merit of the program." She tried to smile, but it was hard when she didn't believe the words she was saying.

"That's the spirit." Justin pulled her close and wrapped his arms around her. His smile faltered as he looked behind her.

Crystal turned to see a group of people making their way toward them. It was clear that they had been drinking and were yelling in their direction. They were still far enough away that Crystal couldn't make out what they were saying, but she doubted it was friendly.

"We should be heading back to the embassy. This isn't the safest part of town after dark," Justin said and started to lead her down the street away from the river and the group of drunks behind them.

Crystal looked over her shoulder again. She wasn't afraid of them. She could probably take them all on by herself if it came to it, but Justin was right. There was no reason to draw any unwanted attention to themselves, and she wouldn't want to miss the hearing because she had been thrown in jail.

Chapter 6

The scene outside the Pentagon was drastically different than the day before. Yesterday, they had been able to pull right up to the gate without any issues, but today their car was swarmed by reporters the second it slowed down. Desi shot Justin a look of concern but didn't say anything. She hadn't had a chance to talk to him since the argument with Wolf at the embassy the day before. She wanted to bring it up during the car ride over, but she had been waiting for him to start the conversation. He didn't.

"Do you think they're all here for us?" Justin slid away from the window.

"It certainly seems that way." Desi was glad that the car's windows were tinted. Their driver laid on the horn as he slowly inched the car through the gate. Desi figured once they were on the other side, they would be free of the media. She was wrong. Up ahead she could see reporters waiting on the steps to enter the building.

"Maybe Crystal was right, and this really is just a sunt for the government to try to discredit Neophia," Justin said. Desi wasn't sure why he was surprised. Of course this was a stunt to cast LAWON—and Neophia by extension, since it seemed no one understood the difference—in bad light.

"Then we'll just have to make sure that doesn't happen. Now come on." Desi opened the car door and the reporters surged at her.

"Lieutenant Flint, do you think we should continue relations with Neophia after the attacks of the NIA?" one reporter asked and shoved a microphone toward her.

"Do you think Neophians are dangerous?" another one asked.

"Do you think the exchange program should continue?"

"Will you return to Neophia when the hearings are over?"

Desi ignored them all and kept walking. Her eyes were fixed on the door in front of her. She hoped Justin was doing the same, but she couldn't risk turning around to check, in case any of the reporters took it as a sign of weakness. The onslaught of questions stopped once she crossed the threshold of the Pentagon. At least the reporters weren't allowed inside, though it was odd to have them there at all.

Wolf, Price, and Grady were waiting for them in the lobby. There was no one from the U.S. military with them. Desi wondered if anyone had even been sent to greet them. They were guests here after all.

"Glad to see that you made it through that in one piece." Desi gestured over her shoulder toward the reporters waiting outside.

"I have a lot of practice ignoring reporters," Wolf said

with half a smile. Wolf eyed the other people in the lobby. She was nervous, something Desi had rarely seen from her before.

"Do we know where we're supposed to go?" Justin asked.

"Not yet," Grady said. "Most people here seem to be going out of their way to avoid us actually." He nodded to the person closest to them, who quickly picked up their pace and passed by them with their eyes fixed ahead of them. "See what I mean?"

"Maybe that's just how things are here," Wolf suggested. "We don't know the customs. Try to have an open mind."

"Look who became the little politician overnight," Grady teased.

"Trust me, there's nothing normal about the way you're being treated," Justin growled. "I'm going to go find out where we need to go. Why don't you two come with me?" Justin patted Grady and Price on the shoulders, and the three of them walked away. Desi saw Justin turn back and shoot a knowing smile at Wolf.

"Now that we have a minute," Wolf started, she looked around the room to make sure they weren't being overheard before giving Desi her full attention. "I want to apologize for yesterday. I know you wouldn't betray us, and this is your home, and you have every right to want to return to Earth."

"And I get why you could view that as me turning on you, but that was never my intention," Desi said.

"I know. You need to do what's right for you. I get it." Wolf blew out a frustrated breath. "Part of me wishes that you were coming back to Neophia for *Journey's* second tour, but I understand if that's not the case. The boat won't be the same without you though."

A wide grin broke out over Desi's face. "You're going to miss me."

Wolf held up a finger. "That's not what I said."

Desi threw her arm around Wolf's shoulders. "Yes, it is. Who would have thought I would've wormed my way through your emotional steel wall straight to your heart?" Desi wiggled her finger at Wolf, bringing it to rest on her chest.

Wolf shook her head, but she had a smile on her face. "You know what? I take it back. Stay on Earth."

"Let's go kick some ass together, one last time." Desi led Wolf over to where the guys were waiting for them. She didn't remove her arm until someone finally showed up to escort them.

The hearing room was packed when they entered. Crystal expected to see it full of military personnel, but only about half the people in the room wore uniforms. The rest were dressed in civilian clothing — a lot of them hadn't even bother to dress up. Crystal wished she had known this was going to be an open hearing. They were already going to be fighting an uphill battle; she didn't need an angry audience to contend with on top of it.

Tyler turned around as they walked to the front of the room "Are these things normally televised?" He pointed toward the two people in the front corners of the room setting up camera.

"No, they're not." Flint shot Crystal a look, but didn't elaborate. She didn't need to; Crystal was thinking the same thing. They were only here to be the bad guys in the story the U.S. government wanted to tell the public. Well, wouldn't they be disappointed when they realized Crystal didn't fold that easily?

"These are real classy." Grady picked up a paper nametag off their table in the front of the room. "Apparently I've been demoted."

Crystal took a closer look at the name tag, which looked like an intern had printed at the last minute. Sure enough, it read Chief Grady. She picked up her own name tag. "I don't even have a rank." She rolled her eyes and threw it back on the table.

"At least your names are spelled right." Tyler held up a piece of paper that said Ensign Rice.

"I'm sorry guys." Flint looked genuinely embarrassed.

"It's not your fault. We all knew this wasn't going to be friendly terrain. At least now we know what we're up against." Movement on the other side of the room caught Crystal's eye. The LAWON officers that had been serving on Earth entered through a side door. They didn't make eye contact with anyone and went directly to their table to sit down. Crystal didn't know any of the them, but it didn't seem like the kind of behavior she expected from people that had volunteered to serve in a war zone. "If you'll excuse me for a minute, I want to go introduce myself to the other LAWON officers here."

It was only five steps from their table to the one opposite them. Crystal could see two of the LAWON soldiers tense up with every step she took in their direction. The third seemed more relaxed, but none of them turned to look at her. Crystal didn't understand it. These were her people.

"Hi. I'm Lieutenant Commander Wolf." Crystal held out her hand, but none of them moved. She would need to take a more direct approach. It's a good thing she had spent some time going over their files last night. She moved so that she stood directly in front of them. Good luck avoiding her now. "You're Lieutenant Tricia

Plourde, LAWON Air Force, right? You flew the chopper on the wildfire rescue mission in Kincaron two years ago. That was some impressive flying."

"Thank you, ma'am," Plourde said, still refusing to make eye contact with her.

Crystal decided to move on. "Ensign Vega, I believe you graduated from the Academy with Ensign Price." Crystal nodded toward Tyler and noticed that the rest of her team was watching her closely. "Did you two know each other?"

"We had a few classes together." Vega's voice was barely more than a whisper. It was like he didn't want anyone to notice that he was talking to her.

Crystal shook her head and moved on to her last hope, Commander Dominick Brinkman. She searched her mind for something that would make him engage with her, but it wasn't needed. He rose to his feet and held out his hand. "Commander Wolf, it's an honor to meet you."

"Likewise, Commander Brinkman." Crystal shook his hand. She looked over at the other two and noticed they had slumped down in their chairs, as if they were trying to make themselves as small as possible. Crystal turned her attention back to Brinkman. "How has your time on Earth been?"

Before Brinkman could answer a U.S. solider materialized next to them. He stood uncomfortably close to Crystal and puffed out his chest. She was sure he meant to intimidate her, but it wouldn't work. "Can I help you with something?" She turned to face him.

"I believe your table is over there." He pointed behind her.

Crystal didn't move. "You can't stop me from talking to my people."

"Oh can't I?" A side door opened, and the panel members started to file in. The hearing was about to start. Crystal needed to return to her seat, but she didn't want to give this guy the satisfaction. "Bye now." He mockingly waved in her face.

Crystal reluctantly turned and walked back to her side of the room. She sat down next to Flint. "Do you know that guy?" Crystal nodded toward the U.S. solider that had confronted her.

Flint's face was grim. "Yeah that's Captain Lance Corwin. We were SEALs together before I left. He's a real jackass."

Crystal couldn't stop herself from looking over at the other table as the members of the panel took their seats. Vega and Plourde looked as if they feared they would be attacked at any moment. She had never seen a LAWON officer behave like this. What had happened to them on Earth to make them so afraid? Brinkman, on the other hand, radiated frustration, which Crystal could understand. She needed to find a time to talk to him alone, especially since Corwin seemed so determined to keep her from him.

Desi couldn't believe that Corwin was here. Of all the people they could have chosen to represent the U.S. military, why did they have to choose him? He had done everything he could to undermine Desi's career. She had been forced to serve under him during her first year as a Navy SEAL. She was the only women on the team, and he made sure to single her out every chance he got. It didn't matter that she was a better soldier than every other member of the team, she was different, and in Corwin's eyes, that made her easy prey. It probably didn't help that she had shot down his advances on more than one occasion and had to file an official harassment complaint in order to leave his team. She knew he was pissed about that, even though it didn't affect his career. He was promoted just days after her transfer.

"If everyone could take your seats." The room went silent almost instantly. Desi recognized the man standing in the center of the head table. It was General Sloan. She had never served under him, but she knew people who had. He was one of the toughest, no nonsense generals in the military. Everyone she knew feared him.

"I want to thank everyone for taking the time to attend this hearing. Given the current climate, we have decided to open these proceedings to the public, so that they can get a better understanding of the government's relationship with Neophia," Sloan said. Desi shook her head. She knew damn well the only reason they opened the hearing up was to try and embarrass Neophia.

"We will be spending the next three days discussing the value of the officer exchange program with the Lands and Waters of Neophia Organization and whether it is in the best interest of the U.S. to continue it. We will begin with introductions. Ms. Wolf if you would be so kind to start us off." Sloan looked down at the tablet in front him as he spoke. Desi could feel her anger starting to grow. Was it really too much to ask that he have enough common decency to look at Wolf while he was addressing her?

Wolf slowly rose to her feet. Desi could feel the tension radiating through her. "It's Lieutenant Commander Wolf actually, though Commander is fine, if you prefer." There was a collective intake of breath from around the room. Wolf stared at Sloan until he was forced to look up from his tablet and make eye contact with her. No one else in the room had the guts to correct Sloan. Desi had no idea who would back down first. Every minute that passed felt like an eternity, and still Wolf didn't break eye contact. Desi sometimes forgot how much of a badass Wolf really was.

"My apologies Commander Wolf," Sloan finally said. There was no denying the sense of shock that filled the room. Wolf had managed to level the playing field a little. Desi couldn't understate how important the victory was. The U.S. military valued one thing, strength, and Wolf had made it clear to everyone that they wouldn't be intimidated.

"Now would you please introduce yourself and the rest of your team?" There was just a hint of anger in Sloan's voice that made Desi smirk.

"It would be my pleasure, General. As I said, I'm Lieutenant Commander Crystal Wolf. I'm third in command of LAWON's most advanced military vessel, the mega submarine *Journey*, a ship that I designed and oversaw the construction of. In addition to serving as the ship's head engineer, I also lead one of *Journey's* two combat team. Prior to serving on *Journey* I lead a counterterrorism team that was responsible for bringing down several of the most dangerous terrorist groups on Neophia."

Desi had never heard Wolf speak about herself like that before. She usually tried to downplay all that she had accomplished in her career. It was impossible not be impressed by her resume. The military would have a hard time discrediting her.

Wolf gestured to the rest of the table. "With me are two other officers from LAWON's military that serve on *Journey*. Ensign Tyler Price is our chief computer programmer and is by far the best programmer in LAWON. He has also been serving as a member of the ship's combat team under Lieutenant Flint, who appointed him as her second in command. Then we have *Lieutenant* Grady." Desi noticed that she put extra emphasis on his title. "Grady is a weapons expert, a subfighter pilot, and my second on the combat team. He has also spent several years working counterterrorism and special ops missions. Finally, we have the two U.S. officers that have been serving with us on *Journey*. Ensign Justin Anderson is our head pilot and member of my combat team, and of course Lieutenant Desiree Flint, who I'm sure needs no introduction here."

"Thank you, Commander," General Sloan said. Wolf nodded and took her seat. Sloan turned toward the other table, but Desi wasn't about to let them off the hook that easily.

"Before you move on General," Desi rose from her chair, "I'd like to say something."

"Yes, Lieutenant Flint," Sloan said through gritted teeth.

She thought about backing down, but if Wolf could stand up to him then so could she. She picked up the name tags on the table in front of Wolf, Price and Grady. "This is disgraceful." She threw the name tags on the floor. "These people were asked to come here and speak. They are your guests, and you can't even bother to get their names and ranks correct. You should all be embarrassed. I know I am." Desi sat back down.

"If you're finished, I'll let the other team introduce themselves," Sloan said.

Desi didn't pay attention as the others were introduced. They were from a ground force serving in Europe. There was another U.S. officer at the table with

Corwin, but it seemed Corwin was the one running the show. Their introduction didn't go beyond name and rank, except for Corwin, who felt the need to point out that he was once her commanding officer.

"Thank you, Captain." Sloan turned to address the room at large. "Today we would like to get an overview of how each of the teams feel the program has worked for them. We'll start with the team serving on Earth."

One of the officers stood up. "I've been serving on Earth for three months," he said with a shaky voice. He looked down at his hands briefly as if looking for notecards that weren't there. Had he been told what to say?

Wolf leaned over to Desi. "That's Ensign Vega. This is his first assignment." Desi nodded, as if she agreed that was the cause for his nerves. She noticed that Wolf had balled her hands into fists under the table.

Vega took a deep breath and looked at Corwin out of the corner of his eye. Desi would have sworn she saw Corwin nod. "I feel I was not prepared for service on Earth. The tactics of the military here are beyond what we are taught on Neophia. I've spent my time here feeling like I was constantly playing catch up and was a burden to my team."

Desi was shocked. After serving on Neophia, there was no way she could say that they were so far below the U.S. military in regards to training that having a LAWON officer on the team would be a burden. Sure, they might focus on different things at the LAWON Military Academy, but that didn't mean it was any less valuable.

Desi leaned over to Price, who was sitting on her other side. "You knew him right?" she whispered. "Was he a bad solider?"

"No," Price murmured. "He graduated in the top half of the class. I didn't know him well—he was always a little too full of himself for my taste." Price leaned forward to try to get a better look at Vega, who had reclaimed his seat.

The second LAWON officer stood. She stared at the blank wall in front of her. Her message was similar to the one before. She was not prepared for war on Earth, and she did not feel that she added any value to the team. Her voice was robotic. There was a broken-down quality to her that Desi couldn't place. It was different than the effects of war she had seen in other soldiers. Wolf was right; she was scared.

"She's a helicopter rescue pilot," Wolf muttered under her breath. "She never should have been placed with a ground unit." Her arms were now crossed over her chest, and she was shaking her head. There was no way the panel hadn't noticed.

The third LAWON officer stood—the one Corwin wouldn't let Wolf speak to. He didn't start speaking right away like the others had. Instead he looked from Wolf to Corwin, and then back again. Desi couldn't see Wolf's face, but she was sure that Wolf's gaze was boring into him. Desi had been on the receiving end of that stare a time or two, and she didn't envy the guy. In her experience, it almost always ended with Wolf getting what she wanted.

The solider took a deep breath and turned to Sloan. "My experience here has been vastly different from the others. I feel like I had a lot to offer my team, however I was met with resistance at every turn. The soldiers I worked with were not willing to listen to my suggestions or learn a different tactic that could have resulted in lives saved. I will agree that war here is unlike anything we have faced back on Neophia, but that doesn't mean our experiences are not valid. I feel that the military did not take full advantage of the program."

Voices erupted as soon as he finished speaking. Wolf shot Grady a smirk, but Desi didn't join in their celebration. She was too busy watching the panel. This would be the moment they would know for sure if this hearing was legitimate or just an excuse to embarrass Neophia. Sloan was motioning for quiet in the room, but it was a woman Desi didn't know who spoke first.

"Commander Brinkman, do you honestly feel that you could have saved lives if your suggestions were taken on the battlefield, even though you have zero wartime experience prior to your service on Earth?"

"Yes, ma'am, I do," Brinkman said, with the same confidence he had spoken with earlier. Desi sighed. Couldn't he see that she was just trying to set him up?

"That's funny, since units with a LAWON officer have seen an increase in deaths since the start of the program," the woman continued angrily. "In fact, a large percentage of the LAWON officers serving on Earth have been killed in action. That doesn't give a lot of confidence in your military's ability."

Desi glanced over at Brinkman; he seemed to be at a loss for how to respond. That was ok, because she had plenty to say. "That's not fair." Desi rose to her feet. "The units that hosted LAWON officers were sent to some of the most dangerous warzones on the planet, so of course they have higher death counts. If anyone had actually bothered to listen to the LAWON officers, those death counts would probably be a lot lower, since they are taught to value life over the mission — a lesson we could use here."

"Are you finished Lieutenant Flint?" Sloan asked

through gritted teeth.

For a second Desi thought about sitting down, but she looked down at Wolf who nodded. If anyone had a chance of getting the panel to listen, it was her. "No, I'm not. It seems to me that the military set the LAWON officers up for failure from the moment they set foot on Earth. Did you even consider their past experiences before placing them? I mean, Lieutenant Plourde is a helicopter pilot, and you have her serving with a ground unit. What moron thought that was a good idea?"

"That's enough, Lieutenant," Sloan said, not giving her the opening to continue. "I believe now is a good time to take a short recess. We will reconvene in thirty minutes." Sloan got up and walked out of a door on the side of the room. The rest of the panel followed quickly behind him.

Chapter 7

Crystal headed directly to the bathrooms once the panel was gone. The whole morning had been so mentally taxing she needed a few minutes alone to get her head straight before they continued. She couldn't understand why the officers from LAWON had spoken so poorly about themselves and their training. She had no doubt that the LAWON Military Academy would have prepared them for anything they faced on Earth. The only reasonable assumption she could make was that they had been forced to make those comments. She just needed to find a way to prove it.

The morning hadn't been an entire loss. Crystal was sure that Brinkman's testimony, at least, had been honest, though it still bothered her that Corwin had prevented her from speaking to him. She would have to find some time to talk to him in private to find out what he knew about the others. Flint had been a surprising bright spot. Crystal never expected her to speak so candidly about the U.S. military, especially since Crystal was pretty sure Flint would take the promotion they'd offered her when this was all over. She felt guilty for ever questioning Flint's loyalty to them.

The bathroom was empty. Crystal went over to the sink and splashed water on her face to help her focus. She would give anything for a cup of kiki. She needed to prepare to tell their side of the story. She had no doubt she could make the panel see that the U.S. soldiers brought value to Neophia. What she really needed to do was convince them that there was also value in it for the U.S. military.

Crystal looked in the mirror and pushed a stray lock of hair behind her ear. That's when she noticed someone standing behind her watching her. A woman leaned against the wall behind her. Crystal didn't turn around. All she wanted was a few moments alone to recharge for the coming fight; the last thing she needed was a confrontation in the bathroom with some random woman. Crystal washed her hands and hoped the woman would leave.

"I know who you are," the woman said to Crystal's back.

Crystal sighed. There was no getting out of it now. She grabbed a towel to dry her hands before turning around to face the woman. "Have we met?" Crystal was certain she had never seen the woman before in her life.

"No, but I was in the hearing room this morning. I don't know what you're trying to prove in there. You'll never be as good as us." The woman didn't move. Crystal looked her over. She had lieutenant stripes on her naval uniform. Her name tag read O. Ruiz. She was small in stature, but her body language was fierce.

Crystal took a few steps closer to her. She tossed the

paper towel in the trash next to her. "You know, I've only been on this planet for two days, and I'm already tired of people who know nothing about us telling me that we are weaker than Earth, when anyone with common sense would be able to see that Neophia is the superior planet. We have clean water, air we can breathe without machines cleaning it for us first, more natural resources than you could dream of, and peace. But sure, we're the weaker ones." Crystal rolled her eyes and tried to step around Ruiz, but the women moved to block the door.

"That's just a testament to our strength," Ruiz protested. "This planet tried to kill us, but we wouldn't let it."

Crystal knew she should have walked away, but if LAWON wanted a politician to represent them, then they should have sent someone else. She couldn't pretend to be someone she wasn't. "What do you have against Neophia anyway? We provide Earth with resources they wouldn't have otherwise, and still you act like we are so far beneath you. Let me remind you that Earth needs Neophia a lot more than we need you."

"I lost someone I love to Neophia, and the damn officer exchange program," the woman raged. "You people stole him from me, and I know I'll never get him back now. So, excuse me if I'm not going to bend over backwards to welcome you here. Just go home and leave us alone before you ruin any more lives." The woman stormed out of the bathroom.

Crystal was at a loss for words. As far as she knew, they hadn't lost a single member of the exchange program on Neophia. In fact, there have been very few deaths over the last year — one of LAWON's best years since the end of the Great War. Crystal could only assume that Ruiz was trying to mess with her. To get in her head before she had to speak again. Crystal wouldn't let it work.

Desi stood in the hall outside the hearing room with Justin. She had pulled him away from the other people congregating so they wouldn't be overheard. "What do you make of it so far?" she asked in a hushed voice.

Justin sighed. It wasn't a good sign. Had the military finally broken her enteral optimist? "I'm not buying any of it. The LAWON officers had to of been coached on what to say. It was nice to see Brinkman go rouge though."

"I hope he doesn't pay for it later." Desi glanced around the people in the hallway, but found none of the LAWON officers out there.

"I hope you don't either," Justin said. "Calling them out like that was pretty risky, especially if you stay."

"Someone had to say something, and I figured the panel would listen to me more than if any of the others spoke up."

A door behind Desi slammed open, and she turned to see Olivia Ruiz storming out of the bathroom. Their eyes locked, and Olivia stopped dead in her tracks. It was like she had seen a ghost. Only Olivia wasn't looking at Desi anymore—she was looking at Justin.

A second later Olivia's arms were draped around Justin's neck. "I've missed you so much." Desi thought she saw a tear rolling down Olivia's cheek.

"Hi Liv," Justin said weakly. Desi knew Justin and Olivia had dated for years, but she had never gotten a clear answer from Justin on how things ended. She guessed it hadn't been that bad of a breakup, given that

Olivia had hugged him instead of slapping him.

Olivia finally pulled away, but kept her hands on Justin's shoulders. She looked him up and down. "I'm glad to see you're in one piece. I hated that you were on that planet, and they could do god knows what to you."

"You make it sound like they were using us for target practice," Desi said. She looked up and down the hall for Wolf. The last thing Desi needed was for Wolf to see Justin in another woman's arms. She wasn't sure if it would cause Wolf's anger to flare up or if she would shut down completely. Neither was a good option. Desi wasn't even sure if Justin had told Wolf about his past relationships.

"Who knows what those savages are capable of?" Olivia continued fiercely.

"They aren't savages." Justin took Olivia's hands from his shoulders and put them down at her side. "What happened to you? We used to talk about going to Neophia all the time, and now you're talking like they're the enemy."

"They are." Olivia looked from Justin to Desi. "You guys weren't here. You didn't live through the attacks. I lost two of my cousins in the subway attack. Seven and ten years old. They were on their way to school. So, don't go telling me the Neophians aren't the enemy."

"You can't lump them all together like that," Justin protested. "A small group claiming to be from Neophia did terrible things, but that doesn't make the rest of the planet evil."

"That's easy for you to say. You've been brainwashed, Justin. It's time for you to open your eyes to how things really are." Olivia had clearly lost her mind. It was a shame—her fiery personality had been what Desi liked best about her.

"He's not the one that sounds brainwashed," Desi said under her breath. Part of her felt like she should leave, but the longer Olivia talked, the more Desi thought Justin might need some backup. Besides, one of them had to keep an eye out for Wolf, and Justin was a little distracted.

Olivia ignored Desi's comment and gave Justin her full attention. "You'll see now that you're home. We'll start over, and I'll help you understand how things are now." She reached for Justin's hand, but he pulled it away. Maybe their breakup hadn't been all that clean. How could Olivia think they were getting back together? As far as Desi knew, Justin hadn't spoken to her since they left Earth six months ago.

"I'm not staying. I'm going back to Neophia to serve another tour. I'm only here for a six-week leave." His voice cracked slightly as he spoke.

Desi looked over Justin's shoulder and saw Wolf coming out of the bathroom. Now they were in for a showdown. She tried to get Justin's attention, but it was like she wasn't even there. He only saw Olivia, and the hurt in his eyes caused Desi to pause. Did Justin still have feelings for Olivia? Desi wasn't sure if she was relieved or disappointed that Wolf walked right by them without even glancing in their direction. There was a look of pure determination on her face. Desi knew Wolf was preparing for battle.

"And what if the panel decides to shut the exchange program down? What will you do then?" Olivia asked.

"I'll figure out another way to get back there," Justin said. "If you had seen it, you would understand. None of the things being said about Neophia are true. The planet is beautiful, and the people there are so welcoming. It's everything we ever dreamed it would be."

Olivia shook her head. "I don't have time for dreams anymore. It's time to grow up, Justin."

"I have grown up, Liv." Justin tapped his chest. "Enough to believe the information I've gotten from my own experience, not some trumped up propaganda the news casts are pushing. And if you can't see that, you're not the person I thought you were."

The tension was becoming too much for Desi to take. She looked down at her watch and was grateful to see that the hearing was going to start back up in five minutes. "We better get back inside." Desi grabbed Justin's arm and pulled him away from Olivia. She stopped just before the doors. "What happened between the two of you? Did you guys ever actually break up?"

Justin looked down at his hands. "Not really. We hadn't seen each other in over a year when I took the assignment on *Journey*. Our deployment schedules just hadn't lined up. We both agreed that it was better to take a break until we were both in the same place again. The long-distance thing wasn't working. So when I went to Neophia I figured that was it."

Desi shook her head. Poor naive Justin. It was no wonder Olivia thought they would get back together once he was home. "Does Crystal know about her?" Desi nodded toward where they had left Olivia but she was gone.

"No." Justin looked ashamed. "Crys knows I had a girlfriend on Earth but not much else. I honestly didn't expect to ever see Olivia again."

"Take my advice. You need to tell her, before she finds out on her own." Desi patted him on the back and walked into the hearing room.

Crystal took her seat with a renewed sense of purpose. She wasn't just fighting for the exchange program anymore, she was fighting for the respect of her whole planet. The perception of Neophia was so far from the truth that she decided to take it upon herself to change it. No one else from her team was at the table when she got back, but she did notice that all their name tags had been fixed. She would take whatever win she could get at this point. The panel members started to file in, and the rest of her team reappeared at their table. They all looked a little beaten down and distracted.

General Sloan scanned the room, and everyone quickly took their seats. Crystal looked over her shoulder. There seemed to be even more spectators there than before the break. If they had come to see the U.S. military try to humiliate them, they were going to be in for an unpleasant surprise.

"We will now hear from the LAWON team. Please give an overview of how you found the exchange program," Sloan said.

Crystal rose to her feet. "I was extremely skeptical of having officers from Earth on *Journey*. Everyone on Neophia knows of the constant wars on Earth, and I thought having them on the team would be a determent to our role as the head of LAWON's peacekeeping mission. The people of Neophia view people from Earth as violent, arrogant, and short tempered."

"That's just ridiculous," said a member of the panel. He looked down at Crystal in disgust. Crystal tried to stay calm. She needed to speak rationally if she was going to have any chance of having them listen to her.

Crystal was about to respond when she noticed Flint rising to her feet. "Is it too much to ask to show a little respect? Besides, all you're really doing is proving

Commander Wolf's point." Flint's reputation must give her more leeway than Crystal realized.

"My apologies Commander Wolf, please continue," Sloan said.

"Thank you, sir," Crystal nodded. "As I was saying, I was unsure how the officers from Earth would fit in. I was pleasantly surprised to find that my concerns were unfounded. While it did take some time for them to learn our ways, they brought a lot of strengths to our team. The key to our success has been in allowing the officers from Earth to offer their input and really listening to it—something that sounds like it has been lacking from the program on Earth. Our two planets are much more alike than you realize, and the exchange program has allowed us to have a better understanding of our two cultures."

"Of course, you would think that," the panel member said shaking his head. "Neophia has taken so much from Earth you probably don't even know what your planet's culture even is."

Flint was on her feet again. "This is supposed to be our chance to give our views of the program, and we don't need the running commentary trying to undermine what we have to say. We have so much to learn from LAWON, if only we could keep our mouths shut long enough to hear it." Crystal slowly sat back down. If Flint wanted to fight this battle, then she wouldn't stop her.

"Since you seem so eager to talk, Lieutenant Flint, why don't you tell us your thoughts on the exchange program. And I ask that the panel please keep all comments to yourself." Sloan looked pointedly up and down the table at the other panel members.

"I only signed up for the exchange program as a last resort to try to stay in the field," Flint admitted. "When I arrived on Neophia, I thought there was nothing they could teach me. I was the best, after all." Flint paused as a small chuckle echoed through the room. "I had never been more wrong about anything in my entire life. There is so much that we don't know about Neophia and what they can do. Their military strategies might be different than ours, but that doesn't make them any less effective. In a lot of ways, their policies are so much better than ours. The LAWON military values the lives of their soldiers far more than the U.S. military. They put procedures in place to protect those lives, even if it means losing a mission. That's why there have been no deaths of U.S. soldiers while serving on Neophia, because LAWON goes out of their way to protect their people. If the U.S. military did the same thing, maybe you wouldn't have the retention problems you do now."

Crystal couldn't believe what Flint was saying. This was her military she was speaking about. A military Crystal suspected Flint would be returning to after her leave. Flint hadn't come out and said she'd be taking that promotion yet, but Crystal knew that's what she wanted. Earth was Flint's home, and she had to miss it, even if Crystal couldn't see the appeal.

"If anything, we have more to learn from the Neophians than they can learn from us," Flint said. "We just have to be smart enough to see it. It's a shame you have squandered that opportunity by not taking full advantage of the soldiers that have been serving here. How many lives could have been saved if you would have gotten past your collective egos and listened?" Flint stared down each member of the panel, as if she was daring them to respond. No one did. With a satisfying nod Flint took her seat.

Sloan took a deep breath. "I think that's a good place to leave it for today. Tomorrow we will begin the question and answer portion of the hearing." Sloan got up and left the room. The second he was out of sight the room erupted in conversation. Crystal heard the word traitor thrown out more than once from the rows of people behind here. Did Flint realize the target she had put on her back?

Crystal leaned over to the others. "We need to leave, now." She could feel the anger of the spectators baring down on them. They needed to get out of there before anyone decided to act on it. The others nodded and together they made their way out of the room, doing their best to ignore the insults being hurled at them.

Chapter 8

No one said anything on the drive back to the embassy. Grady and Tyler looked as drained as Crystal felt, and they hadn't even had to speak yet. Crystal was looking forward to turning in early for a change.

"So, what's the plan for the rest of the night?" Grady asked as they got out of the car and started to make their way up the front steps to the house.

"I have a debriefing call with Craft. You two have the rest of the night off. Feel free to go out and soak up more of the local culture if you want. I'm staying in." Crystal gave Grady a pointed looked before he could even suggest they go find a bar.

"I think I've had enough of that for one day." Tyler held the door open for them.

Natasha was waiting for them in the entryway, holding a tablet she kept checking every few seconds. "Oh good, you're back. No one was sure how long the hearing would go. I've been too busy getting things ready here to watch any of the broadcast. How did it go?" She tapped her tablet a few times before giving them her full attention.

Grady slid forward so that he was in Natasha's line of sight and flashed her a smile. "It was rough, but I'm confident we'll win them over in the end."

Crystal was about to say something when she noticed a flurry of activity in the large room behind Natasha. The furniture was being moved out and replaced by several high-top tables. A band was setting up in the corner and a huge buffet was being laid out in the dining room next to them. "I'm sorry, getting ready for what exactly?" Crystal asked.

"For the welcome ball my father's hosting tonight in your honor." Natasha looked from Grady, to Tyler, and back to Crystal. "It's been planned ever since the hearing was announced two months ago. He even cleared it with Admiral Craft to make sure he wouldn't get you in trouble." Her shoulders slumped. "I take it from the looks on your faces that you don't know anything about it."

"No we didn't." This was the last thing Crystal wanted. She had already spent the whole day playing politician; she didn't want to spend the rest of the night doing the same thing. Parties called for small talk and pleasantries. Two things Crystal hated.

"Well if you need anything to wear, or your uniforms pressed, just let me know and I'll make sure it's taken care of." Natasha glanced down at her watch again. "People should start arriving in about three hours, so you still have plenty of time to get ready."

"We should be fine. I just need to call Admiral Craft." Crystal took a few steps toward the staircase.

"Of course. I'll make sure no one disturbs you."

"Thank you." Crystal made her way up the stairs with Grady and Tyler. When they reached the landing, she turned to Tyler. "Can you call Flint and Anderson and tell them about the party?"

"Sure thing. Do you want us to stick around while you call Craft?"

"No, I'll handle it. You guys go get ready." Crystal turned and entered her room. She pulled out the signal booster and set it up on the desk in the corner of the room. She took a deep breath before sitting down and dialing up Craft.

It took longer than usual for his face to appear on her screen. "Commander Wolf, I'm glad to see you made it to Earth in one piece," Craft said with a huge smile. He was still in the office. Crystal tried to figure out what time it would be on Neophia, but she couldn't remember the conversion. "Tell me how the first day of the hearing went."

"It's been more challenging than I expected," Crystal answered. "It seems like the main goal of the hearing is to discredit and embarrass Neophia. My guess is that it's in response to the attacks by the Neophian Integration Alliance."

"Yes, I saw your messages about them. I have people looking into it, but so far we haven't found anything credible about them here." Craft shook his head in frustration.

"Lieutenant Flint has been able to make a little headway with the panel, but I'm not sure it'll be enough to persuade them to continue on with the program," Crystal continued. "Our people that have been serving here aren't going to be much help. Their behavior suggests they are afraid of retaliation from the U.S. military if they say anything besides what they've been told to say."

"That is disappointing."

Crystal wiped her hands on her pants under the desk. She had always had a good relationship with Craft, but that didn't make what she wanted to say any easier. "Sir, may I speak freely?"

"Of course."

"Given the number of LAWON officers that have been killed while serving on Earth, I'm not sure that it's in our best interest to continue with the program." Crystal felt a knot in her stomach form as the words came out of her mouth. She thought of Justin getting ready for the party on the other side of town. He always looked so amazing in his dress uniform. If Craft agreed with her, this might be the last time she would see him in it.

"I understand why you would think that," Craft acknowledged, "but I need you to focus on the bigger picture. There is so much tension between the two planets that we need some sort of bridge if we ever hope to get past it. The exchange program can be that bridge. I need you to help them see that."

"I understand, sir," Crystal said with a nod.

"Now don't you have a party to go get ready for?" Craft asked with a sly smile.

"Yeah about that," She slipped into a more casual tone of voice. She had known Craft for most of her life and had grown close to him while she was dating his son at the Academy. Even though things hadn't worked out with Ryan, Craft never held that against her. "Why didn't you tell us?"

"Because I know you, Crystal, and if I had told you ahead of time, you would have found some reason to get out of it." Crystal could feel her cheeks turning red. Craft was right, of course. She had already tried to think of an acceptable excuse to skip it.

Craft gave her a gentle smile. "I'm doing this for your own good. You need to know how to deal with politicians if you ever want to captain your own ship. Consider this a training mission."

"I'll do my best." Her voice lacked the enthusiasm she knew Craft was hoping for.

"And try to have a little fun while you're at it. Jax knows how to throw a good party." Craft ended the call. Crystal leaned back in her chair and eyed the bed longingly. It felt like this day would never end. She took a deep breath and forced herself out of the chair. She pulled out her dress uniform and made her way to the bathroom.

"Mom, I have to go. This is my job." Desi adjusted her uniform in the mirror. She always liked how her dress whites looked on her. She was excited when Price called to inform them of the party the ambassador was throwing in their honor. It would be a great way to unwind from the stress of the hearing. And who knew — maybe after a few cocktails, people might be more willing to listen to truth about Neophia. Though Desi wasn't sure anyone from the panel or the other team would show up to a party meant to welcome and celebrate Neophians.

"You're going to a party, not some important mission," Desi's mom protested.

"No, I'm attending an event my commanding officer requested my presence at." Desi pulled out her makeup and started applying some eyeshadow. She wondered if she should head over to the embassy early to help Wolf with her make up. Desi was pretty sure the last time Wolf had worn any was when Desi helped her get ready for her first date with Justin. It was hard to believe that was six months ago, or that the two of them were barely even friends at the point.

"A request, not an order." Her mom stood behind her in the mirror and crossed her arms. "You could skip it if you wanted to."

Desi looked at her over her shoulder. "Well I don't want to." She turned back around and picked up her lipstick.

"Do you have to go in that car with the flags they keep sending over?"

"The LAWON embassy is on the other side of town. You don't really expect me to walk, do you?" Desi stood up and gave herself a quick once over. She looked fabulous. She brushed past her mom on her way out of her bedroom.

"You could take the bus." Her mom followed her into the living room.

"Mom." Desi whipped around to make sure her mom could see the annoyance on her face. This was getting out of hand. Desi was grateful that her mom had been working this afternoon and hadn't seen the broadcast of the hearing. She might have tried to lock Desi in her room if she had heard what Desi said to the panel.

"At least have the driver take the flags off the car," her mother pushed. "It's putting a target on you. What if something were to happen to you or Justin because they thought you were from Neophia?"

"You're being ridiculous."

"Desi, they're dangerous."

"Who's dangerous mom? The Neophian terrorists or the humans targeting anything even remotely associated with Neophia? You can't have it both ways." Desi let out a deep breath and shook her head. "This isn't like you," she said in a calmer voice. "You raised me not to judge people that are different, and here you are doing just that. I expected more from you." Desi picked up her jacket and walked to the door. She grabbed the handle, but turned back to face her mom. "You'd better be pleasant when you meet them tomorrow night."

"I'm not meeting them."

"Yes, you are. We're all having dinner at the Andersons' tomorrow. So, you'd better get over whatever all this is," Desi said, gesturing toward her mom. "These people are important to me, and if you're rude to them, maybe I'll have to rethink my decision to stay on Earth." Desi opened the door and slammed it behind her.

Desi's anger disappeared as soon as she saw Justin standing next to the car in his dress whites. He opened the door for her and bowed. "Your chariot, my lady."

"Why thank you, kind sir," Desi drawled with a chuckle. She got in the car. Justin gently closed her door. A second later he entered the car from the other side. "You're awfully chipper this evening," she said.

"Well, why not? How often are we the guests of honor at big government party? I say we live it up."

"I'm all for it. Today was insane, and I could use a distraction."

"Yeah, but you kicked ass today." Justin playfully reached over and gave her a little shove. "I thought a few of panel member were going to have a heart attack after your little speech."

"That was pretty great, wasn't it?" Desi said with a huge grin. She hadn't really let herself celebrate what she had accomplished today.

"So why are you so distracted?" Justin turned in his seat so that he was looking at her.

"It's my mom." Desi sighed. "She's changed so much since I've left. She is so prejudiced against anything having to do with Neophia that she actually suggested we would be safer taking the bus than riding in a car with LAWON flags on it."

"After everything we've seen over the past two days, are you really surprised?"

"I am. Growing up she always taught me to accept others. I guess I want her to be better than everyone else. To not let all the negative press cloud her judgement."

"Speaking of the press." Justin nodded his head toward Desi's window. They had just pulled up to the embassy. Even though they were an hour early for the party, the press was already lined up along the steps to the house.

"Are you ready for this?" she asked Justin.

"I'm not the one they want to talk to." Justin got out of the car first and made his way around to her side. While a few people took his picture, most of the reporters didn't pay him any attention. Desi knew that would change as soon as she stepped out of the car.

She took a deep breath, then nodded at Justin to open the door. The press was on her the second her feet hit the sidewalk. She braced herself for the questions. It felt like they were throwing stones at her. She knew standard protocol was not to engage with the press, though she was tempted to respond. She heard the word traitor being thrown out more than once. It took everything in her to ignore it. She focused on the front door. She knew the media wouldn't be allowed inside. Once she made it there, she would be safe

Chapter 9

Crystal had been dressed for the last half hour but was putting off heading downstairs for as long as possible. She was not looking forward to the party. She groaned when she heard a knock at the door, assuming it was someone coming to force her downstairs. She was pleasantly surprised to see Flint on the other side when she opened it.

"I came to see if you needed any help getting ready." Flint held up a cosmetic bag. "But I see someone's already beat me to it."

Crystal stepped aside to let her in. "Yeah, Natasha, the ambassador's daughter, sent a team of professionals."

Flint walked around her, inspecting her hair and makeup. "They did good work." Flint turned her gaze to take in the rest of the room. "Maybe we should have stayed here with you guys. This is a pretty nice room they set you up in."

"It's all a little excessive if you ask me. The cars, the

party, all of this." Crystal motioned toward her hair.

"Hey, at least someone is happy to have you here. You should enjoy it."

Crystal sat down on the edge of the bed. "Have people started to show up yet?"

"A few. The guys are already down there hitting up the bar. I suggest we go join them." Flint held out her hand.

"If we have to." Crystal grabbed her hand and let Flint pull her up off the bed. The two went downstairs arm in arm. It didn't take long to spot the guys standing around one of the high-top tables in the back corner of the room. They didn't look eager to mingle either. Crystal wondered if they could get away with passing the evening unnoticed, but then she remembered what Craft told her. She would never be given her own ship if she couldn't learn to talk to politicians. She would have to mingle at some point.

"These are for you." Grady picked up two glasses of wine from the table and handed them to Flint and Crystal.

"They didn't have anything stronger?" Flint took her glass of wine and took a big sip. Crystal was tempted to do the same.

"I thought it best to pace ourselves. Jax mentioned the party is likely to go pretty late," Tyler said.

Crystal rolled her eyes and took a sip of her wine. "Fantastic." She turned her attention toward the people slowly filing in the door. Jax and Marcell were there to greet each of them. It looked like they knew everyone personally. If that's what it took for her to get her own ship, it would never happen. She had a hard enough time remembering people's names, let alone personal details about each of them.

She turned back to the table, but the conversation had moved on without her. From what she could tell, the others were in the middle of a very heated conversation about which planet had better food. Crystal thought there was a clear winner, but didn't have the energy to join in. The band had started to warm up. She wondered if anyone would dance or if it was just there to provide background noise. She probably should have spent her downtime researching party etiquette on Earth instead of begrudging the fact that she had been forced into attending.

"Excuse me, Commander Wolf." Jax was by her side. She hadn't noticed him leaving his post at the door. Crystal quickly scanned the room again. There were a lot more people there than she realized. "Would you do me the honor of the first dance of evening?" Jax held out his hand to her.

The last thing Crystal wanted was to be the center of attention, but she took his hand anyway. "It would be my pleasure." See she could totally do this politician thing if she needed to. She let Jax lead her to the center of the room. People moved aside to give them space.

Jax took her in his arms and nodded to the band. A moment later the room filled with music unlike anything Crystal had ever heard before. It was slow and sweet. It had an ancient quality to it. It was nothing like the up-tempo songs she normally danced to with Grady on the rare nights he could convince her to go out. Jax moved her gracefully across the dance floor. She focused on the footwork so she wouldn't notice all the people in the room watching her. People she was pretty sure hated her because of the planet she'd been born on.

She noticed someone dancing next to them. Flint was dancing with Marcell. Crystal glanced around. Several other couples filled the dance floor. Crystal was surprised to see Tyler dancing with Natasha. She looked around to see if she could spot Grady sulking somewhere. That's when she noticed Justin dancing with someone. The woman's back was to Crystal, and she couldn't tell who the woman was. From the way Justin was laughing, Crystal assumed the two of them knew one another.

"I'm sorry if all of this is a little much," Jax said pulling her attention away from Justin.

"All what?" Crystal asked, slightly embarrassed that she wasn't giving the ambassador more of her attention.

Jax slowly spun her. "This party. Natasha told me that you didn't know anything about it. I assumed Admiral Craft had told you about it."

Crystal gave him a soft smile. "It's all right. The Admiral thought it would be good for me to learn how to act in this type of environment without a lot of preparation."

Jax chuckles. "That explains why he asked me to give you some advice on how to deal with politicians."

Crystal fought the urge to roll her eyes. "That's always been my greatest weaknesses. I'm sorry he gave you an impossible task."

"Oh, I don't know about that. You held your own just fine at the hearing today." Jax spun her in a slow circle.

Crystal scanned the room as she spun. Justin was still dancing with that woman. They looked completely enthralled with one another. Before Crystal could give it much thought, she was facing Jax again. "I'm not sure Admiral Craft would be happy with the way I behaved today. He sent me to strengthen relationships, not add to the tension."

"You might not have made any friends today, but you

certainly earned the panel's respect, which is more important. They value strength here, and you showed them that you have it."

"You think that will make tomorrow's hearing any easier." Crystal looked over Jax's shoulder to where Justin was dancing. She still hadn't gotten a good look at his partner's face, but something about her was familiar.

"If anything, it will make it harder," Jax admitted. "The panel will try to see if they can break you. Don't let them."

A knot started to form in the pit of her stomach. She knew Jax was right. They had barely started to fight. She would need to call upon every ounce of strength she had to get through the next two days. "I'll do my best." The music ended and the room erupted in applause. "Thank you, Mr. Ambassador."

"It was my pleasure Commander. Now go enjoy the party." Jax released her. Crystal turned to see Justin waiting for her a few feet away. His dance partner was nowhere to be found.

Justin bowed slightly and held out his hand to her. The smile on his face made her forget about her search for the woman he had been dancing with. "May I have this dance?"

Had this been a different time, he would have made the perfect fairytale prince. "Of course." Crystal took his hand, and a moment later they were dancing. Lost in the sea of people on the dance floor, to Crystal they were the only two people in the room.

"Did the Ambassador have anything interesting to say?" Justin asked.

Crystal glanced over at Jax, who was now dancing with Marcell. The two of them looked so comfortable in one another's arms. It was different than how she felt with Justin. It was a comfort that had to be earned over a lifetime of love. Crystal shook her head slightly and returned her gaze to Justin. "He said that it's only going to get harder, but that he thinks we're on the right track."

"That's something, I guess." Justin pulled her a little closer, but Crystal put out her hand to stop him.

"Speaking of dance partners, who was that woman you were dancing with?" She flashed him a wicked smile.

Justin's smile faltered for a moment, before it returned to normal infectious brilliance. "She was just an old friend. Now how about we go get some drinks?"

Crystal wasn't sure want to make of his response, but she decided not to push it. She leaned forward and gave him a kiss on the cheek. "That sounds like an excellent idea," she whispered in his ear.

Desi excused herself from Marcell the second the song was over and made a beeline in the direction Olivia had gone. She would have liked to confront Justin first, but he was waiting for Wolf, and Desi didn't want to draw attention to the fact that Justin had been dancing with his old girlfriend, in case Wolf hadn't noticed. Though Desi felt confident that she had.

Olivia had disappeared into the crowd. It took Desi a few seconds to spot her in the corner of the room, holding a drink. Oliva was watching something behind Desi. She turned to see Justin and Wolf dancing. The carefree expressions they wore assured Desi that she was doing the right thing.

"What are you doing here?" Desi demanded the moment she reached Olivia.

Olivia jumped, nearly spilling her drink. She took a deep breath and tore her eyes away from the dance floor. "I was invited. I work for General Sloan."

"General Sloan's here?" Desi asked, momentarily forgetting her mission.

"Yes, most of the panel and their staff are here." Oliva glanced back at the dance floor.

"So, the Neophians are good enough to drink with, but not good enough to serve with."

"They're a couple, aren't they?" Olivia clearly hadn't heard what Desi had said, but it didn't matter; they were back to the topic Desi was there to discuss.

"Yes, they are." Desi turned her gaze to the dance floor just in time to see Wolf whisper something in Justin's ear. "Which is why you shouldn't be here. I thought Justin made it pretty clear that he didn't want anything to do with you."

"He only said that out of anger. He even apologized to me while we were dancing."

Desi rolled her eyes. Of course, Justin had apologized even though as far as Desi was concerned, he hadn't done anything wrong, yet. "That doesn't mean he wants you back."

"No, but he's letting me in, and that's a start," Olivia countered. "Maybe Justin and your Commander aren't as serious as you think they are." Olivia turned to face Desi as Justin and Wolf left the dance floor and headed to the bar.

"Trust me, they're serious," Desi snapped. "The last thing Justin needs is you butting in where you aren't wanted and screwing everything up. If you really care for him, the way you say you do, then leave him alone." Desi turned sharply on the spot and strode away in the direction Justin and Wolf had exited the dance floor.

They were no longer at the bar, but Desi knew they couldn't have gone far. She found them making small talk with someone Desi didn't recognize.

She walked up behind Justin and firmly gripped his arm. "I need to borrow you for a second," she said, as sweetly as she could while squeezing his arm so he knew she was serious.

"Ok," Justin stuttered. He looked helplessly to Wolf, who was busy shooting daggers at Desi. This was for her own good. If Wolf knew what had been going on, Desi was sure she would forgive her. Desi pulled Justin out of the room and into the library. She wanted to make sure they wouldn't be overheard.

"What the hell were you thinking?" Desi yelled, finally releasing his arm.

Justin rubbed his arm where she had been gripping him. "What are you talking about?"

"I saw you and Olivia on the dance floor, and I'm pretty sure Wolf saw it too." Desi waved her hand toward the door.

"That was nothing." Justin shook his head. "It was completely innocent. You're making a big deal over nothing." Justin took a step toward the door, but Desi moved to block him.

"What did Wolf say when you told her you were dancing with your ex-girlfriend?" Desi held up her hands as she blocked the door.

"She didn't say anything."

"Why?" she pressed.

"Because I didn't tell her it was my ex-girlfriend." Justin looked down at his feet and turned away.

"Sounds completely innocent to me." Desi crossed her arms as she watched Justin. She took it as a good sign that he looked guilty.

"What was I supposed to do? Turn Olivia down when she asked me to dance?"

"Yes."

"That would have been rude." Justin made it sounds like Desi had suggested he shoot Olivia or something.

"Then be rude." Desi couldn't believe she had to tell him this. Justin's need to always be the good guy was going to end up costing him one of these days. Desi wanted to make sure that today wasn't that day.

"You're making a big deal out of nothing. It was just a dance. No different than when Crystal dances with Grady."

"It's completely different." Desi threw her hands up in frustration. "You and Olivia were in a serious romantic relationship. One that she wants back. There's never been an ounce of romance between Wolf and Grady and you know that."

Justin didn't say anything.

"Is this worth losing Wolf over? 'Cause that's what's going to happen if she finds out you lied to her."

Justin gave her a pointed look. "I didn't lie to her."

"No, but you didn't tell her the truth either, which is just as bad." Desi softly shook her head, all the anger gone from her voice.

Justin started to say something but stopped. Desi could see she had gotten her point across. "Tell her who Olivia is." Desi gave him a weak smile and left the room. Now that Justin's love life was out of danger, she set her sights on another target. She was out to find Sloan.

Crystal wasn't thrilled that Flint stole Justin away from her; he was so much better at small talk than she was. Jax had told her to be herself, but if she did that, she would be hiding in her room upstairs at the moment. Instead, she was listening to some work story, told by a person whose name she couldn't remember, surrounded by people who looked down on her home planet. She waited for a break in the conversation before excusing herself to get another drink. She ran into Justin on her way to the bar. He held out a glass of wine to her.

"You read my mind." She took the glass and took a sip. It was like medicine for her soul. "It's the least you could do after abandoning me like that."

"It wasn't like Flint gave me a choice." Justin wrapped his arm around her waist. Crystal leaned her head on his shoulder and looked out over the party. She needed Justin by her side if she was going to get through the rest of the evening.

"What was that all about anyway?" Crystal didn't remove her head from his shoulder. She wished the two of them could sneak away to her room, but she knew they'd never get away with it.

"You know Desi always making a big deal out of nothing," Justin said, a little too quickly.

Crystal picked up her head and looked at him. "It seemed like it was pretty important."

"She wanted to talk about some of the people here," Justin started. "Actually, I did have something I wanted to talk to you about."

"Hold that thought." Across the room Crystal had spotted Commander Brinkman in the back corner of the room. He was watching her intently, and the moment their eyes locked he lifted his glass to her. Crystal knew that if she wanted to talk to him without interference this would be the only chance she got.

She removed herself from Justin's arms and started to make her way across the room toward Brinkman. Before getting ready for the party, Crystal had spent some time going through Brinkman's, Vega's, and Plourde's files in more detail. She wanted to review their service records on Neophia. She figured it would be the only way to get an accurate representation of their character, since she refused to believe they were the meek submissive people she saw at the hearing today. She was surprised to see that Brinkman had graduated in the top ten percent of his class at the Academy. He had a strong service record with good references from his superiors and even a few medals to his name. He could have had his pick of assignments if he'd stayed on Neophia.

"Mind if I join you for a drink?" Crystal approached the table he was standing next to. She set her glass of wine down and scanned the room quickly to make sure no was going to try to stop her from talking to him again.

"Not at all," Brinkman said casually. "I was hoping to get the chance to speak to you tonight. That was the only reason I accepted the ambassador's invitation." Now that she was here, he no longer appeared interested in her. She assumed it was just for show. Crystal wished they could go somewhere more private to talk, but she feared that would draw too much attention.

"I noticed that Plourde and Vega aren't here," Crystal said looking out over the dance floor. This conversation felt far too much like her covert meet ups with Grady when he was working undercover gathering intel on whatever terrorist group they were tasked to take down. It was her least favorite part of that assignment.

Brinkman took a moment to respond. It was clear that he was choosing his words very carefully. "It was strongly suggested that our appearance here might be detrimental to our health."

"Are you saying they were threatened?" Crystal turned to face him. She wanted to see his face when he answered. It would be the only way she could trust that she had heard him right.

"Not in so many words, but it's been made very clear to all of us that we need to be loyal to the U.S. military or something bad could happen." Brinkman finally turned to look at her. "Showing up here would make our loyalties to LAWON and Neophia clear, which is risky."

Crystal had to assume they had been threatened since she first saw them at the hearing, but Brinkman's confirmation sent a jolt of anger through her that she wasn't prepared for. It was wrong to demand they choose the U.S. military over Neophia, just like it was wrong for Crystal to blame Flint for choosing to return home. "Then why are you here?"

"I'm going home after the hearing. I should be able to keep myself safe until then. Besides I needed to talk to you, and I doubted I'd be able to do that with Corwin there."

Crystal was about to comment on what a jerk Corwin was when something else Brinkman said stuck out to her. "What do you mean *should* be able to keep yourself safe?"

Brinkman pick up his glass and took a sip. "I'm sure you've realized by now that the exchange program has a high fatality rate on Earth."

"I'm aware. What I can't seem to get a straight answer on is how our people were killed." Crystal turned and looked out over the party. Peppered among the tuxedos and evening gowns were several formal military uniforms. She wondered which one of them held the answers to how her people died. And more importantly, what purpose those deaths served.

"I'm not surprised. I'm sure once the official reports are finally released it will say that they were kill in action by enemy fire, but I don't believe it. The U.S. military is bent on discrediting us, and if anyone should speak up, they find themselves transferred to the front line not long after. At that point, it's hard to say which side the bullet came from."

Crystal noticed that Brinkman got paler as he talked. She could only imagine what he's seen while serving here. If what he was implying was true, and Crystal didn't have any reason not to believe him, then the U.S. military was intentionally killing their people. The idea made her blood boil with rage. How could the LAWON brass ask them to fight to keep a program going that was just sending their people to be murdered? "You've managed to make it out in one piece, and I don't take you for one to hold your tongue." She needed to know how he survived. She needed him to give her some small shred of hope to keep her fighting.

He gave her a small smile. "No, I'm not. I just got lucky. The captain I've been serving under protected me from some of the harsher backlash. It hasn't been easy, but at least no one on my team has tried to kill me."

Crystal set her drink down on the table and looked Brinkman in the eyes. "Tell me honestly, do you think the exchange program should continue?"

"No, I don't. Thanks for the drink." Brinkman set his empty glass down on the table and walked away.

Crystal wasn't sure what to think. She had orders to get the program extended, but she wasn't convinced that those orders were right. The LAWON brass might be willing to accept the current fatality rate, but she wasn't sure she could. If she got the program extended and more people died, she would be responsible. She looked over the room hoping to find an answer among the crowd. Her gaze came to rest on Justin and Tyler chatting by the bar. There was one reason to save the program, even if it was a completely selfish one.

Desi worked the room slowly, all the while keeping her eyes peeled for Sloan. She didn't want to miss an opportunity to talk to anyone that might be able to help their cause. Not to mention she was going to be returning to service here shortly, and it couldn't hurt to make a few connections. She wasn't sure how much weight her name had lost while she was serving on Neophia. Unfortunately, no one seemed very interested in talking to her. More than once, people obviously changed directions to avoid crossing her path. She had tried to insert herself into a few conversations only to have them break up and the people scatter moments later.

Undeterred she kept moving around the room until she saw Sloan laughing with Jax near the bar. They looked like they were old friends. She went to the bar to get a fresh drink while she waited for their conversation to end. When Jax was pulled away she made her move. "I was surprised to hear you were here," she said as a greeting.

"Lieutenant Flint." He turned to look at her. His face was hard, but there was a friendly undertone in his voice that threw her off guard. "My wife works with Marcell at the hospital. Besides, the Donnellys' parties are some of the most important social events in town. I'd be a fool to miss them."

"Even though this is technically Neophian soil, hosted by LAWON officials? An organization you went out of your way to disrespect at the hearing today?" Desi took a sip of her drink while she waited for him respond.

"Don't judge me to harshly Flint," Sloan chuckled. "This afternoon was a test, one you and your Commander passed with flying colors. You know as well as I do that our military only respects strength. The panel knows *you* have it — what they needed to see was if the rest of your team has it too. Even I was a little taken aback when Commander Wolf stood up to me. I'm not sure anyone has ever done that before," he said with a small smile. Sloan glanced across the room. Desi followed his line of sight to see Wolf talking with one of the LAWON officers from the hearing on the other side of the room. "Commander Wolf is an impressive young woman."

"Yes, she is," Desi said as confusion washed over her. Was Sloan on their side? Desi had a hard time believing he had put on a show at the hearing in order to give them a chance to prove their strength to the rest of the panel. It seemed more likely he was just trying to save face after Wolf had called him out. Sloan was a military officer, but at this point in his career, Desi knew he was more politician than solider.

Sloan turned back toward her. "Believe it or not, I want the exchange program to continue. Unfortunately, the majority of the panel doesn't. Your team needs to make them see that there is a lot that we can learn from LAWON's military if we give them a chance. But the only way that's going to happen is if the LAWON officers that are serving here start demanding that they are heard, and that's not happening. So, the U.S. officers are taking advantage of them."

"If you're really on our side, why didn't you say anything during the hearing about the LAWON officers from Earth being told exactly what to say? You could have pushed them to give honest responses."

"Sure, I could have, but then my loyalties would be been called into question, and I would have likely been pulled from the panel. If that happened, the program wouldn't stand a chance. You should know better than anyone the value of a respected reputation in the military. It's what let you get away with your little speech today."

Desi scoffed "I see. You're hoping we'll do the hard work for you. That way if things go south, your hands won't be dirty." Desi shook her head as Sloan looked away without saying anything. "If you aren't going to help us, the least you can do is give me some advice to get us through the hearing tomorrow."

"Just keep doing what you're doing," Sloan answered. "You're a fighter Flint. It shouldn't be that hard for you." Sloan started to walk away.

"Sir," Desi called after him. He turned to look at her. "Do you know what's the best thing about serving on Neophia? They don't play game."

"Then it's a shame we aren't on Neophia." Sloan raised his glass to her before walking away.

Chapter 10

Crystal had been in the embassy dining room for a little over an hour. No one else was awake yet. She had managed to sneak away from the party shortly after her conversation with Brinkman, though she could hear music playing downstairs until the early hours of the morning. She had no idea when the others had called it a night. She could only hope they hadn't stayed up too late. They were in for another long day. Today would begin the question and answer portion of the hearing, and Crystal was pretty sure most of the time would be spent grilling her team. They needed to be at the top of their game if they were to get through this.

The ambassador's staff had laid out a small breakfast for them. Crystal poured herself a black coffee. She looked into her cup in disappointment. She would have given anything for a cup of kiki right now. She had spent most of the night digging further into the circumstances surrounding the deaths of the LAWON officers serving on Earth. The reports were so vague that she suspected that Brinkman had been right. They'd probably never know for certain who had killed their people.

"So, are you ready for today?" Grady asked.

Crystal looked up from her tablet where she had been going over an email from Stiner with the latest repair list for *Journey's* drydock. "I guess." Crystal got up and joined Grady where the food had been set out. She grabbed a plate and started to fill it. "Commander Brinkman was at the party last night. We were able to have a nice chat."

Grady looked up from the food and gave her his full attention. "Did he have anything interesting to say?"

"He doesn't think the program should continue."

"That's just fantastic." Grady finished putting food on his plate and went to sit down at the table.

Crystal refilled her cup of coffee and retook her seat. "I don't think we can expect any help him today."

"That's not really that surprising. Did he give you a good reason at least?" Grady started to pick at the food on his plate.

"He believes that the LAWON officers who've been killed in the program were the victims of friendly fire, and the more I look into it, the more I think he's right."

"That's awful," Grady said through a mouthful of donut. "Have you tried these? They're great."

"Focus," Crystal said.

Grady set the donut down on his plate and folded his hands in front of him on the table. "Sorry. I'm listening. Friendly fire. I can understand why he wants the program canceled."

"Me, too. Which is why I've been wondering if we should be fighting so hard to keep the program going. I mean would it really be that bad to fail this mission?"

Crystal looked down at her plate. She never imaged there would be a time when she would suggest intentionally failing a mission.

"You can't be serious. What about Anderson and Flint? Without the program they won't be able to come back to *Journey*."

"I don't think Flint's coming back even if the program is renewed," Crystal said avoiding his question. The only way she could think about this whole thing rationally was if she took Justin out of the picture. She losing him would break her heart, but it wasn't her job to think with her heart. She had made him agree when they started their relationship that the job would always come first, and that's what she was doing now.

Grady leaned forward. "Crystal, answer the question," he said with an even tone, as if he were talking to a child who didn't understand what they were saying. "Have you thought about the impact it will have on our team if the program is canceled? The impact it will have on you?"

"I haven't thought of anything else," Crystal answered, "but I keep coming back to the same thing. Is it worth it? I don't want to lose Justin, but can we really keep sending our people down here so the U.S. military can use them as target practice?" She could hear the desperation in her voice, but she didn't care. She needed Grady to tell her what the right answer was.

"Of course not."

"So what do we do? Our orders are to get the program extended, but if we do that, we'll be responsible for sending more of our people to their deaths. Deaths that would never happen if they stayed on Neophia." Crystal rested her head in her hands.

"We could talk to Craft. Maybe he doesn't know how

many fatalities there's been," Grady suggested.

"He knows. I brought it up in the debriefing call before the party, and I left him a message explaining what Brinkman told me at the party. Though I didn't know they were friendly fire deaths at that point, so I didn't push it as hard as I should have."

"Did he change our orders?" Grady asked hopefully.

Crystal looked up at him. "He did not. He said that I need to look at the bigger picture, that the exchange program is the only way to keep a bridge open between our planets so that our relationship doesn't get worse." She looked into her coffee, wishing again it was kiki. "The new information doesn't change that. The message I got back from him this morning said that if we are successful the sacrifice would be worth it."

Grady picked up his donut again and took a bite. Crystal could tell he was trying to come up with a solution. "There *is* still a chance that a lot of good could come from the exchange program. If we can get the U.S. military to listen to us, maybe we can convince them to treat our people better."

"Who sounds like the politician now?" Crystal said with a smirk.

"It's the best I got. It was a long night."

"And you sure did make the most of it, didn't you?" Crystal's smirk grew to a wicked smile.

"You bailed early," Grady protested, putting his hand on his chest and giving her his best puppy dog face. "I thought it would be rude if I didn't stay. I really did it for you."

Crystal pointed her butter knife at him. "You better be ready to back me up today. I can't be the only one fielding their questions. I might snap, and no one wants that."

"When have I not had your back?" It was true. Grady was the only person Crystal knew she could count on no matter what. He would follow her into any battle without question.

The hearing room was full when Desi and Justin arrived. They were even early, something Desi was not known for. Grady and Price were standing up front by their table, but Wolf was nowhere in sight.

"Aren't we missing someone?" Desi asked.

"She needed a minute to get her thoughts together," Grady said, giving Justin an awkward glance.

"Thoughts about what?" Desi asked looking from Grady to Justin.

"She learned some new information last night that has her questioning if it's really in our best interest to keep the exchange program going," Grady said carefully.

Desi whipped around to look at Justin. He had gone pale. Desi wondered if this was the fallout from him finally coming clean about Olivia. "Is this because of you?" Price and Grady gave them an odd look, but Desi didn't care.

"I didn't tell her anything," he finally said. Desi was floored. After everything she had told him last night, he still hadn't told Wolf about Olivia.

"It's because she found out that our people were likely killed by friendly fire, and she thinks if we convince them to keep the program going and more people die that it will be on her," Price murmured.

"That's insane," Desi said.

"That's Crystal." Grady raised an eyebrow and sat down at the table. Desi wasn't sure what to think. She wished she could say something to convince Wolf that the LAWON officers killed in action were just part of war. It was insane to think that the military would kill its own people. Even if they weren't great soldiers, their main concern had always been enlistment numbers, so why would they intentionally lower their own numbers. But the more Desi considered it, the more she knew in her heart that Wolf was probably right. She had heard rumors of the U.S. military disposing of troublemakers by sending them to the front line where they were killed shortly after. The deaths were too common to all be enemy fire. If she took the promotion, would the same thing happen to her?

Desi turned toward the table to see Ensign Vega timidly making his way over to them. "Hey Price," he said, while he looked around the room like a scared child.

"Vega." Price nodded at him and folded his arms across his chest.

"It's good to see you. Sorry I didn't get a chance to talk to you yesterday." His voice was shaky.

"You could have if you weren't so busy being Corwin's mouthpiece," Desi accused. "Tell me, did he give you the exact words to say or just the general idea and let you go from there?" Desi probably should have felt sorry for him, but she was too angry to feel sorry.

"It's not like that," Vega protested. "It risky not to do what they tell you to do. I had my orders." Vega rubbed his hand along his other arm as he looked around the room.

Tyler stood up and leaned on the table. "What happened to you man? You used to be so confident when we were at the Academy."

"Look, I'm just trying to make it home in one piece, and the only way I can do that is if I do what they tell me to."

"Then you better run back over to your table before anyone sees you talking to us." Desi waved him away.

"What was all that about?" Wolf asked, joining them at the table as Vega retreated. She looked calmer than Desi expected based off what Grady and Price had said.

"Nothing." Desi glanced over at the other table and shook her head.

"Vega wanted to say hi," Price said.

"I guess that's a good sign." Wolf brushed a stray strand of hair out of her face. Desi noticed that she hadn't so much as made eye contact with Justin since she got there. She knew the two of them tried to keep their relationship private, especially when working, but this was different. It was like she was actively avoiding him.

"Grady mentioned you're having second thoughts about the program. Does that mean you're going to change our orders?" Desi figured it was better to get it out in the open before the hearing started. It wouldn't look good if they weren't all on the same page once the panel started interrogating them.

Wolf's eyes slid toward Justin. "I have my concerns, but our orders remain the same. We will convince the panel to keep the exchange program going, and more importantly, we will make them see that our people have a lot to offer and should be treated with respect and dignity."

"That should be easy." Price rolled his eyes and looked over at Vega. He seemed to be taking it personally that Vega hadn't done more to help their cause.

Desi looked up at the empty panel. "We might actually get some help with that."

"What do you mean?" Price asked.

"I had a conversation with General Sloan at the party last night."

"Sloan was at the party?" Wolf asked.

"Yes, and he claims he's on our side." Desi didn't completely believe what Sloan had told her last night; he was a politician after all, and she knew better than to take anything he said at face value. Still, given their current situation she would take whatever help they could get.

"He has a funny way of showing it," Grady said.

"He claimed yesterday was a test. A test that we apparently passed."

"What kind of test?" Price asked.

"The U.S. military values strength above all else. When we pushed back yesterday, we showed the panel that we have that strength," Desi explained. "He said the reason most of the LAWON officers aren't respected is because they aren't standing up for themselves. That's why the military sees them as useless. We can start to change that today."

"By fighting back?" Wolf asked.

"Yes."

"I think we can do that." A small smile formed on Crystal's lips. Desi could almost see the gears turning in her mind. She had no doubt that her team was up to the challenge. Sloan had no idea what he had unleashed.

After the first two hours of the hearing, Crystal was exhausted. Easily eighty percent of the questions had been directed at her team. The LAWON officers on the other side were barely allowed to speak, and when they did it was only to reinforce the claim that they were not able to provide value to the U.S. military. Crystal had hoped Brinkman would speak up to defend them, but he sat with his arms crossed and mouth shut. He was holding fast to his belief that the program shouldn't be renewed.

Justin had just finished explaining what is was like to be a pilot on *Journey*. The panel had been mostly interested in hearing about the technological advancements Crystal had designed for the ship. Justin had done a decent job explaining the full body chair that was used to drive that ship without actually giving anything away.

"That all sounds very impressive. What I want to know is who designed the drive mechanisms for the ship and how much help they had from engineers from Earth," said a member of the panel in an off-handed way.

Crystal glanced at Sloan and could have sworn he raised his eyebrows at her as if he was challenging her to speak up. "I designed it, as well as the rest of the ship, without any help from Earth." Crystal stared down the panel member who had posed the question, but they suddenly seemed very interested in the tablet in front of them. Crystal just shook her head.

"I think it's time we turn to what we are all really interested in. Combat," said another panel member. Crystal took a deep breath. This was where LAWON's military policies varied the most from the U.S. military. If they were looking for something to use as proof that Neophia was the weaker planet, this would be it.

"I find it interesting that your ship had two separate combat teams, one led by a respected officer from LAWON," Sloan nodded toward Crystal, "and the other by a respected officer from Earth." Sloan turned his gaze to Flint. "How did that power dynamic work? Which team was the lead team?"

Crystal glanced at Flint who gestured for her to answer. Crystal took another deep breath. "There's wasn't a lead team. Both teams were considered equal. The lead would go to whichever team was best suited for the mission. Most of the time, we would run two different operations at the same time. There were always multiple objectives that needed to be met, and each team would tackle different things to make the mission as a whole a successful."

"What do you mean by multiple objectives?" The panel member who had first steered the conversation toward combat leaned forward in his seat with a disapproving look.

This was where she was going to lose them. Crystal knew from working closely with Flint over the last six months that the U.S. military only had one objective for their missions: secure the resource. They never really gave a second though to the civilians they encountered along the way. "Saving lives is always our primary objective, so that would be the sole focus of one of the teams. The other would tackle whatever was putting the civilians' lives in danger, whether that be an invading government or an issue with an underwater colony's life support system." Crystal noticed that Brinkman was nodding his head at the other table, even though he didn't speak up.

"Why not put all of your resources on fixing the problem first?" Sloan asked.

Crystal squeezed the bridge of her nose while she tried to get her frustration in order. She knew they would ask something like that. To anyone on Neophia, it seemed so obvious—why was it so hard for the panel to understand? She was about to answer when Grady beat her to it. "Because if we failed, we would lose everyone," he said firmly. "This way if we failed, at least we saved as many lives as possible. Saving lives comes above anything else."

"That policy will won't win you a war," someone on the panel chimed in.

Flint pressed the palms on her hands on the table. "Neophia isn't at war." It was strange hearing those words come out of Flint's mouth. Crystal had needed to remind Flint of the same thing several times when she first came to Neophia.

"Then what purpose do LAWON's military forces serve, if not to defend their land and gain resources for their people?" Sloan asked. Crystal could see that he was trying to steer the conversation, she just wasn't convinced that it was in a direction that would help them.

"LAWON's primary mission is to maintain the peace that was established during the end of the Great War. To ensure that we don't have another war," Crystal said. She tried to put as much passion and feeling into her words as she could, but one look at the panel and she could tell she had fallen short. They weren't interested in preventing wars, only winning them. She looked to Flint for help.

Flint nodded. "War costs lives on both sides. All the governments of Neophia have agreed not to declare war on one another. LAWON values the lives of their soldiers and their enemies in a way that the U.S. military can't even begin to comprehend." The members of the panel shifted uncomfortably in their seats.

"Let me see if I understand you Lieutenant Flint," Sloan interjected. "You're saying that you never felt like the U.S. military valued your life?" Sloan was having a hard time hiding the trace of a smile that had formed on his lips. Either Flint was making the point he had hoped, for or they were in big trouble. Even though Flint had said Sloan was on their side, Crystal didn't trust him.

Flint leaned back casually in her chair. "That's exactly what I'm saying. I'm just another cog in the war machine. You don't care if your soldiers live or die. That's why you didn't even bat an eye over the deaths of fourteen LAWON officers who came here to help you. You know how many U.S. officers died while serving on Neophia? None, because LAWON cares about their people's safety, and the U.S. military doesn't." If Flint's goal was to piss off the panel, she had succeeded.

"That's a pretty bold allegation," one of the panel members yelled at her.

Flint just shrugged. "It's one I'm sticking to. If you don't like it, then maybe it's time to take a good look in the mirror and figure out how to change the culture of the military. Until then, you'll have to accept that the LAWON military cares about their people more than you do."

"Which is why, even during the Great War, we never had mandatory enlistment in the military," Grady added. "We never had any problem getting people to join and make lifetime careers out of military service."

"In fact, the LAWON military had to reject more people from their military academy last year than applied for yours," Tyler said. Crystal had no idea where he had found the statistic, but given the fact that his tablet was on the table in front of him, she we sure it was true.

"Let's get back on topic," a panel member said. Crystal guessed she didn't want to get into a debate over enlistment numbers, especially since LAWON would easily win that fight. Numbers didn't lie. "I want to discuss LAWON's weapon policies, particularly the one stating that all weapons are to be set to stun for combat missions."

"It all goes back to the concept that LAWON makes preserving life their top priority," Crystal said. "The policy to set weapons to stun was agreed upon by all Neophian nations in the Peace Treaty at the end of the Great War. Violating it would be construed as an act of war, but it goes deeper than that. While LAWON's military is completely voluntary and its members are treated well no matter their rank, this is not the case for every county on Neophia. We recognize that the people we are fighting might not be there by choice. Is it right to take their lives when their government is forcing them to fight for a cause they might not believe in?" While she was referring to Teria, it wasn't lost on Crystal that the same principles applied to the U.S. military.

"Do you really find this method effective?" the panel member demanded, doubt clear in his voice. "Wouldn't it be better to simply weaken your opponent further through the use of lethal force? That way you are protecting your people by keeping the other side from being able to strike back." The panel member slammed his fist into the palm of his other hand with aggression to a general round of applause from the room. Crystal glanced behind her to see most of the audience nodding in agreement. They were in a room full of people who saw murder as a solution. Crystal didn't know how to respond. How could she possibly make them understand?

"Absolutely not." As promised, Grady had her back. "The idea that you can save lives by taking them is idiotic at best. The other side, as you call them, are people just like you and me. They have family and friends back home that care about them. Killing only turns those people against you. So you haven't so much as taken down one enemy as you have created a handful more in their place."

"It's amazing you get anything accomplished," the aggressive panel member responded, his condescension clear.

"Without the constant fear of death hanging over everyone, the LAWON military is able to accomplish more, and in a shorter time period, than the U.S. military could ever dream of," Flint countered. "You might have been able to experience it if you had chosen to listen to the LAWON officers serving here instead of sending them to the front line to be slaughtered every time they disagreed with you." Flint banged her hand on the table and rose out of her chair. Crystal was afraid that she would pounce on the panel, but she only stared them down. Behind them the room erupted in chaos. Crystal wondered if this time Flint had gone too far, as threats were hurled at her from the audience. If Flint was really planning on staying on Earth, she wasn't making it easy on herself.

Chapter 11

"Well we either got our point across or pissed off a lot of powerful people," Flint said.

"I'm just glad it's over." Crystal was standing outside of the pentagon with the rest of her team, waiting for the embassy car to come pick them up. They had a few hours to kill before dinner with Justin's parents. Part of her felt that going another round with the panel would be less stressful.

"I think the most important question is: Where can we get a few drinks before dinner?" Grady said.

Flint put her arms around Grady and Price. "I believe I can be of assistance with that."

Justin gently grabbed Crystal's elbow and pulled her away from the group. "I was hoping you and I could have some time alone before dinner tonight."

Crystal wrapped her arms around Justin's neck. "I like that sounds of that. What did you have in mind?" Crystal gave him her best seductive look. A few hours alone with Justin was exactly what she needed to destress before meeting his parents.

"I want to take you somewhere important to me." Justin's eyes lit up with childish joy.

"Sounds great." She gave him a quick kiss and then released him. It wasn't exactly what she had in mind, but she could tell what it meant to him. Besides, she doubted she would ever have the chance to see places from Justin's past first-hand again. If it was up to her, she would never set foot on Earth again once this mission was over.

Justin squeezed her hand in excitement and turned back to the others. "You guys don't mind if we pass, do you?"

"Nope, you two would only slow us down anyway," Grady said.

"Remember, we still have dinner with Justin and Desi's parents tonight. You better behave yourselves." Crystal looked from Grady to Flint. The two of them were such a bad influence on one another.

"I'll keep an eye on them," Tyler said with a sigh. Crystal knew he would have his hands full trying to keep the two of them in check. After the stress of the hearing. She was sure they were ready to cut lose.

"Why don't you two take the car. If Justin is taking you where I think he is you'll need it more than we will," Flint said. "Now, come on boys, there are drinks to had." She pointed down the street as if she was leading a charge. Grady and Tyler followed dutifully after her, though Tyler did glance back over his shoulder to give Crystal a look that made it clear he thought he was being led into a trap.

Crystal watched them walking away with amusement. "Do you think there's a chance of them showing up to your parents' sober?"

"No, not at all," Justin said with a chuckle. "Now, shall we?" He put his hand on the small of her back and escorted her over to the LAWON car that had pulled up.

"So where are we going?"

"It's a surprise." Justin held open the door and waited for her to get in, before heading to the front of the car to give the driver directions. A few moments later he joined Crystal in the back seat.

They drove to the outskirts of town, Justin pointing out landmarks as they went. Crystal tried to pay attention, but honestly, she hadn't ever heard of any of them. She had given Flint a hard time for not knowing anything about Neophia when they first met, but the truth was Crystal knew next to nothing about Earth. She liked to think that if she had been given more notice, she would've learned some basics, but she wasn't sure that was true.

An hour later the car stopped in front of a large domed building. A faded sign out front read Last Edan Nature Sanctuary. Justin looked absolutely giddy as he sprang from the car. Crystal could barely keep up with him. "I used to volunteer here when I was in high school and whenever I was home between deployments."

They entered a small lobby, which was really nothing more than a concrete box. The desk was empty, but that didn't deter Justin. He walked right over to the door in front of them and keyed in a code. A huge grin was plastered across his face as he pulled open the heavy door and motioned for Crystal to enter. It was like she had stepped onto another planet. The air was filled with moisture, and trees sprouted all around them. Flowers and grasses covered the ground. It almost felt like home.

Crystal spun slowly to take it all in. Justin was

standing in front of the door, watching her. "This place is incredible," she breathed. "Thank you for showing it to me."

"You're welcome." Justin came over, pulled her close, and kissed her. "Come on there's more to see."

Crystal took his hand and let him lead her down a dirt path as she tried to take everything in. It was such a contrast to what was outside.

"The sanctuary is privately funded, and most of the workers here are volunteers," Justin said as they walked toward the center of the dome.

"Why do they do it?" Crystal hadn't seen much selflessness in the few days she had been on Earth; she was starting to think it might be a purely Neophian trait.

"Because if we didn't, then all of Earth's beauty would be lost forever. This is a tiny glimpse of what the planet used to be." He pushed opened a glass door that led to the heart of the sanctuary. "Close your eyes and listen," he said once they were on the other side.

Crystal did as he asked. The electronic hum that had filled her ears since they landed was gone. She had almost forgotten that is wasn't a natural sound. Now she heard birds singing in the trees overhead and the sound of water flowing somewhere nearby. She ached to be near the water again, and not that sludge flow they called a river Justin had taken her to. "I love it here," Crystal said as she opened her eyes and turned toward him.

"I knew you would." Justin took her hand. They started to walk the dirt path in front of them.

Crystal was enthralled by the beauty of this place. The beauty that Earth had lost a long time ago. "What did you used to do here?" She had a hard time imagining Justin working in a place like this. He seemed so at home at *Journey's* helm.

"I helped take care of the wolves. Their enclosure is over here. We have to keep them separate since they are one of the few predators we have." They rounded the corner to an open grassy area with a fence along one side. In the middle of the field was a blanket with a picnic basket waiting for them.

"What's all this?" Crystal smiled they walked over to the blanket. As much as she hated surprises, she loved this. Justin always knew exactly what she needed.

"I know we have dinner in a few hours, but I thought a little private appetizer couldn't hurt." He sat down on the blanket and motioned for Crystal to join him. She watched as he pulled a bottle of champagne and two glasses from the basket. He popped the cork and poured her a glass. "For you."

"Thank you." She took a small sip and let the bubbles play in her mouth before swallowing.

"And in case you need something a little stronger." He pulled out a bottle of whiskey. "I know the past few days have been tough."

Crystal leaned forward and kissed him. "You know me so well," she said as she slowly pulled away. She leaned back on the blanket as Justin pulled out an assortment of fruits and cheeses and placed them on the blanket next to them. Crystal soaked in the moment. It was the thing dreams were made of.

She watched the enclosure as she sipped her champagne. She didn't really expect to see anything, but three large animals appeared. Crystal set her glass down and leaned forward. She had never seen anything like them. They were larger than she imagined they would be, their bodies covered with beautiful gray and white fur. They came right over to the fence closest to them.

"Hi there." Justin got up and walked over to the fence. He crouched down so he was at eye level with them and held his hand up to the fence for them to sniff. "I know it's been awhile, but you remember me, don't you?" Justin said to the wolves and a calm even voice. Crystal watched as one of them rubbed its face against his hand through the fence. "That's a good girl." Justin turned back to her. "Would you like to meet them?"

"Is it safe?" Crystal tentatively got up and walked over to him. He had said they were predators, and she had never been great with animals to begin with.

"You'll be fine as long as you don't climb over the fence," Justin said with a small laugh. Crystal crouched down next to him, though she made sure to keep her arms tucked in just in case.

"This is Luna," Justin pointed to one of the wolves, "and that one there is her sister Skyler. The darker one is Shadow; he's the alpha of the pack."

"They really seem to like you." Crystal pulled her eyes away from the animals so that she could watch Justin as he looked at the wolves. She was in awe of him.

"I was here when they were first brought in. They were just pups at the time. I watched them grow up." Justin cracked a smile.

"They're beautiful." Crystal watched as the wolves walked back into the heart of their enclosure.

Justin tucked a loose strand of hair behind her ear. "You're beautiful."

Crystal cocked an eyebrow at him. "How many people are working here?"

"Only two. Why?"

"Do you think they will be in this area anytime soon?" Crystal couldn't keep the sly grin off her face.

"I doubt it. They knew I was brining you here. They

were the ones that laid out the picnic."

"Good." Crystal reached over and started to unbutton his shirt. She had to have him. Here. In the place that was so special to him. A place where the real Justin rose to the surface and shined.

"Here?" Justin gently put his hands on hers, stopping her from unfastening the last few buttons on his shirt.

"Yes." Crystal finished unbuttoning his shirt and pushed it off his shoulders. The next thing she knew his lips were pressed against hers as he gently pushed her back onto the grass.

Desi took Grady and Tyler to a bar not far from the Pentagon. It was a popular hangout for SEALs. She tried to stop in every time she was in town. It would be fun to show off her old stomping ground. The place was fairly empty when they entered. It was still early. Maybe she would bring them back after dinner so they could fully experience its charm. They had kicked off their tour on *Journey* with a night out; it would be nice to end it the same way.

"You guys grab a table, and I'll get the first round," Desi said.

"Works for me." Grady clapped Price on the shoulder and the two of them took off toward an empty table in the corner.

Desi made her way to the empty bar, scanning the room for anyone she knew as she went. She was usually treated like a hero here and honestly, she missed the feeling. Especially after having to fight to even be heard at the hearing. "Three beers please," she said when she reached the bar. She didn't recognize the bartender. She tried to think back to the last time she had been in here.

It had to have been over a year ago. She shouldn't be surprised that there were some new people working here.

The bartender looked her over without saying anything. She watched as his gaze shifted to Grady and Price sitting on the other side of the room. So much for being treated as a hero; Desi wasn't even sure she could get him to serve her. "Hey, I'm over here." She pulled out her credit card and threw it on the bar. "I said three beers."

The bartender grabbed her card and went to pour their drinks. He still hadn't said a word to her. He returned a few minutes later. He threw her card back on the bar and placed the drinks in front of her. He walked away without a word.

"Jackass," Desi muttered under her breath as she gathered her drinks and headed over to the table. "Here." She set the drinks down and took a seat. Her eyes kept returning to the bartender as she sipped her drink. The bartender was now chatting away with someone at the bar.

"This place is nice." Price picked up his beer and took a sip. Desi could tell from his tone of voice that he was lying.

"It's changed." Desi couldn't shake the feeling that they were being watched. Maybe it was a mistake to come here.

"We don't have to stay if you don't want to," Price said.

"No, it's fine. I'm just still on edge from the hearing." Desi tried to smile. She wanted to show them a good time.

"That was pretty brutal." Grady took a long sip of his beer. He held the glass away from him to look at it. "I guess it'll do." He took another sip.

Desi smirked. "I'm sorry it's not up to your high standards. I'll gladly take it off your hands if it's not good enough for you."

"No, no, I'll manage." Grady held out his hand to block Desi from grabbing his glass. He quickly downed the rest of it.

"I'm surprised you'd show your face in here, traitor," said someone behind Desi.

She recognized that voice. She took a deep breath. "Go away Corwin," she said without turning to look at him.

Corwin stepped around the table and leaned on the empty chair across from her. "You don't belong here. This is a bar for Navy SEALs and their friends. That no longer applies to you."

Desi tried to keep calm even though she wanted nothing more than to jump across the table and punch the smug look off his face. "Last I checked I'm still a SEAL. So take your cronies and move along." Desi waved at the two guys that were standing a few feet behind him.

"I don't care what the brass calls you, to the rest of us you stopped being a SEAL when you chose to side with enemy over us." Corwin motioned toward Grady and Price.

"I'd watch it son," Grady said. Desi saw his fists clenching on the table. She knew Grady could take Corwin down without even breaking a sweat.

"You have a bodyguard now." Corwin turned to look at his friends standing behind him and laughed. "Going to Neophia make you too soft to fight your own battles? Or have you always been this weak?"

Desi slowly rose to her feet and leaned over the table.

"I could take you, but you're not worth the energy." She sat back down. She wouldn't sink to his level. "Why don't you run back to whatever hole you crawled out of and leave us alone?"

"You think you're so tough. The untouchable Flint. Too bad the whole country now knows what you really are: a traitor to your country and your species. I wouldn't be caught dead associating with anyone from Neophia, and here you are flaunting it for the world to see." Corwin motioned toward Grady and Price. "You really are a disgrace to your species."

"I seem to remember you abandoning your team during a mission last year. Didn't they all die?" Desi said through gritted teeth. "If anyone here doesn't deserve to be a SEAL it's you." Desi lunged toward Corwin, but Price grabbed her and pulled her back into her seat. Desi could see the veins starting to pop on Corwin's neck. She had hit a nerve. She smirked at him, trying to push him a little further.

"At least I don't spend my time defending the scum of the universe. Neophia is so far below us they can't even lick the bottom of our shoes," Corwin spit at them.

Price's attention was focused on Desi, but he should have been worried about Grady, who had jumped to his feet. "Would you like to test that theory?"

"You think you can take me?" Corwin laughed. He didn't know who he was dealing with. Desi shot Grady a warning look.

"I was referring to all three of you actually. I want to give you a fair shot." Grady shrugged but didn't sit back down.

"You're a cocky son of a bitch. Let's take this outside and see what you got, you piece of shit." Corwin cracked his knuckles while staring Gardy down.

Desi could tell Grady was about to snap. Part of her really wanted to let him do it, but what good would come from that? All they would accomplish was to further the thought that Neophians were dangerous. As much as it pained her, she knew they needed to be the bigger person. She got to her feet and turned Grady to face her. "They aren't worth it."

"Someone needs to teach them some manners." Grady jerked his head toward Corwin.

"I agree, but it's not going to be you," Flint ordered. "What would Wolf say if we missed dinner with the Anderson's because we were too busy bailing you out of jail?"

"Fine." Grady picked up Price's beer, downed it in one sip, then slammed the glass back down on the table. "Let's go." He nodded toward Price and started to make his way toward the door, kicking his chair to the ground as he went.

Corwin turned to his buddies. "I knew they were all a bunch of cowards. I bet none of them even know how to throw a punch."

That did it. Desi causally walked over to Corwin, pulled back her fist and punched him square in the jaw. Corwin hit the ground with a satisfying thud. She stepped over him without saying a word and made her way to the door where Grady and Price were waiting for her.

"Nice punch," Price said with a smile.

"I bet that felt amazing," Grady added.

"It really did. Now let's go get some dinner." Desi left the bar feeling better than she had since coming back to Earth.

Chapter 12

Crystal sat awkwardly in the Andersons' living room. Her backup hadn't arrived yet. Justin had gone into the kitchen to get them drinks, leaving Crystal alone. She wasn't sure what she was supposed to do. His parents had fussed over her when they first entered, smothering her in uncomfortable hugs that she wasn't sure how to get out of, but after the introductions they had retreated to the kitchen where dinner prep was in its final chaotic stage.

She passed the time studying the room. Every available space was filled with pictures of Justin and his family. He was a cute kid, even though he was pretty scrawny. As kids, all his sisters were bigger than him. From the picture, it looked like he had a major growth spurt in high school. She carefully picked up Justin's graduation picture from the end table and traced his face with her fingers. He was just starting to resemble the man she knew.

The front door opened. Crystal quickly put the picture back and looked to the door for salvation, but instead she saw a woman she didn't know walk in. There was no doubt that it was Flint's mom. Crystal rose to her feet and looked toward the kitchen; no one was coming to save her. The women stopped when she saw Crystal.

"Hi. I'm Lieutenant Commander Crystal Wolf." She wasn't sure why she had given her full name and rank. She had thought the overly familiar greeting with Justin's parents had been bad, but this was so much worse.

"Ms. Flint," the woman answered, without looking at Crystal. "Is my daughter here yet?" She tried to look over Crystal's shoulder, as if Crystal was hiding Flint in the other room.

"Um, no she isn't. She should be here soon." Where was Justin with her drink?

Ms. Flint didn't say anything. The tension between them grew. Crystal wasn't sure if she should keep standing or sit back down. Ms. Flint didn't move either. "Your daughter is an amazing officer." Crystal had to do something to break the tension.

"Thank you." Ms. Flint relaxed a little. "Are the two of you close?" She took a seat on the couch across from Crystal.

"We weren't at first, but we are now." Crystal retook her seat and looked toward the kitchen again for Justin. How long did it take to pour a few glasses of wine? She turned her attention back to Ms. Flint. "We share a cabin on *Journey*. I'm really going to miss her if she decides to stay here."

"Why wouldn't she be staying here?" The look Ms. Flint gave her sent chills down her spine. Crystal had thought it was an innocent comment. All she was trying to do was make small talk. She realized she wasn't any good at it, but Ms. Flint's reaction was a little extreme.

"I'm sorry," Crystal offered. "I didn't mean anything by it. I didn't think she had made her decision yet. But maybe she has and just hasn't told us yet. There's some paperwork involved, and I know she'll put that off for as long as she can." The words fell out of Crystal's mouth as she retreated. The last thing she wanted to do was start the evening off by offending Flint's mom.

"Hi Ms. Flint," Justin said. Crystal whipped around to see him finally emerging from the kitchen with two glasses of wine. He handed one to Crystal and then went over to give Ms. Flint a kiss on the cheek. "I didn't realize you were here already. Can I get you something to drink?"

"I'm fine for now. Thank you dear."

Ms. Flint was much warmer now that Justin was in the room. He sat down next to Crystal and took her hand. Ms. Flint gave them a stern look that Crystal was sure Justin was oblivious to. She glanced at the front door, no longer wishing that the rest of her team would appear, but that she could escape through it. The food wasn't even ready, and she was already in over her head. How was she going to make it through the rest of the night?

"I see you've met my girlfriend," Justin said.

Ms. Flint forced a smile on her face. "Yes, we were just getting to know each other."

"She's an extraordinary woman." Justin looked at Crystal with admiration in his eyes. A pang of guilt shot through her as she tried to force down the urge to run for the door.

"I'm sure she is, but aren't you worried what people will say when they realize you're dating someone from

Neophia?" Ms. Flint asked, as if Crystal wasn't even in the room. She could feel the muscles in her arms start to tense. People had been implying that she was worthless since she arrived on Earth, and she was sick of it. Crystal could see where Flint had gotten her bluntness from. Crystal had no problem putting Flint in her place when she first arrived on Neophia, and she was prepared to do the same with her mom now.

Crystal was about to speak when she felt Justin squeezing her hand and gently pulling her back into the couch. She wasn't aware that she had leaned forward while preparing for battle with Ms. Flint.

"Of course I'm not concerned. Other people's misguided opinions never mattered to me before; why should they now?" Justin took a sip of wine. Crystal was always amazed by how he could let things roll right off his back. If it wasn't for him, she probably would have ruined the whole evening.

The front door opened, and Flint walked in with Tyler and Grady. They all looked a little annoyed, but otherwise in the good spirits. "Sorry we're late." Flint walked over and gave her mom a kiss on the cheek.

Justin's parents emerged from the kitchen for another round of introductions. Justin went to grab everyone drinks as they got settled. "Your timing is amazing," Crystal said to Grady and Tyler. They were standing off to the side of the room away from Flint and her mom.

"Why what was going on?" Tyler asked.

"Flint's mom was asking Justin if he had considered the risks of dating someone from Neophia." Crystal glanced over at the woman. She looked a lot more at ease now that her daughter was here, though Crystal could have sworn she was going out of her way not to look in their direction.

"Are you serious?" Tyler asked.

Crystal nodded and took a sip of wine from the glass in her hand.

"Where were you when this was going on?" Grady asked. She could see his muscles starting to tense already. She expected him to be shocked by Ms. Flint's behavior, maybe even a little defensive, but this was a little extreme.

"I was sitting next to Justin on the couch. He shut her down pretty fast. It probably wouldn't have happened if you guys hadn't been late," Crystal said changing the subject.

"We had a little run in with Corwin at the bar," Tyler said.

"That couldn't have ended well."

"Flint put him in his place," Grady said.

"I would've liked to have seen that," Crystal said with a smile.

"How have Justin's parents been?" Tyler asked. He seemed genuinely concerned as he glanced across the room where Ms. Flint was talking with Mrs. Anderson. Crystal wondered if she would ever get used to having her older brother play such an active role in her life.

"They've been fine, though I haven't really talked to them much. They've spent most of the time in the kitchen getting dinner ready."

Justin came over, put his arm around her waist, and pulled her close. "You all right?"

"Of course." Crystal flashed him a smile she hoped he would believe.

"Don't let Desi's mom get to you. I'm sure she didn't mean anything by it. Just trying to get a reaction out of us. Desi had to get it from somewhere, right?" Justin gave her a quick kiss on the cheek.

Crystal wasn't sure he was right. After all the anit-Neophian sentiment she had seen the last few days, she believed Ms. Flint meant every word she had said. She couldn't tell that to Justin, though; it would break his heart. So instead she smiled and said, "It's forgotten."

Tyler looked around the room. She wondered if he was putting off going over to meet Flint's mom. Crystal had suspected that Tyler's feeling for Flint went beyond the normal teammate bond, though he hadn't acted it on yet, as far as she knew. "Is this everyone?" he asked.

"We're still waiting on my sisters," Justin said. "They should be here any minute."

As if on cue, the door opened, and three women walked in looking a little disheveled. "Sorry, it's my fault!" the oldest of the three women said. "My train was late." She set down a bag at the door as her parents enveloped her in their arms. "Where is he?"

The room parted as she made a beeline for Justin, who handed Crystal his glass. She had never seen him with a bigger smile on his face. "Hey little sis." He wrapped his arm around his sister and pulled her close. The two embraced for a long time.

"It's been too long."

Justin released his sister and turned to Crystal. "Ava, I'd like you to meet Crystal."

"So this is the woman you won't shut up about in all your messages." Ava came over and offered Crystal her hand.

Crystal tried not to blush as she shook Ava's hand. She was the same age as Justin's sister, but she felt like a nervous child in her presence. She knew Justin and Ava were extremely close, especially because they were only a year apart. If there was anyone that Crystal needed to impress tonight, it was Ava. She took a deep breath to steady her nerves. "How long has it been since you two saw each other?"

"A little over a year," Justin said. "Ava was deployed when I signed up for the exchange program, so I didn't get to see her before I left for Neophia."

"I was excited when I heard he was going to be coming home for the hearing." Ava wrapped an arm around her brother's shoulder. "I only have four days of leave, and I was afraid I was going to miss him."

"You might have been the only one excited about the hearing," Crystal said nervously. Thankfully, Ava chuckled.

"Well I didn't have to testify. I was able to catch a little bit of today's Q and A session. That was brutal."

"At least we only have closing statements in the morning, and then it will be over. Then it will be in the panel's hands to determine what's right." Crystal glanced in Justin's direction. He didn't seem to notice that her smile faltered as she spoke. She still wasn't convinced that renewing the program and sending more LAWON officers to Earth was the best decision for her people.

"All right everyone, the food's ready," Mrs. Anderson called over the noise in the room. "Come grab a plate and find somewhere to sit."

Crystal followed Justin and Ava to the kitchen. She was surprised that she recognized several of the dishes that had been placed out. She hadn't realized how badly she needed a taste of home until that moment. The last two days had taken more of a toll on her than she realized. She gently grabbed Justin's shoulder and turned him to face her. "Did you do all this?"

Justin beamed with pride. "I wanted to give my family a little taste of Neophia. We couldn't find everything I needed, but it should be pretty close."

"It's incredible." Crystal spooned a large helping of her favorite Neophian noodle dish on to her plate.

"Seriously Justin?" Flint yelled. Crystal turned to see her standing at the other end of the kitchen surveying the buffet the Andersons had put out. "You couldn't leave well enough alone, could you? And to think, I've been looking forward to this meal all day."

"Don't worry, I made your favorite dishes too. They're at the end," Mrs. Anderson said.

"That's why I like you so much better than your son." Flint wrapped an arm around Mrs. Anderson and gave her a quick squeeze. Flint always said she and Justin were family, but seeing them here really drove the point home for Crystal. She couldn't help but be a bit envious of them. To have two moms to love and look after you must be an incredible feeling.

Crystal turned back to the food. Once her plate was overflowing, she followed Justin into the other room where she found herself seated at a large table with Justin's parents, Ava, Flint, and her mom. Justin's younger two sisters, both still teenagers, had attached themselves to Grady and Tyler. Grady was eating up all the attention, but poor Tyler looked like he had been forced to chaperone the kids table. The four of them took a seat on the couches in the family room.

Crystal caught Tyler's eye through the open doorway and mouthed, "Sorry." She wished she could go over there and save him, but she didn't want to offend Justin or his parents. She was supposed to be getting to know them after all.

"So Ava, how are things on the home front?" Flint asked between bites of food.

"It's been worse, that's for sure. We haven't had an

attack in the last few months at least." Ava shrugged her shoulders.

"Where are you station now?" Ms. Flint asked.

"I'm on the *USS Obama*, currently patrolling the Pacific."

"I wish you could have come to Neophia with me," Justin said.

"You applied for the exchange program?" Crystal didn't really know a whole lot about Justin's sisters. He talked about Ava more than the others, but it was usually about their childhood. He never mentioned what she did as an adult. He probably still saw her as his baby sister tagging along after him.

"I did, but I was rejected." Ava took a bite of food. "This is really good. I've missed your cooking, Mom." She motioned toward the food on her plate with her fork.

Crystal set down her fork so that she could give Ava her full attention. She hadn't considered that there were U.S. soldiers that had applied for the program and didn't get chosen. "Do you know why you got rejected?"

"I'm a translator. I'm fluent in ten different languages, but none of the Neophian languages. They said they couldn't find a placement where I could be of use. I've been studying the Neophian Common Tongue on my own though," Ava said.

"I've been trying to teach Justin the Common Tongue," Crystal said, starting to eat again.

"I'd say I could help you, but you probably already know more than me," Justin laughed.

"It's for the best, if you ask me," Ms. Flint said. "It was hard enough on your mother to have one child on another planet. I can't imagine how tough it would have been if two of you went."

"We would have managed," Mrs. Anderson said with a small smile. "We just want what's best for them."

"I plan to apply again if you guys managed to get the program renewed," said Ava.

"We did what we could, though I'm not sure it will be enough. The unfounded hostility toward anyone from Neophia was an unexpected challenge." Crystal watched Ms. Flint as she spoke. She seemed perfectly happy to ignore Crystal's comment and focused instead on her plate.

"Crystal, how does your family feel about your being on Earth?" Mr. Anderson asked. The table shook slightly. Crystal was pretty sure Mrs. Anderson had just kicked him.

Crystal tried to stifle a laugh. She loved Justin's mom already. She looked toward the living room where Grady was regaling Justin's sisters with some story. It must not have been anything too bad, as Tyler looked amused by the whole situation. "Tyler's really the only family I have left."

"Of course, Justin told us about your parents. I'm sorry." Mr. Anderson reached down to rub his shin.

"It's all right. This is my family now. For what it's worth, I never dreamed I'd be on Earth," she said with a smile.

"And what do you think of it?" Ms. Flint asked.

"It's been an eye-opening experience." Crystal picked up her glass of wine and took a sip without breaking eye contact with Ms. Flint. If she was waiting for Crystal to go on about how great Earth was, she would have to keep waiting.

Justin leaned over and whispered in her ear, "You're really getting the hang of this politician thing."

Much to her mother's disappointment, Desi gathered the guys after dinner and herded them up to her apartment. She wanted to give Justin and Wolf some time alone with his family. She did notice the look of panic on Wolf's face as they left, but Desi knew she would be fine. The Andersons were the most welcoming people on the planet. They would go out of their way to make sure Wolf was comfortable.

Desi showed Grady and Price into the living room, then went to the kitchen to get them all drinks. She noticed that her mom headed straight for her bedroom without saying a single word to their guests. So much for her mom getting to know them. At least she wouldn't be around to insult them or their planet anymore. Desi opened the fridge and then called out to the guys, "We have beer or bourbon."

"Bourbon," Grady said.

"Beer for me," Price said.

Desi grabbed the drinks and rejoined them in the living room. She turned the television on out of habit. She had spent so much time alone in the apartment growing up, she started to turn the TV on just to have some noise. It made the apartment seem less lonely when her mom was working late.

Price took his drink from her. "The Andersons seem nice."

"They are, and don't worry they already love Wolf because Justin does. She'll be fine down there alone," Desi said, answering his unasked question.

"Well now that's settled, can we talk about you?" Grady raised his glass to her.

Desi plopped down on the couch next to Price. "What about me?"

"Are you coming back to Neophia for the next tour, or have you decided to stay here?"

Desi sighed. "I haven't decided yet." Movement in the hallway caught her eye. Her mom was standing in the shadows, listening to them.

"Come on Flint, you have to have some idea of what you're going to do." Price nudged her with his shoulder. "Don't try to spare our feelings. Just tell us."

"I really don't know," Desi insisted. "If you had asked me before the hearing, I was sure that I would be staying here. Believe it or not, I miss this place."

"And now?" Grady pressed.

"Now, I don't know. I do know that I can't get on board with the Neophian bashing the military seems to be so fond of. And I'm sure I didn't make a lot of friends with my testimony." The incident with Corwin at the bar flashed through her mind. If she decided to stay, she would have to deal with shit like that on a daily basis.

"It sounds like you're leaning toward coming back for *Journey's* next tour." The smile on Price's face caused Desi's heart to skip a beat. Price had been quiet about the whole topic, but Desi couldn't help but wonder if he was hoping she would come back. The two of them had developed a good friendship over the last six months—maybe there was more between them than she realized. She certainly hadn't been thrilled to see him dancing with Natasha last night.

"I wish it was that simple." Desi looked at her mom's shadow in the hallway. The last thing she wanted to do was disappoint her mother. Whatever her decision, someone would end up upset with her. She needed to figure out whose disappointment would be easiest to live with.

The sound of the front door bursting opened startled

Desi. Wolf and Justin ran into the room. Justin dove at the remote and pointed it at the TV. "You need to see this," he said as he changed the channel.

A breaking news report flashed on the screen. The scroll on the bottom read "Neophian Integration Alliance attacks hospitals across the country." This couldn't be happening.

Justin turned up the volume as the picture changed from chaos outside of a hospital to a news desk. "We can now confirm that one hundred and fifteen hospitals across the country have been targeted by the terrorist organization known as the Neophian Integration Alliance. In a coordinated attack, toxic gasses were released into each of the hospitals within a five-minute span. First responders have not been able to enter any of the buildings. Across the country, hazmat teams are assembling to try to get into the affected hospitals. We cannot confirm how many are dead at this time."

"Holy shit." The words escaped from Desi's mouth without her realizing it.

"We take you now to Ronnie Aptner who is standing by outside of Capitol Health hospital here in D.C."

The screen changed to show a young man standing outside a hospital. Behind him was a sea of emergency response vehicles. "Thanks Judy. The hazmat team has just arrived on the scene and are putting together a plan to safely enter the building without releasing the gas. Authorities here have not been able to identify what chemical was released or the method used for distribution. We'll be standing by and will report back when we have new information."

Desi turned away from the screen. She couldn't process what she was seeing. Why had they targeted the hospitals? Even in the deadliest wars, medical facilities had been untouched. This was horrific, even for Earth.

"Is that the hospital where Marcell works?" Wolf asked, her hand covering her mouth.

"Yeah, I think it is." Justin put his arm around Crystal's shoulders.

The picture on the TV suddenly went black. When it returned it showed the silhouette of a person in front of a Neophian flag.

"This isn't good," Grady said. Desi noticed that he was exchanging looks with Wolf. She tried to interpret their silent conversation to distract her from what was coming.

"People of Earth, I come to you on behalf of the Neophian Integration Alliance." The voice coming from the TV was robotic. It was impossible to tell if it was a man or woman talking. "You claim not to see the people of Neophia as your equals. You think you are superior to us because you value violence and force over peace and understanding. We are learning to speak your language. Our acts tonight might seem brutal, but in actuality, we are only helping you to live the value you claim is the most important: physical strength over anything else. We have done what you could not and eradicated the weakest portion of your population. You are welcome. Since violence is the only thing that you respond to, we will continue to get your attention in the only way we can. You have the power to stop this. Convince your government to acknowledge the debt it owes to the people of Neophia and the violence stops." The screen went black again.

"This is really bad," Wolf muttered under her breath.

When the picture came back, they were once again looking at the newsroom, only this time it was a flurry of activity as people tried to figure out what had happened.

After a few seconds things seemed to calm down and the anchor was back at the desk. "Ladies and gentlemen, we apologize for the interruption. We're not sure how we lost control of our feed, but it appears we have it back now."

"They must have highjacked the satellite feed for every news station in the country," Price murmured in awe.

"I'm getting word that we are going live to the White House, where the president is about to make a statement," the anchor said.

The screen changed again, and now they were looking at an empty podium in the White House press room. A moment later the president took the podium. "The actions of the Neophian terrorist group will not be tolerated. We have lived in fear of them long enough, and it's time we take action. I am prepared to dedicate every resource at my disposal to catching the people responsible for these horrific attacks. Until that time, I'm ordering anyone with Neophian blood to immediately report to the designated detainment center for their area. Anyone who fails to do so will be assumed to be working with the terrorists and arrested." The president walked off the stage without another word.

The screen flashed back to the newsroom. "We have received the list of detainment centers for our area. You'll find them on the bottom of the screen."

Desi watched in horror. The whole situation was insane. Every Neophian in America was to be held until the terrorist were caught? How had things gotten this bad in the six months they were gone? She looked at the rest of the team. Justin and Price seemed to be in shock. Wolf and Grady were another story. Desi could almost hear the gears turning in their minds as they formulated a plan.

"We need to get to the embassy." Wolf turned off the TV and moved toward the door. "There are going to be a lot of terrified people heading there, and we need to be there to provide support. We can't expect local law enforcement to offer them any kind of protection."

Grady jumped to his feet. "Let's move out."

Desi was about to follow when she felt her mom grab her arm. She had been so focused on the news that she hadn't noticed her mom was in the living room with them. "You can't go."

"I have to." How could her mom suggest she not go help? This was what Desi was good at, the whole reason she had stayed in the military. She needed to protect those who couldn't protect themselves.

"No, you don't. They aren't your people. It's going to be dangerous out there. You're going to be targeted just for being with them." Her mom motioned toward the open door her team had gone through.

Wolf stuck her head back into the apartment. "Flint, are you coming?"

"Yeah." Desi pulled her arm from her mom's grasp and left the apartment.

Chapter 13

Desi had the others wait inside while she went out to assess how bad the situation was. She knew people had to be angry, but she was hoping that most people would still be at home watching the news. She was wrong. The street was filled with people, most of them shouting things like, "Death to Neophia!" and "Bring down the terrorists!" At least they hadn't started organizing yet. Once that happened, her team would really be in trouble. Mandatory enlistment had been in place for the last seventy-five years, which meant that everyone on the street had at least some level of military experience.

For a second, Desi considered flagging down a cab to take them to the embassy but thought better of it. If the driver recognized them, it would be all over. He could drive them straight to one of the detention centers, or worse hand them over to the police. Taking the car Jax had been allowing them to use would be even worse. For once Desi agreed with her mom: driving around in a car with LAWON flags flying from the hood would be dangerous. They would have to get to the embassy on foot. Desi had no idea how they would make it all the way across town without being recognized.

Desi went back inside where the others were waiting. She looked at Wolf and shook her head. "It's worse than I imagined out there. We can't go out that way. You guys will be caught in a matter of minutes."

"Is there a back entrance?" Wolf looked from Desi to Justin.

"This way." Desi pushed past the others as she made her way to the back of the building. "We'll need to stick to the alleys as much as possible. Making it to the embassy without being seen isn't going to be easy." Desi disconnected the security alarm that was attached to the back door before opening it. She peered outside and was relieved to see that the alley was empty. "Come on."

They made the first few blocks easily. It felt strange to Desi to be moving through her neighborhood as if she were a criminal instead of the hometown hero she used to be. She guessed is some ways she was a criminal. The president had ordered all Neophians to turn themselves in or be arrested; she assumed that humans trying to help Neophians would be arrested, too.

Desi held out her hand to stop the others as they reached the end of the alley. They had to cross the street before slipping into the next alley for cover. They would only be in the open for a few minutes, but it was risky. They needed to time it right. She peered around the building into the street. It was fairly empty, but there was a group of people coming toward them. She noticed a few of them carrying baseball bats. As they got closer, she saw two people with their hands tied in front of them being dragged down the street. Their faces were bloodied and bruised.

"We need to wait here for a minute." Desi tried to move the group further back into the alley so that they could stay hidden in the shadows. She didn't mention the group approaching them or the Neophians they had taken prisoner. There was nothing they could do for them now.

Desi's stomach dropped as Wolf slipped past her to survey the street for herself. There was no way she would miss what was happening. Desi moved closer to her. One look at Wolf's face and Desi knew what she was going to do. The moment Wolf lifted her foot to enter the street, Desi grabbed her and pulled her back into the alley. She put her hand over Wolf's mouth to keep her quiet. The two women struggled, but Desi was winning. She dragged Wolf back into the shadows where the others were waiting. Desi didn't release Wolf until the mob had passed.

"What are you doing?" Wolf pushed Desi off her and got to her feet. "They are going to kill those people. My people. We have to help them." Wolf pointed angrily toward the street. Thankfully, she had enough sense to keep her voice down.

"I know, but we *can't*," Desi pleaded with her. "You're not being rational. There are probably thirty people in that mob, and we're unarmed. We can't help anyone if they kill us."

Grady had moved to the entrance and was looking down the street after the mob. "They're only carrying bats. The five of us can take them."

"The bats are just the weapons we can see. This is America—there's a good chance at least half of that group has a gun on them," Justin said.

"And they won't be using a stun setting," Desi said.

Wolf looked longingly to the street. Desi knew she was trying to come up with a plan to save those people. "We can't save everyone. You said yourself, we have to get to the embassy. I don't like it any more than you do, but there's no other way."

Wolf sighed and nodded. She looked down the street at the mob one last time. "How much farther to embassy?"

"At least another two miles, and the closer we get, the more populated the streets will be. Are you sure you're ready?"

"Yeah," Wolf said, reluctantly. "Lead the way."

Desi nodded and took off running across the street. She could hear the others following behind. She had no idea how she was going to get them all to the embassy in one piece.

Flint got them within a mile of the LAWON embassy, but that was a walk in the park compared to what they were about to face. The only way to the embassy was to cross a major intersection next to an open park that appeared to be the epicenter of the riots. There was nowhere left for them to hide. Cars burned in the street, windows to storefronts were smashed and the stores' contents strewn into the street. Crystal would bet good money they were Neophian owned businesses. This was what the NIA really wanted, to make the people turn on each other.

"Just like the good old days." Grady was by her side surveying the street.

"I don't know where you were serving because I've never seen anything like this." She shook her head as she took in the scene. "I would give just about anything for my side arm," she added under her breath as another mob of people moved past the alley's entrance. At least this one hadn't taken anyone prisoner.

She turned back to her team. "Turn your uniforms inside out," she said as she started to unbutton her shirt.

"Why?" Tyler asked, even as he followed her lead.

"Do you really want to walk out there with the LAWON flag over your heart?" Crystal gestured to the chaos in the street. She turned her shirt inside out before putting it back on. It looked ridiculous, but at least you couldn't tell where she was from at first glance.

"Point taken," Tyler said.

Crystal looked over her team to make sure all signs of Neophia were gone. She wished she had something to block out their faces. Anyone who had watched the broadcast of the hearing would be able to recognize them. She had to hope no one was paying close attention to those around them. With a final nod to her team, she stepped out of the alley and into the chaos on the street. She was immediately engulfed by people. She kept her head down and tried to avoid calling any attention to herself as she worked her way through the crowd. When she made it to the center of the street, she turned around to check that the rest of her team was with her. Big mistake.

"A Neophian, right there!" a woman yelled, pointing at Crystal. All around, people stopped and searched the crowd. It wouldn't take them long to hone in on her. A moment later, Grady and Tyler were by her side. Crystal sighed. She wished they had scattered. She was the only one that had been IDed. They could have gotten away.

"What do we do now?" Tyler asked with a hint of panic in his voice.

Crystal fought not to roll her eyes. If he hadn't tried to

come to her aid, he wouldn't be in this position in the first place. "Run." She scanned the mob closing in on them. There had to be a weakness somewhere, some way for them to escape. But there were too many people on the street, all pushing in on them. There was no way out. It was too late.

They went after Grady first. He fought them off as best he could. At least none of them had weapons, from what Crystal could tell. She tried to keep an eye on Grady to make sure he didn't cross a line they couldn't come back from, but someone grabbed her. She turned and punched them without looking to see who it was. Under any other circumstance, she wouldn't go after civilians, but mobs were dangerous. Things could turn deadly quickly if they didn't defend themselves.

She was a much more skilled fighter than any of the people coming at her, but there were so many of them, Crystal was having a hard time keeping up. It wouldn't be long before they overpowered her. She had to hold on as long as possible and hope for some kind of miracle to calm the mob. Someone behind her swept her legs, and Crystal fell to the ground hard. Her whole body ached as people descended on her, feet connected with every inch of her body. She fought to get back up but was pushed back down every time.

That's when she heard it. Whistles blowing all around the crowd. Suddenly the sea of people around her started to thin. Crystal quickly clambered to her feet to see two dozen police officers working their way through the crowd. She wasn't sure if this would make things better or worse for them.

She looked to Grady and Tyler. The mob had backed off from them too. They looked a little beaten up and out of breath, but nothing too serious. The police were moving in on them quickly now, their guns drawn and pointed, not at the mob, but at them. Crystal put her hands over her head. She wouldn't fight the police. "Don't fight it," she yelled to Grady and Tyler, who put their hands up.

Now that she was sure Grady and Tyler were relativity safe, she turned her attention to the officer closest to her. "We are LAWON military officers here by the request of the U.S. government to participate in a military hearing," she called out. "We need to get to the LAWON embassy." She wasn't sure it would work, but it was the best chance they had.

"Thanks for the admission of guilt," the officer barked as he approached. "It makes things so much easier." The officer grabbed Crystal's arms and twisted them painfully behind her. A second later they were secured with a pair of cold metal handcuffs. "By order of the President, you're under arrest for acts of terrorism against the United States of America."

He pushed Crystal through the mob to the line of police cars. Crystal scanned the crowd for Justin and Flint. She hadn't seen them since they left the alley. She spotted them standing off to the side, watching, Flint holding Justin back. Good. The last thing Crystal wanted was for them to be arrested, too. She needed them free if she was going to have any shot at getting them out of this. Crystal locked eyes with Justin. He lunged toward her, but she shook her head no. He stopped dead in his tracks.

The next thing Crystal knew, she was being shoved into the back of a police car with Grady and Tyler. At least they were alive. Now all she had to do was find a way to get them back to Neophia before that changed.

Chapter 14

Desi and Justin watched in horror as the rest of their team was pushed into police cars, the mob around them cheering and calling for their deaths. It turned Desi's blood cold. This was unlike anything she had ever experienced before. What had become of her people while she was serving on Neophia? She felt like she was in some alternate reality.

"What do we do now?" The look on Justin's face mirrored what she was feeling. She knew they were kidding themselves if they thought their friends would be safe in police custody.

Desi didn't have an answer. The only thing she could do was stand by and watch the chaos unfold around her. She thought things would have calmed down now that the Neophians had been arrested, but the energy from the crowd had increased. "I don't know."

"Do we go after them?" Justin voice was an octave higher than normal. He was holding back tears. This was bad. As in touch with his emotions as Justin was, he rarely cried. No matter how bad things got, he was always able to find the positive, until now.

Desi had to come up with a plan. Justin was counting on her, and she had never let him down. "No. I don't think that will help them. We might end up in jail right next to them if anyone recognizes us." The mob was moving on in search of its next victim. They needed to act quickly. "We head to the embassy as planned. Maybe they'll be able to help. There must be some kind of diplomatic immunity, right?" Desi knew she was grasping at straws, but at least it was a plan.

"Ok." Justin nodded his head. Any sign of tears Desi thought she had seen in him were gone. He was ready for battle.

"We're only a few blocks away. We just need to get past this mob without anyone realizing we work for LAWON."

"I think we should spread out. That way if one of us is caught, the other will still have a shot." Justin watched the mob carefully as he talked. Desi could see Wolf's influence coming through.

"Sound good to me. Meet up in the alley behind the embassy. I suspect the scene out front to be even crazier than this."

Justin nodded and took off. She lost sight of him within a few seconds as he merged with the crowd heading down the street. It was a good idea. Use the crowd as camouflage. She waited a minute to make sure there was enough space between her and Justin before she joined the crowd. Her group splintered off from the main mob. Their general direction was right, so Desi stuck with them.

Desi tensed as someone behind her grabbed her

shoulders. She fought the urge to turn around and punch him. The hands clapped her shoulders in triumph once and then were gone. The mob started to chant "Death to Neophia!" Desi put her fist up in solidary, though it made her feel like a traitor. She needed to blend in. The mob was headed toward the embassy; she prayed that it wouldn't be their destination. How many people really knew where the LAWON embassy was located? She certainly hadn't until three days ago, and she had grown up in the city. Thankfully, they marched right past the street the embassy was on. Desi quickly slipped from the crowd and ran down the alley.

Unfortunately, the alley wasn't as empty as she hoped. A handful of people were trying to get in the back gate. Desi wasn't sure if they were there looking for help or if they were there to cause trouble. She scanned them quickly, looking for Justin. With his head start, he should be here by now. What would she do if he didn't make it? She couldn't do this without him.

Her heart almost stopped when she saw him emerge from the shadows. He quickly made his way over to her, glancing back at the gate as he went. "How are we going to get in?"

Once again, she didn't know what to say. She hadn't been able to think that far ahead. Her mind was only capable of operating one step at a time right now. The crowd at the back gate was getting agitated. Someone would need to intervene soon. Surely the embassy had a security detail. Where were they?

Desi watched the house as if she would find some secret entrance they could slip through. Instead she saw Natasha emerge from the back door and make her way to the gate. She was alone, and Desi feared for her safety. If anyone there wanted to harm her, it wouldn't be hard to do.

"Everyone, please stay calm," she called to the group. "My father is working with LAWON to try to get everyone back to Neophia as quickly as possible. Until then please return to your homes, lock your doors, and monitor the LAWON news alert frequency for directions."

"We can't go home. They know where to find us," someone yelled.

"I'm sorry we're working on making arrangements as fast as we can," Natasha called. Why was she the one out here? There had to be someone better equipped to handle this. No one left. Desi watched as Natasha sighed and turned back toward the house.

They were about to lose their chance of getting inside. "Natasha!" Desi yelled after here. She hoped that Natasha would remember her.

Natasha turned back and made eye contact with Desi. Relief washed over her face as she rushed toward the gate again. Desi and Justin tried to push their way to the front of the crowd.

"Please let them in," Natasha called in desperation. Her calm demeanor starting to crack.

"Why do they get to come in and we don't?" someone yelled. It was a valid question.

"Please, we are LAWON military officers. We need to get in to help." Justin quickly took off his shirt and turned it the right way before putting it back on. Desi followed suit. The LAWON flag was now an asset instead of a target.

A few people moved aside, but for the most part, everyone rushed forward as Natasha started to unlock the gate. She quickly closed it. Panic was visible in her eyes. Desi motioned for her to come to a part of the fence away from the crowd.

"What do I do?" Natasha asked, the panic raising in her voice.

"Where are your fathers?" Desi asked. This girl shouldn't be the one out here handling this.

"Jax has been holed up in his office since the attack happened. The phone won't stop ringing, and his whole staff is gone for the day. And Marcell...." Natasha's voice faded away as tears started to form in her eyes. Desi had been hoping that Marcell had the night off, but clearly that wasn't the case. Desi looked to Justin for help. He was better at handling emotional people than she was.

"Is there any way to prove that those people are Neophian citizens?" Justin looked over his shoulder at the people at the gate. Desi was pretty sure a few more had arrived since they started talking.

Natasha took a deep breath and nodded her head. Desi noticed that no more tears fell from her eyes. Justin had been right not to bring up Marcell. Right now, Natasha needed something to do to keep her mind off her father, and that was something they could help with. "It should be indicated on their IDs."

Desi could feel the fear coming from the crowd at the gate. The longer they talked to Natasha the more restless they became. "You have to let them in," Desi said.

"But how do we make sure none of them are here to hurt us?" Natasha asked. It was a valid point, but looking over the crowd, Desi didn't think they had come here looking to cause problems. They were scared and looking for help. The only place they would be safe was on the other side of that fence.

It was time for Desi to take charge. "We'll verify everyone's citizenship and search them for weapons.

Once they are on the other side of that gate, they're technically on Neophian soil and can't be arrested. It should start to ease the panic."

Natasha nodded and started to make her way back to the gate.

Desi took a deep breath and walked back over to the crowd that was watching her intently. "Everyone, listen up. Form two lines and have your Neophian identification ready. We need to search everyone for weapons before you can be let inside. If you have any kind of weapon on you, please hand them over to me or Ensign Anderson so we can get you inside quickly."

She was shocked by how fast everyone organized themselves per her instruction. A few people flagged her down to hand over guns and knives. Tools that had probably been key to getting them to the embassy safely were given up without question. She knew that would never happen if these people were humans. It only solidified in Desi that they were doing the right thing by letting them in. Desi took one of the lines, while Justin took the other. Forty-five minutes later everyone was IDed, searched, and through the gate. Finally, Desi and Justin were let inside. Natasha quickly relocked the gate and brought everyone into the house.

"We need to speak to Jax," Desi said to Natasha as they watched the people they had let inside milling around the large living room. A room that had been filled with Neophians and U.S. politicians drinking and dancing the night before. What a difference a day made.

Natasha nodded and led them upstairs to Jax's office. She knocked quietly, but didn't wait for a response before opening the door and showing them inside. Jax was standing with his back to them behind his desk on the phone. Desi shifted her weight from one foot to the other as they waited for Jax to turn around an acknowledge them.

"You can't do this!" Jax yelled into the phone. "My people didn't do anything wrong. You can't go rounding them all up just because you think someone from Neophia is guilty." He paused and ran his free hand through his hair. "How do you even know that this group is actually from Neophia? Shutting down the portals could be exactly what they want, and you're playing right into their hands." Jax slammed the phone down on his desk.

He was muttering under his breath when he turned around and saw them. "You don't know how happy I am to see you. We need help. I can't get my staff here without putting them in danger, and I know people will start showing up here if they haven't already."

"They helped me get a group of Neophians inside," Natasha said. "I hope that's ok."

"Of course, that's the only way we're going to be able to keep our people safe. Are Commander Wolf, Lieutenant Grady, and Ensign Price downstairs?" Jax looked from Desi to Justin.

Desi shook her head. "They were arrested while we were trying to make it here."

Jax let out a string of profanities that belonged in her line of work instead of his.

"We were hoping you could help us get them out," Justin said.

"I wish I could. I've been trying to get the detainment order reversed for the last hour with no luck. If anything, the U.S. government seems to be doubling down, arresting anyone they can. Doesn't matter if they were on their way to turn themselves in or not. We aren't safe anywhere. Neophians are being hunted down and killed all over the country." Jax started to pace around the room.

"Daddy," Natasha said quickly as she took a step closer to Jax. "Is there any word from the hospital?"

Jax went to her and grabbed her hands in his. "Not yet." He leaned forward and pressed his forehead to hers. "Stay strong baby girl. We'll get through this." He kissed her forehead. Natasha nodded and left the room quickly. Desi could see the tears starting to form in her eyes as she went.

"Mr. Ambassador, I'm sorry for what you're going through right now, but what about our people?" Desi didn't want to be insensitive, but she needed to get her people out of police custody before something happened to them. Jax said Neophians were being killed across the country, and none of them had spent the last two days insulting the U.S. military on television.

"I'm not sure there is anything I can do for them at this point."

"Fine." Desi turned toward Justin. "We'll head over to the police station and see if there's anything we can do there." She took a few steps toward the door.

"You can't," Jax called after her. "I've been told military police is taking authority over all Neophians that have been arrested. They won't let you in. If anything, they'll arrest you for trying to help them."

"Then we're screwed." Desi threw her hands up in the air and sat down on the chair near the door. She had failed her team.

"Maybe not," Justin said with a wicked smile.

"What do you mean?" Desi looked up at him.

"You said the military police is in charge of all arrested Neophians, right?"

"I don't see how that helps," Jax said.

"Well, we're military." Justin's eyes gleamed as he looked at Desi. She couldn't believe he was suggesting this.

"It won't work. Too many people know who we are."

"It will if we're convincing enough. The cops will have to let us in to see them. We might even be able to trick the cops into releasing the prisoners into our custody."

"You'll have to be smart about it." Jax turned to his desk and started to dig through the drawers. "You can't head over there right away. Wait an hour or two at least so your team can be processed and put into the system. If you show up before that happens, you'll give yourselves away. They'll be recording all interrogations, so you'll need this." Jax handed Justin a small silver clip with a button on it. "It'll create enough white noise on the video so they won't be able to hear what you're talking about."

"Thank you." Desi got up and shook Jax's hand.

"If there is anything I can do for your friends, I will," Jax said.

"You take care of your people Mr. Ambassador, and we'll take care of ours." Desi left the room with Justin in tow. This was going to be risky, but it was the only chance they had.

They left the embassy the same way they had come in. There was a new crowd of people at the back gate, double the size of the last one. Natasha was back at the gate with a few of the people they had let in earlier, checking IDs and searching everyone for weapons. Desi nodded to Natasha as she and Justin slipped through the gate. She looked back over her shoulder as they made their way down the alley. She wished there was more she could do for them.

The force the officers used to pull Crystal out of the car nearly brought her to her knees. They would get no protection from the cops. She wasn't sure if they were in more danger now than when the mob closed in on them. At least out there they could defend themselves. Now they were helpless.

They were brought in the front door of the station. The front desk was empty, and the silence of the building gave her the chills. Where was everyone?

"Got a few more for you to process," the officer holding her yelled into the heart of the station.

"Yeah, one second. I'm just about done with this one," a voice responded, though Crystal couldn't find its owner. Next to her, Grady's handcuffs were clinking together. She knew he was trying to get out of them, though she wasn't sure what good it would do. They would all be shot before they reached the street.

They waited five minutes before a male middle-aged officer appeared. Crystal expected the face of the police force to look more professional, the least he could do was tuck in his shirt. "Three at once, nice catch. And what's this?" The officer walked over to Crystal and pulled at her shirt to reveal the inside of her uniform. "Military officers. We've been waiting for these celebrities. Bring them back. I'm going to need some help processing them. Between the scene down at the hospital and what's going on out in the streets, we're severely understaffed here."

He grabbed Crystal and pushed her through the station. The officer that had brought them in followed behind with Grady and Tyler. They stood silently while the processing officer put them into the system. Every once in a while, Grady or Tyler would shoot her a look. She knew they were looking for some clue as to what her plan was. Too bad she hadn't figured out what that was yet.

Crystal gave her information in a robotic voice as she memorized the layout of the police station. She glanced down at the computer as she answered his last question. That's when she realized they already had a lot more information on her than she had provided. Someone had reported them to the police. According to the time on the file, it was only a few minutes after they had left Flint's apartment. Crystal was having a hard time comprehending the name that was listed as the source. All it said was D. Flint. There was no way Flint would have done this, but her mother would. Ms. Flint had been making some pretty anti-Neophian comments all night. What would Flint say if she knew her mother had betrayed them? Crystal vowed never to speak a word of it.

Once they had all been processed, they were led back to the holding cell. Finally, the handcuffs were removed as one after the other they were pushed into the cell. Crystal's eyes locked with the person on the other side of the cell immediately. She couldn't believe what she was seeing. It wasn't possible.

Crystal rushed at him and pushed him against the back wall of the cell, ramming her forearm against his neck as she held him there. "Was it you?"

Ryan smirked at her. She couldn't process it. Ryan Young, Teria General, who hated all things human, was on Earth. And not only that, but in the same place as she was. It was too big a coincidence.

"No," he answered, his voice coming out as a growl.

Crystal pushed her arm into his neck harder. "I don't

believe you." He had to be connected to the attack somehow. She could think of no other explanation for him being on Earth.

"Why would I lie?" he asked breathlessly. She was cutting off his windpipe, but she didn't care. Anger that had been building up inside her over the last three days had finally found an outlet.

Behind her she heard the officer that had brought them back laughing. "Should we stop her?" one of them said.

"Nah, if she kills him, that's one less person we have to keep track of," the other said. The next thing Crystal heard was the door leading back into the station closing. The officers were gone.

Crystal didn't want to give them the satisfaction of doing their dirty work for them, but she couldn't let up either. "What are you doing here Ryan?" She maintained a steady pressure on his throat. Not enough to completely cut off his oxygen supply, but close.

"That's none of your damn business," he choked out.

"Crystal." Grady was standing behind her. She felt him place a hand on her shoulder, but she didn't turn around. This was between her and Ryan. "Crys. That's enough."

Reluctantly, she pulled her arm away from Ryan's throat. She was glad to see him bend over as he fought to catch his breath.

"I'm fine." She held up a hand to stop Grady and Tyler and walked to the other side of the cell. That's when she heard it. A soft whimper coming from the back corner of the bottom bunk. There was someone else in the cell with them. Crystal bent down but still didn't see anyone. She moved closer and saw a mound of blankets moving in time with the whimper. She slowly pulled the blanket away to reveal a little girl with tears in her eyes.

"Hey, it's ok," Crystal said in an attempt to calm her down. The best she could tell, the girl was no more than seven or eight years old. Where were her parents? How could the police throw her in here alone? She was just a child. "I'm Crystal. What's your name?" She tried to keep all the anger that was still coursing through her veins out of her voice.

"Melody," the girl squeaked out. It was better than Crystal had hoped for. If she had been in the girl's position, she wasn't sure she would have been able to talk at all.

"Melody. That's a really pretty name. Do you know where your parents are?" Crystal reached out and brushed a tear from the girl's cheek. Melody shook her head, but didn't start crying again. "Can you tell me what happened?" Crystal sat on the edge of the bed and motioned for Melody to come sit next to her. Slowly the girl moved forward and sat with her legs pressed against Crystal's. She fought the urge to move away — as much as Crystal didn't like being touched she knew that was what Melody needed right now, so Crystal wrapped her arm around the girl pulled her close.

"I was out to dinner with my mom and dad, when something bad happened on the TV. I hadn't even finished eating yet when they grabbed me and we ran from the restaurant. They said bad people were going to try get us and that we needed to hide. We were in the park when the bad people found us." Melody looked at the floor the whole time she talked.

Crystal exchanged a look with Grady. They both knew how this story was going to end. Tyler was sitting on the bench next to the bed with his head in his hands.

"My dad threw me into the fountain and told me to

go to the bottom and not let anyone see me," Melody finished between tiny sobs.

"So you're Aquienian and Sertex?" Crystal said trying to keep Melody from completely breaking down again.

Melody nodded.

"My friend Jim is also Aquienian and Sertex." Crystal pointed at Grady who crouched down in front of them and smiled. Crystal felt the girl started to relax a little.

Melody looked at Grady. "I heard a lot of noise above me, but I didn't move. I was scared. When the noise stopped my mom and dad were gone."

Out of the corner of her eyes Crystal saw Ryan run a finger across his neck. She should have cut off his air supply a little longer.

"Then the police came and took me."

Melody climbed into Crystal's lap and started to cry into her chest. Crystal didn't know what to do. She wasn't the maternal type. She looked to Grady and Tyler for help, but they didn't do anything. Crystal wrapped her arms around Melody and stroked her hair while she cried. For the first time in her life Crystal had no idea how she was going to get her team home safely, let alone protect the child that was somehow finding comfort in her.

She noticed Tyler had moved to the cell's door and was trying to examine the keypad lock without being noticed. Crystal felt a surge of hope course through her veins. "Can you get it open?"

Tyler looked at her and all hope was dashed. "Not without alerting someone. The only way to get it open is with a physical key with a chip imbedded in it. If I try to bypass that, they'll know instantly."

Crystal nodded and continued to stroke the girl's hair. The stream of tears rolling down her cheeks had not slowed. Crystal knew she had to get Melody out of here, she had to get them all out of here, she just didn't know how to do it.

Chapter 15

Desi had no idea how long it would take for Wolf, Grady, and Price to be processed at the police station, but she figured three hours would be long enough to avoid suspicion. They just had to hope that no one from the actual military police showed up while they were there.

Justin hadn't said a word since they left the embassy. She knew he was taking Wolf's arrest hard. She wanted to tell him that it would be all right, but she couldn't lie to him. It was entirely possible that their friends had already been killed. It happened all the time to people in police custody, and that was when everyone wasn't out for Neophian blood to begin with.

When they arrived back at their apartment building Justin headed directly to his parent's apartment. Desi didn't argue. She knew it would be safe to talk freely in front of the Andersons, something she wasn't sure they could do in front of her mother. Justin slammed the door shut behind them before he started to pace in the living room.

Mr. and Mrs. Anderson were sitting in the living room waiting for them. Ava, Isabell, and Reanna were nowhere to be seen. "Did you get them to the embassy all right?" Mr. Anderson rose to his feet as he watched his son carefully. Justin looked at his dad and then headed to the kitchen. He returned a moment later with a glass of whisky. This wasn't like him. She needed him to snap out of it. She could only handle one crisis at the moment.

"No," Desi answered Mr. Anderson. "They were arrested." She watched the color drain out his face.

Justin set the drink down without taking a sip. If he didn't stop moving, she was going to lose it. She needed Justin to be in control if they were going to have any chance of getting their friends out of this. "We're going to break them out though."

Desi turned to face him. She must have heard him wrong. "I'm sorry, we're going to do what now?"

"We're going to break them out of jail." Justin crossed his arms and stared her down. He was challenging her to contradict him.

"I never agreed to that."

"Yes, you did." Justin pointed at her as he talked.

"No, I agreed to go down there so we can talk to our team and figure out where we go from here," Desi said evenly, trying not to push Justin closer to the edge. It was like Justin had been part of an entirely different conversation than her.

"That's a waste of time. We both know the longer they are in there, the more danger they are in. We need to break them out now." He slammed his knuckles into the palm of his other hand to accent each word.

"Justin, be reasonable. We can't break them out until we know what we're up against," Desi argued.

"The police are distracted with everything else going on. I bet they aren't even guarding our people." There was a manic look in Justin's eyes she had never seen before. "We could easily sneak a few guns in, take out the guards and free our team." Desi looked to his parents for help, but they looked just as shocked as she was.

"Justin you know you can't do that." Mrs. Anderson got up and walked over to him. "Those officers didn't make the law. It's not their fault. You can't go in there and just start killing people."

"And you don't think Neophian's are being killed all across the country right now?" Justin waved his arm at the window. Desi thought back to the people they had seen being dragged away by the mob on their way to the embassy. She hoped they hadn't suffered.

"We have to be better than that," Desi said. She couldn't believe that she had to be the voice of reason right now.

"Then what do you suggest we do? Because we both know they aren't going to let our people go," Justin said.

"Your idea to pose as military police is a good one, but we're going to use it to get in there and talk to Wolf. She'll know what our next steps should be."

"Then you'll need these." Ava was leaning against the wall near the front door holding up three MP patches. Desi had no idea how long she had been standing there. "Mom, can you grab your sewing machine?" Mrs. Anderson smiled and left the room.

Desi went over and took the patches from Ava. "How did you manage to get these?" The military uniform stores were tightly guarded to prevent people from trying to pass themselves off as a higher rank than they were. In a country full of soldiers, there was a lot of prestige that came with officer bars.

Ava blushed slightly. "I'm dating a guy who works in the distribution center. I called him right after you headed to the embassy. Just in case."

"You're brilliant." Desi ran her fingers over the stitching on the patches. With these, they would have no issues getting in to see their people.

"Ava, why are there three patches?" Justin looked from the patches in Desi's hand to his sister.

"Because I'm going with you."

"No. No way." Justin crossed his arms over his chest. "Crystal's life is already in danger for no reason; I'm not putting you at risk, too."

"I'm not a kid anymore," Ava said, jutting out her chin. "I'm more than capable of protecting myself. I'm a solider, too." Ava stood her ground. She had grown up a lot from the little bookworm Desi had known.

"You're a translator, not a combat solider." Justin looked longingly at the glass of whiskey sitting on the table, but didn't move to pick it up.

"The fact that I'm a translator is the very reason you need me to go with you," Ava pressed. "My cover is better than yours. Besides you don't know how bad things have gotten over the last six months." Ava crossed the room and put a hand on his shoulder. "I do. You need me."

After a few seconds, Justin looked at her. "Fine. But if things start to go south, I want you to get out of there and let Desi and me handle it, ok? I'll never forgive myself if something happens to you."

Ava smiled and nodded. "Do you guys have an old set of uniforms we can add the patches on?"

"I should have some upstairs. I'll be right back." Desi

left the Andersons' apartment, hoping she would be able to slip in and out without her mom noticing. She couldn't afford any distractions; there were too many lives in her hands.

Crystal knew that it was only a matter of time before Justin and Flint would show up, and she wanted to make sure they were ready. She had started to develop a plan to get them out, but it was risky. She was sure the entire U.S. military would be after them the moment word of their escape got out. They wouldn't be able to do anything without a way off the planet. Having Melody with them only further complicated things. Crystal had never had to factor an eight-year-old into her combat plans before. The other issue was Ryan. She would need him to corporate if her plan was going to work. They had been a good team once, but there was so much bad blood between them now. Crystal didn't know if it was possible to work with him. If he betrayed her again, they would be killed. But that problem was farther down on her list. The first thing she needed to figure out was how to get a message to Flint without the cops finding out.

"Does anyone have paper and pen?" Crystal was sitting in the corner of the cell with Grady and Tyler. Melody hadn't allowed more than two feet of distance between them since she told them what happened to her parents. She was currently sitting on Crystal's lap. Melody had grabbed Crystal's arm and wrapped it around her. Crystal wasn't entirely comfortable with the contact, but at least Melody had stopped crying.

"Sure, how much do you need?" Grady rolled his eyes. "We were all searched together remember. We don't have anything to work with." Crystal shot him a look. She knew Grady never did well when contained like this, so she'd let his snark slide for now.

"Why do you need it?" Tyler asked.

"I want to get a message to Flint without the cops overhearing." Crystal lowered her voice. Ryan was watching them intently from the other side of the cell.

"Do you really think they're coming?"

"Of course they are, and we need to be ready."

"So you have a plan?" A flicker of hope returned to Grady's eye.

"I have the start of a plan. There are a few things I need to work out before we can execute it." She looked over at Ryan, who winked at her the moment their eyes locked. Maybe she could figure out a way to pull this off without involving him.

"I had a coloring book and some colored pencils in my backpack when they brought me here," Melody said. It hadn't occurred to Crystal that Melody was listening. Kids were not one of her strengths. She looked around the cell hopefully, but of course the bag wasn't there. These were the same people who threw a child in a cell alone with a bunch of adults. Why would they let her keep her bag?

Crystal shifted the girl so she could see her face. "Melody, do you think you can do me a really big favor?"

"I can try. What do you want me to do?"

"I want you to cry really loud. If we can get one of the officers in here, I might be able to convince him to give you your bag back. Do you think you can do that?"

Melody nodded. Crystal watched as she closed her eyes and scrunched up her face. A few seconds later large tear started to run down her cheeks. Crystal was impressed. She wouldn't have been able to do that if she tried for an hour.

Crystal motioned for Grady and Tyler to spread out so it wouldn't look suspicious when the cops came in. "That's great, Melody," Crystal whispered. "Now I need you to be louder so they hear you in the other room."

Melody cried harder and added in a piercing scream that made Crystal's ears ring. This kid knew what she was doing. Crystal kept one eye fixed on the door, but no one came. How heartless could these people be? Melody sounded like she had been mortally wounded. It should have been more than enough to cause some level of concern for the police in the other room. Maybe this wasn't going to work. Crystal would need to come up with a different plan to pass a message to Flint. She was about to tell Melody she could stop when one of the police officers finally came back to check on them.

"What the hell is going on in here?" the cop demanded as he walked to the front of their cell.

"Can you do something to shut the kid up?" Ryan yelled over Melody's screams. Crystal spun around to see him pressing a finger into his ear with the trace of a smirk on his lips. So he had been paying attention to them and was willing to play along — for now anyway.

Every muscle in Crystal's body tensed as the cop pulled out his night stick. She gently moved the girl off her lap so she was sitting on the floor behind Crystal. She needed to be ready to spring into action. Crystal hadn't wanted to hurt anyone, but if he made a move toward Melody, she would take him out. It wasn't the escape plan she had in mind, but if it came down to it, she would make it work. She shot Grady and Tyler a look to get ready.

"Hey kid," the cop yelled and banged his nightstick against the bars. "Knock it off." Crystal relaxed slightly as he returned the stick to his hip.

"Brilliant," Ryan said as Melody turned up the volume.

Crystal got up and went over to where the cop stood. She wanted to make sure she was between him and Melody in case he decided to do something drastic to quiet her. The cop's hand went back to his nightstick as Crystal got closer. She held up her hands and made sure to stand a foot away from the bars so he wouldn't perceive her as threat. "She's scared. She lost her parents today and has no idea what's going on. Maybe if she had something to do, I would be able to get her to calm down."

"What did you have in mind?" The officer rubbed his ear as he eyed the girl.

"I don't know." Crystal slowly lowered her hands. "Did she come in with anything? A toy or something. Maybe a coloring book to keep her busy?" She let the words spill out of her mouth as if she was coming up with things off the top of her head and not fishing for the item she needed.

"It's against the rules for prisoners to have personal items. You need to find a way to keep her quiet on your own, or I'll be forced to intervene." The officer started to turn away. Crystal felt all hope slipping away.

"There has to be something you can do," Grady said in desperation. "This is torture."

Tyler rushed forward. "Come on man, don't you have kids?" The officer paused with his back to them. "How would you feel if someone was treating your kid like this when they could do something about it? What harm could she really do with a coloring book?"

"I'll see if I can find something." The cop left.

Crystal breathed a sigh of relief. She turned to Melody

and gave her a quick thumbs up. "You're doing great," she murmured. "Keep it up a little longer." Melody nodded and kept crying, though she stopped screeching for the moment, which Crystal was grateful for.

The police officer returned a few minutes later and threw a notebook and few colored pencils on the floor of the cell. "Now shut her up."

Crystal gathered the items and took them over to Melody. She rubbed the girl's back and whispered for her to start calming down. She expected the officer to leave, but he pulled a chair over to the cell and sat down. How was Crystal going to write her message to Flint with him watching them? She looked to Grady and Tyler for help, but they both shrugged their shoulders. Did she have to figure everything out on her own?

"I think she's all right now. Thanks." Crystal hoped this would be enough to get him to leave, but he sat there and looked at them. She sat down on the cold concrete floor next to Melody and pretended to watch her color. Melody kept looking up at Crystal expectantly. The kid wanted to help, but if she wasn't careful, she would give them away.

"Do you speak common tongue?" Crystal asked in her native language.

"Ke," Melody responded back in the Neophian Common Tongue.

This was good. Given the general lack of knowledge about Neophia on Earth, Crystal assumed the cop wouldn't be able to understand what they were saying. This could work. Crystal started to dictate a message to Melody, making sure to insert directions for Melody to smile and laugh along the way. They had to make it look like they were only playing. After a few minutes Crystal noticed that the cop was paying closer attention to them than before. Had she been wrong in assuming he couldn't understand them? They were too far in to stop now, so Crystal kept going trying hard to ignore the eyes fixed on her.

"Hey, you two." The cop stood up and walked over to the side of the cell where Melody and Crystal were. "Enough with the weird noises."

They only had half of the message down on paper. Crystal needed more time. She stood up and walked over to the bars directly in front of where the cop was standing, never breaking eye contact.

He started to fidget, and his hand went back to the nightstick on his hip. Now all she needed was something to push him over the edge. She started to chant in the Common Tongue while waving her hands at him. She felt ridiculous, but it was the only thing she could think to do.

Melody gasped as soon as Crystal stopped talking. The kid's timing was perfect. Grady had come over to her, but Crystal maintained eye contact with the cop. If she acknowledged him, she wasn't sure she would be able to keep up the effect.

"I don't need this shit today." The cop threw his hands up. "If she does anything with those pencils, I'm taking it out on you." He pointed at Crystal and left.

Crystal didn't move until the door had closed firmly behind him.

"What was that?" Tyler asked.

Crystal didn't answer. She was back on the floor with the notebook and pencil in her hand, writing frantically. She didn't know how much time she had before someone came back to check on them.

"You are aware you just told him that purple cows poop rainbows and eat children for breakfast?" Grady said, standing over her watching her work.

"Yep." Crystal didn't look up as she scribbled down the last few details Flint would need to pull off her plan.

Grady folded his arms over his chest. "Why?"

Crystal shrugged, but didn't look up. "I needed him to leave."

"And what if he knows the Common Tongue or has someone translate the video feed?" Tyler asked. The tone of his voice made her look up briefly. His face was washed in concern, like he was afraid she had lost her mind.

"Then they will think they got the translation wrong, because what kind of lunatic would say something like that?" Ryan got up and joined Grady and Tyler. "The hand motion was a nice touch by the way."

Crystal couldn't help but smile. At least someone understood. She had forgotten what it felt like to be on the same page as Ryan. She never had to explain to him what she was doing, because he always knew what she was thinking. She quickly finished writing and ripped out the page. She folded it as small as she could and tucked it up the cuff of her sleeve. Now all she needed was an opportunity to pass it to Flint.

Ryan sat down on the floor next to her, his leg brushing against her knee. It felt comforting and wrong all at the same time. Would she ever be able to get to a place where Ryan didn't affect her? "I take it you have a plan." He nodded to the note in her sleeve.

"Maybe." Crystal needed Ryan for her plan to work, but the last thing she wanted to do was let him know it. She couldn't give him that kind of power.

"I want in."

Crystal made sure her face was void of any emotions before she turned to look at him. "Why would I help you?"

"Because we both know that you need me in order to pull off whatever you're thinking."

She hated how well Ryan still knew her. She had never been able to completely hide what she was feeling from him, no matter how hard she tried. "I don't know about that. Maybe I like the idea of you locked up in a cell on Earth, wasting away the rest of your days." Crystal looked across the cell. She knew if she looked him in the eye, he would be able to tell that she was lying.

"How about we call a truce?" he continued. Was he laughing at her? "Just until we get out of here, of course."

Crystal turned to look at him. For the moment, she had the power, and she wasn't about to give it up. "On one condition."

"What?"

"You tell me the truth about what you're doing here and how you're involved in the attack, because we both know you are."

Ryan leaned back on his elbows so he was stretched out on the floor. "Why not? It's not like you're going to be able to do anything about it anyway."

"So, you are responsible for this?" She wasn't sure why she was surprised. Teria would be the only ones on Neophia that would benefit from a war with Earth. The first move would be to shut the space portals down, which was want Rank wanted.

"Not exactly. It's true I was sent here to try to help the NIA, but by the time I got to them, it was too late. They had already set this attack in motion. The best I could do was offer them a few extra words of encouragement. The speech though, that was my handiwork. Did you like the part about helping Earth eliminate their weak? I personally thought it was a nice touch."

"You're horrible."

"Thank you." Ryan lay down the rest of the way, his head on his arm, relaxing as if he were sprawled out in a field instead of a jail cell floor.

Chapter 16

Desi wished she felt more confident as she walked into the police station. Justin was even closer to the edge than when they arrived at his parents' apartment. Desi thought he would calm down while they worked on their uniforms, but she was wrong. She was afraid that if anything went wrong, he would crack, and she would be on her own. Not that Ava was useless, but she wasn't trained in combat.

"Where the hell is everyone?" They stood at the front desk in the police station, and there wasn't another soul in sight. She peeked through the window on the door leading into the heart of the station, but it looked deserted. Desi had been monitoring the police scanner and had heard that several Neophians had been brought here. Had she heard wrong? If they showed up at the wrong station, their cover could be blown, and they would be back at square one.

"There have been a lot of cuts lately. A lot of people

laid off." Ave looked around the entrance room as she talked, though Desi had no idea what she was looking for.

"Hello," Desi called. "Military Police. We are here to interrogate the Neophians you have in custody." She had rehearsed the line over and over in her head as they made their way to the station. She had to believe it if she was going to have a shot at getting the police to believe it.

"I'm coming," a voice said from somewhere in the station. Desi breathed a sigh of relief. A second later an annoyed looking middle aged officer appeared looking a little aggravated. Desi took in his untucked shirt and arrogant posture. She hated him instantly. "What's that again?"

"We need to question some of the Neophians you have detained here," Desi repeated.

"On whose authority?"

Desi tapped the MP patch on her chest. "The U.S. government."

"You should have received a notice that we were coming," Ava said with a confidence that Desi didn't feel.

"I didn't get anything." He crossed his arms and looked Ava up and down like he was a lion stalking his prey. Justin started to move in an attack position, but Desi reached out to stop him. Ava had this under control.

"Check again if you like, but if you hold us up, you'll have to answer to the military," Ava said. Desi had never realized how intimidating Ava could be. It was hard for Desi to see her as anything other than Justin's kid sister.

The cop took a step closer to Ava. "And who might

you be?"

Ava held her ground. "Ensign Ava Anderson. I'm a translator."

"A translator? Good, we need one of those." The officer's posture started to relax. He waved them over to the back wall of the station where a bank of screens showed security footage. Desi's eyes went directly to the interrogation room. The camera was pointed at small table in the center of the room without a direct shot at either of the seats. She could make that work.

The officer hit a few buttons rewinding the feed from the cell. "There's some crazy bitch locked up that's been speaking all kinds of nonsense. I think she tried to curse me."

Desi ripped her eyes away from the interrogation room. There was no way she heard him right. "She did what?"

"She tired to curse me. She was waving her hands around and chanting in this weird language. Here maybe you can make out what she was saying." The officer hit play and stepped aside.

Desi had to bite the inside of her cheeks to keep herself from bursting out in laughter. She would have given anything to see that. Desi couldn't imagine Crystal doing something as ridiculous as pretending to curse someone. It also didn't speak very highly for the cop if he believed Neophians had the power to curse people.

Ava shook her head. "I think you're right. I'm not an expert on Neophian witchcraft, but it certainly sounds like she has damned your soul and the souls of all your descendants to a life of misery and hardship." Desi had no idea how Ava managed to say this with a straight face. Desi was moments away from bursting and blowing their cover.

"I knew it," the officer said under his breath. "That bitch is going to pay for what she did to me."

"Take us to them." It was the first time Justin has spoken since they entered the station, and there was a hardness there that caught Desi off guard. She hoped that once he saw Wolf he would start to relax.

The cop waved for them to follow him through the empty police station and back to the holding cell. "Which one do you want to question first?"

Desi barely heard the question. She was shocked to see General Ryan Young, Terian terrorist and murderous pain in the ass, sprawled out across the floor of the cell like he was relaxing in the sun. Wolf sat on one of the benches with a child on her lap. Desi wasn't sure which threw her off more.

"That one," Justin said through gritted teeth, pointing at Young. That was not the plan, but it was too late now.

"I'm flattered you thought of me." Young jumped to his feet. He looked from Wolf to Justin with an evil grin on his face. Desi felt her heart plummet into the pit of her stomach. She knew what Young was capable of, and she wasn't sure Justin would be able to handle his mind games right now.

The cop pulled out his side arm and pointed it toward the cell. "All right you four, move to the back of the cell." He waved the gun toward their people. Wolf picked up the child and carried her to the back of the cell with Grady and Price. The cop shifted the gun to Young. "You, put your hands behind your back and walk here slowly." The cop unlocked the cell. He cuffed Young's hands, pulled him out, and quickly relocked the cell door.

He pushed Young down the hall with Justin trailing in his wake. Desi hesitated, turning to look at Wolf. Her mouth was taunt, and her eyes bored in Desi. She knew Wolf wanted to say something, but she couldn't. Desi gave her the most reassuring look she could without giving anything away before following the others down the hall.

Ava was waiting outside for her. "Who is that, and why does Justin look like he wants to kill him?"

"That's Crystal's ex-boyfriend." Desi took a deep breath and opened the door. Young was already sitting at the interrogation table when she entered. The cop lingered in the doorway. "Thank you," Desi ordered, "we can take it from here." She couldn't have him hearing any of what was about to go down. Desi looked at Justin, whose fists were clenched at his side.

The cop shrugged his shoulders and left. Desi reached into her pocket and clicked the chip Jax had given them. She prayed it would work. By the time Desi looked up, Justin had already made it across the room and his fist was inches away from Young's face. He managed to get two punches in before she could get to him.

"That's enough." Desi grabbed his arm, but he pulled it away and landed a third punch.

Young barely flinched, even though Desi knew Justin had put everything he had into those punches. Young's eyes were both bruised, and a thin trail of blood ran from the corner of a mouth that still wore the same smirk it had when he first saw them. "Is that really the best you can do? I was right, there's no way you're strong enough for Crystal. She must be biding her time with you until a real man comes along."

Justin took a deep breath, his nostrils flaring with anger. He lunged at Young, knocking him off the chair. With Young's hands cuffed behind him, there was no way for him to protect himself from the onslaught of

Justin's fists.

"Seriously, Justin!" Desi yelled but she didn't move to stop him. Personally, she thought Young deserved what he was getting, but they didn't have time for this.

Ava rushed forward and somehow managed to get between Justin and Young. "This isn't you." She grabbed his wrist. Justin struggled to free it from her grasp, but Ava's grip held as she stared her brother down. Desi saw the tension finally leave Justin's body. Ava released him and carefully helped Young back into that chair.

Desi took a seat across from Young. "Since we have you here, why don't you tell us how you managed to pull this off?"

"What makes you think I'd tell you anything, especially after that little stunt?" Young leaned over and spit a wad of blood on to the floor.

"Is Teria behind the attacks?"

Young just smirked at her. She didn't know why she was wasting her time on him. She needed to talk to Wolf.

"Are you here to kill Crystal?" Justin asked from behind her.

Young's smirk turned into a large smile. "No. Though if I get the chance, I won't pass it up."

Justin lunged at Young again. Desi managed to catch him before he made contact this time. "Get him out of here," she said, throwing Justin back into Ava, who pulled him from the room. She would get nothing from Young. She called for the cop.

"Well, what happened here?" The cop said as he entered the interrogation room. Desi thought he'd be pissed to see his prisoner hurt, but he was almost laughing.

"Things got a little out of hand."

"It happens. Do you want to talk to anyone else?" The

cop pulled Young to his feet.

"Bring me the woman." Desi folded her arms and leaned back in her chair as Young was removed.

Crystal paced in the cell. They didn't have time for this. She had never seen Justin that angry before. She was sure that he had been surprised to see Ryan in the cell with them, but Justin looked like he had lost it. She had come to depend on his unwavering optimism so much over the last six months that she'd started to believe nothing could break him. Justin was her rock.

The cop returned with Ryan. His face was covered in blood, and bruises had started to form around his eyes. Crystal was furious. Despite how much she hated Ryan the cops had no right to treat him like that.

"What did you do to him?" she yelled.

"I don't know what you're talking about," the cop said with a smirk.

Crystal could feel rage boiling in the pit of her stomach. She would have to fight to keep it there. If she attacked the cop, she wouldn't be able to get her message to Flint. Or see Justin, which she desperately needed. She nearly jumped when she felt something touching her leg. She looked down to see Melody hiding behind her. The girl looked terrified.

"You're next." The cop pointed at Crystal. "The rest of you get back against the wall."

Melody clung to her leg so hard that Crystal had to pry the girl off her. She picked her up and handed her to Grady. "Stay with Jim and Tyler. They will keep you safe, I promise." She stroked the girl's cheek before stepping forward with her hands raised.

The cop opened the cell and pushed Ryan in. "Your

boyfriend has some anger issues he needs to work through," Ryan whispered in her ear in Common Tongue while the cop removed his handcuffs.

Crystal stiffened. Justin had done this. She didn't have a chance to respond as the cop twisted her hands behind her back and secured them with the cuffs. The next thing she knew, she was being pushed down the hall to the interrogation room where Flint, Justin, and Ava waited.

Crystal nearly tripped as the cop pushed her inside. The only thing that kept her from falling on her face was the officer's firm grip on her arm. "This one's a little feisty. Do you want me to stay and help?"

"No," Desi said a little too quickly. "We can handle her."

"Let me know if she gets out of hand. I can always move her to her own cell and spend the rest of the night teaching her some manners." He gently ran his knuckles down her cheek and winked at Justin.

"Touch her again and you're a dead man," Justin growled. Crystal shot him a look. He was going to give them away.

Ava stepped forward, blocking the officer's view of Justin. "What he means is these prisoners are in the custody of the U.S. military, and if anything should happen to them, you'll have to answer to us."

Flint moved forward. "We'll take her from here." Flint grabbed Crystal's other arm and stared down the officer until he finally left.

"I don't need you to project me." Crystal spat the words at Justin. He was going to get them all killed. She prayed they had a way of blocking out the cameras.

"Then how come you're the one in handcuffs, and I'm not?" Justin countered.

"Because they weren't hunting you."

"Wait a second," Flint said, letting go of Crystal's arm. "Are you saying the cops were looking for you before you got caught?"

Crystal sighed. "Yeah, I saw on their computer system that someone turned us in. We would have ended up here one way or the other."

"Who turned you in?"

Crystal looked at Desi and her stomach dropped. She shouldn't have said anything. "I don't know," she lied.

"I'm sorry." Justin took a few steps toward her, but Crystal backed away. If he hadn't already given them away, Justin kissing her certainly would. "You aren't scared of me, are you?"

Crystal looked toward Flint in desperation.

"They can see us, but the sound's blocked out," Flint said reading her mind. She took Crystal's arm and deposited her in one of the chairs.

Crystal breathed a sigh of relief. "Of course, I'm not scared of you. A little shocked by what you did to Ryan though."

"Is that why you don't want to be near me?" Justin looked heartbroken. He wasn't thinking rationally, and that could put them all in a lot of danger. Melody understood the situation, and here Crystal was having to spell it out for Justin. She knew he was hurting, but he had to get his emotions in check.

"It can't look like we know each other, or you'll end up in here with us," Crystal reminded him. "We don't have time to argue about this."

"So you have a plan?" Flint sat down across from her.

"I have a plan to get us out of there, but I'm not sure where we go from there. We need a safe place where we can regroup and a way off the planet."

"The warehouse where my parents met. Remember? I

showed it to you the other day," Justin said, his voice calmer now.

"I do," Crystal had to force herself not to smile. Whoever was watching the security footage might not be able to hear them, but they could still see her. They had to keep up appearances.

"The river is only a few blocks south of here," Justin instructed. "You can take that downstream and come up right around the corner from the warehouse."

Crystal gave one short nod. "There's a note up my right sleeve with the details and a list of supplies that would be helpful to have."

Flint nodded to Ava. "Sorry," Ava whispered while forcefully grabbing Wolf's wrists on the pretext of checking her cuffs. The paper tickled Crystal's skin as Ava removed the note and went to stand next to Justin.

"When?" Flint asked.

"Tomorrow, while you two are at the hearing," Crystal said.

"You can't really expect us to go to the hearing after today." Flint waved her hands at her incredulously. Crystal could tell that Flint wasn't acting, but it would look good in case anyone watched the security footage.

"I do, and you're going to make sure they extend the exchange program. Your government desperately needs a better understanding of Neophia."

"This is crazy," Justin said.

"No, it's not. You two need to be there so you aren't accused of helping us break out." Crystal shifted her gaze from Justin to Flint. She had to make them understand that she was trying to protect them. "You can't be tied to this in any way, or you'll never be able to stay here."

Flint nodded.

"There's one more thing. There's a girl in there with us. Her name is Melody Lambert. I think her parents were killed by rioters. I need you to find out if she has any other family on Earth and get them to the embassy."

"We'll get it done." Flint stood up and walked over to Crystal. "Now, let's get you back to your cell," she said with a weak laugh and pulled Crystal out of the interrogation room.

Chapter 17

Desi felt deflated by the time they got back to their apartment building. She left Justin and Ava to translate Wolf's note. She understood why Wolf had written it in the Neophian Common Tongue, but she would be no help until they translated it. She was hoping to grab a few hours of sleep and then go and check on their progress. Tomorrow was going to be a long day, and she wanted to make sure she was ready for it.

She was surprised to see her mom standing in the kitchen when she walked in. It was late, and Desi was pretty sure her mom had mentioned needing to go to work early the next day. Her mom set her coffee mug down on the counter and rushed over to her. "Thank god you're ok." She wrapped her arms around Desi and pulled her close.

Desi gently stroked her mom's hair as she held her. "I'm fine, Mom." She couldn't remember a time she had seen her mother this concerned, and Desi had been in far more dangerous situations than tonight.

"The news kept talking about all the violence in the streets. I was so afraid that you and Justin had been caught up in all that." Her mom pulled back slightly so she could look Desi in the face. "You two should have never been out there."

"Mom, we're ok. I know how to handle myself." Desi let a small laugh escape. Wasn't her mom supposed to be comforting her in situations like this? She couldn't help but find the role reversal amusing.

Her mom wiped away the tears that were starting to form in her eyes. "You were gone for so long, I thought maybe you had accidently been arrested with the others."

Desi stepped back and looked at her mom in confusion. "How did you know they'd been arrested?" It was possible the arrest had made the news, though the few news trucks she had seen out were covering the riots. Reporters had their pick of big stories; Desi doubted the arrest of three LAWON officers would even break the top ten stories.

"I assumed, since they aren't with you," her mother said quickly. "I mean all Neophians are supposed to be arrested if they don't turn themselves in to one of the detention centers, and your friends didn't look like they were off to do that. It was the only logical conclusion."

Desi knew her mom was lying. She always started to ramble when she wasn't being honest—a trait that her mother had passed down to her. It was one of the reasons Desi was always brutally honest. She'd rather be seen as rude but truthful over nice, but an idiot.

"Mom, how do you know the others had been arrested?" Desi asked again.

"Desi why are you being like this?" her mom asked,

avoiding the question. "I only care about your safety. I don't have time to concern myself with anyone else's."

"You've made that abundantly clear," Desi reproached. "I care about these people. I care about their safety." Desi pointed at her heart for emphasis. She considered Wolf, Grady, and Price to be family. She loved them. She had to make her mother understand. If she couldn't, what was the point of Desi staying on Earth? The thought shot through her like a bolt of lightning.

"You barely know them," her mother dismissed. "You can't possibly care about them."

Desi choked back tears. She couldn't tell if they were tears of anger or heartbreak—maybe both. "Did you turn them in?"

"I don't know what you're talking about," her mother evaded. "It's late I'm going to bed." She moved toward the hallway, but Desi blocked her.

"You did, didn't you?" She couldn't hold back the tears anymore. She could feel them rolling down her cheeks, but she didn't brush them away. She wanted her mom to see how much she had hurt her.

"They're dangerous, Desi. I know you don't see it, but they are. I was doing my civic duty." Her mom put her hands on her hips and planted her foot. It was the position her mom took every time she had scolded her as child. Desi refused to back down this time. This time, it was her mom who was wrong.

"I can't believe you. They're my friends, and you put their lives at risk." Desi's voice cracked as she yelled the words at her mom.

"The police won't kill them." Desi's mom waved her hands at Desi to dismiss the very thought.

"Tell that to the little girl in the cell with them," Desi

spat. "Her parents were murdered tonight by people who believe the same thing you do."

"That wasn't the police," her mother said curtly. "As long as they're in jail, we'll all be safe."

"Oh really?" Desi pushed. "Because I went down to the station where they are holding my people, and I watched the cop causally threaten to rape Wolf, like it was nothing. So please, tell me again how the cops will keep them safe." Desi crossed her arms over her chest.

"They aren't your people. You aren't Neophian."

Desi shook her head and laughed bitterly. It was the only thing she could do. "I'm ashamed to be your daughter." She turned around and headed toward the door.

"Desiree Lucille Flint, where are you going?"

"Out." Desi knew she sounded like a teenager, but she didn't care. She couldn't stay in the same room with her mom any longer.

"You can't. The government set a curfew. If they catch you, they'll shoot you."

"I'll take my chances." Desi slammed the door behind her.

It felt like they had been in the cell for days, even though Crystal knew it had only been five hours. She tried to keep Melody distracted. It wasn't fair for a child to be going through all of this. When she noticed Melody starting to yawn, she tucked the girl in the bottom bunk and sat with her until she fell asleep. There was only the one set of bunk beds in the cell with the five of them. Crystal had considered putting Melody on the top bunk so someone else could use the bottom, but after a quick inspection of the welds, Crystal wasn't convinced the thing would hold. No one said a word about Melody taking the bed, though she half expected Ryan to make a comment, just to piss her off. Thankfully he kept his mouth shut for once.

When Crystal was sure the girl was asleep, she slipped off the bed and went to join Tyler and Grady. They hadn't gotten a chance to talk since Flint and Justin left. Crystal didn't want to discuss the finer details of the plan with Melody there. There was no point scaring her now.

"Did Anderson really do that to Young?" Grady nodded at Ryan sitting along the opposite side of the cell.

"Apparently." Crystal sat down on the wooden bench between them.

"I wish I could have been there to see it." Grady leaned back on the bench with a huge smile on his face. Crystal thought about smacking him, but she didn't have the energy.

"Are we all set for tomorrow?" Tyler asked. Crystal noticed his leg hadn't stopped bouncing since she sat down. She wondered if he even realized he was doing it.

"I have no idea." Crystal shrugged her shoulders. "I was able to get the note to Flint without the cop noticing. Whether or not they are able to pull it all off is another thing entirely. It's not like we're giving them a lot of time to arrange things."

"They'll come through." Tyler nodded as if he was trying to reassure himself.

"That's if they can read the note. Did you really have to write it in Common Tongue?" Grady asked.

"Yeah I did. What if the cops found it? Do you really want them to know what we're planning on doing?" Crystal rubbed her hands against her knees. "I've been teaching Justin Common Tongue for the last few months. He'll be able to figure out what it says. I have faith in him."

"That just leaves one piece of the puzzle to sort out." Grady nodded toward Ryan. He was watching them closely, but didn't make any kind of move to join them.

"He'll do what we need him to," Crystal assure him. "It's the only way he'll get out of this cell. It's not like Rank has any kind of authority here that can save him. If anything, he needs us more than we need him." Crystal locked eyes with Ryan. Something wasn't right about him, but she couldn't figure out what it was.

"So you talked through the plan with him, and he's on board?" Tyler asked.

"He knows I have a plan and that he has a part to play in it," Crystal answered. "I'm not crazy enough to give him all the details up front. I'll fill him in right before it's time to act. That way he can't double cross us."

Grady and Tyler continued to talk, but Crystal was only half-listening. She needed to figure out what was off about Ryan before it drove her crazy. "Do Young's eyes look different to you?"

"I can't say I've spent a lot of time looking at his eyes," Grady said. This time Crystal did smack him.

"They look muted to me," she said trying to pinpoint exactly what was wrong with them.

Tyler shrugged. "It could be the light."

"Maybe," Crystal said. She tore her gaze away from Ryan. "I wish I knew what he was really doing here. He volunteered the information about helping the NIA way to easily."

"He's a cocky son of a bitch. He probably thought it would impress you," Grady said.

"If he did help them, like he said he did, he would

have to know how to find them right?" Crystal turned to Grady, a small smile forming on her lips.

"What are you thinking?" Grady sat up to look at her better.

"If we can find out who the terrorists really are, the government would have to lift its detainment order. We could save everyone, not just ourselves."

Grady shook his head, rejecting her plan before she even made it. "That's not what we're here to do. We don't have the resources to even attempt something like that."

"I feel so guilty." Crystal leaned forward and put her head in her hands.

"Contacts," Tyler said out of nowhere.

Crystal sat up and looked at him. "What are you talking about?"

"I heard a rumor that Teria was developing a microchip that could be imbedded in a contact lens. It allows the wearer to access information through eye motions without anyone else seeing it. That's where Young's keeping the information about the terrorist. That's why his eyes look muted. He's wearing contact lenses."

"Are you sure?" Crystal asked.

"It's just a theory," Tyler admitted, "but if I'm right, all the information the government needs to find the real terrorist is on the other side of this cell."

"Great," Grady said, "now all we have to do is get them out Young's eyes and we'll be all set."

A piercing scream rippled through the cell. Crystal was alert at once. She scanned the cell quickly, before noticing Melody thrashing around on the bed. Crystal extracted herself from between Grady and Tyler on the wood bench where she had been dozing. She was amazed that Melody's cries hadn't woken either of them up. She sat down on the corner of the bunk. "You're safe. It was only a nightmare," Crystal whispered as she stroked Melody's hair. Crystal wasn't even sure if Melody was awake. "Nothing bad can happen to you as long as I'm here. There's no room for bad thoughts here, only happy thoughts." It was what Crystal's grandmother used to say to her after her parents were killed and she started having nightmares. After a few minutes, Melody started to calm down, until eventually Crystal could feel her breathing even out.

Crystal moved to the end of the bed and put her face in her hands. This whole situation was a nightmare. Her plan would put a lot of people at risk, but what else could she do? She knew LAWON would come for them eventually, but that could take months. She wasn't sure they would last that long. The people here were angry and willing to take it out on anyone, regardless of guilt. There was no other way.

"You're good with her," Ryan said.

Crystal looked up. She had almost forgotten he was in here with them. He hadn't said anything since his comment about Justin when the cop was taking her from the cell. He was stretched out on the wooden bench opposite where Grady and Tyler now slept.

"What was that?" Crystal said.

"I said you're good with her." Ryan sat up and turned toward her. "You'd be a good mother, even though I know that's not something you ever wanted." There was no malice in his voice, but Crystal still couldn't decide if he was being nice or if he was trying to screw with her.

"Thanks, I think." Crystal got up and went to sit next

to him. It couldn't hurt to play nice for a bit. "Sorry about all that." Crystal pointed to the bruised on his face.

"I can't blame the guy," Ryan offered. "I mean your first reaction to seeing me was to try to cut off my airway. A few punches are nothing."

"Fair point," she said with a smile she couldn't help. Without the threat of Rank and Teria hanging over them, it was easy to fall back into their old roles and just be themselves.

"So is that what you want?" Ryan nodded his head to the bed where Melody was now sleeping peacefully.

"What? Kids?" Crystal shook her head. "No, it's not what I want."

"Does your boyfriend know that?" Ryan asked with a childish smirk

Crystal folded her arms over her chest. "Of course, he does." She had never come out and told Justin that she didn't want kids, but she was sure it had been implied from the beginning. She had been very clear that her work would always come first, that she was career military. Kids didn't fit into that.

"Is he ok with it?"

She didn't say anything. She knew Justin wanted a family one day. He had told her long before they had started dating. It was one of a hundred reason why she was so hesitant to start things with him in the first place. She knew it was something she could never give him.

Ryan chuckled. "That's what I thought." He turned away from Crystal and looked across the cell. "For what it's worth, I would have been ok with it."

His voice had a soft, far away quality to it that Crystal wasn't sure she had ever heard before. Why did he have to bring up their past? Everything would have been fine if he had left their relationship out of it. "Let's not do this again. Our relationship is done; it's in the past. Let's just leave it that way."

"Fine by me." Ryan put his hands behind his head and kicked his feet out so that he was reclining on the wooden bench.

They sat in awkward silence for a few minutes. Crystal wasn't sure how to get the conversation going again. "Did Rank really send you to Earth to provide aid to the NIA?" It probably wasn't the safest topic of discussion, but she wasn't sure what else to say. It was the question that had been going around her mind since she saw him.

Ryan shrugged. "Their goals aligned with ours, so why not try to help them? Attack the Human infestation from both sides." He turned to look straight at her. His words made her sick, but at least she was able to get a good look at his eyes. They were back to their usual brilliant shade of green. Had she imagined them being a different color earlier, or had Tyler been right about the contacts, and Ryan had removed them without them noticing? If they were out of his eyes, it would be a lot easier to steal them.

"It seems a little below your pay grade," she continued casually. "There wasn't some other lacky Rank could send?" Crystal wanted to keep the conversation going. If nothing else, it was a good distraction.

"This is my punishment," Ryan said stone-faced.

"Punishment for what?"

"For not getting him Stapleton Farms."

Crystal didn't want to talk about Stapleton Farms. She had done everything she could to block the mission from her mind. She didn't need to think about Ryan shooting her father or the fact that she had been forced to mourn him for the second time. "I don't understand why Rank doesn't have you killed."

"I'm so glad you care." Ryan put his hand to his chest, though Crystal could tell from the tone of his voice that he wasn't offended.

Crystal shrugged. "That's how Rank usually deals with people who fail him. That's all I'm saying."

"Rank and I have an understanding. He doesn't try to kill me, and I don't release the information I have on him."

She wanted to press him, to find out what he had on Rank so that she could use it herself to bring his reign of oppression to an end, but she knew no matter how freely she was able to get Ryan talking, he would never give up the ace in his back pocket. "Speaking of understandings, are you sure you know what do to tomorrow?"

"I got it. It's a good plan," he said with his usual cockiness.

"A lot is depending on you playing your part. How do I know I can trust you?"

"You don't," Ryan said, too cheerfully for Crystal's comfort, "but I'll do what you want me to. Like you said, we can't get out of here without the others' help."

"You better. The life of that little girl depends on you." Crystal got up and went back to the bunk where Melody was still sleeping peacefully. Crystal envied her.

Chapter 18

Desi spent the night on the Andersons' couch. She couldn't bring herself to go back upstairs to her mother's apartment. It was one thing to be cold to her friends, but calling to have them arrested was another thing entirely. Desi wasn't sure if she would ever be able to forgive her mom for that.

Desi folded the blankets that Justin had given her as she watched Mrs. Anderson making breakfast in the kitchen. She would be heading to work in a few hours. It was amazing how quickly things went back to normal. They didn't even have a final death count from the attacks on the hospitals, let alone the riots afterward, but those not directly affected were expected to go about their business as if nothing had happened. Desi picked up the remote and turned on the news. There were still hospitals across the country officials hadn't been able to enter. There was no telling how long the aftereffects of this would be felt.

"Do you want to talk about last night?" Justin walked into the living room with his duffle back slung over his shoulder.

"What's that for?" Desi pointed to his bag to keep from answering his question.

Justin set the bag down by the front door. "If everything goes according to plan today, I'm getting on that shuttle back to Neophia. I'm not going to risk staying here for another six weeks, having something else go wrong, and the portals being shut down."

"Do you really think that's a possibility?" Desi asked dubiously. "Earth wouldn't survive without the resources we import from Neophia." Desi sat down on the couch.

"Congress introduced a bill to do just that in an emergency session they held last night." Justin sat down across from her. Desi hoped he had forgotten his original question. She wasn't ready to talk about what her mom had done.

"When did this happen? I feel like that would have been major news." Desi looked over at the television to see if it would confirm what Justin had told her, but it was just a replay of the attacks.

"It broke while we were at the police station. Ava had a message waiting when we got back saying her leave had been canceled and she needed to report back immediately. Everyone's on high alert."

"That's going to be hard on your parents, both of you leaving today." Desi played with the corner of the blanket folded up next to her. It would be hard on her too. With Justin and Ava gone, she would have no one left to talk to. No buffer between her and her mom.

"So, are you going to tell me why you slept on our couch last night?" Justin asked again.

"Breakfast is ready," Mrs. Anderson called from the kitchen.

"We shouldn't keep your mom waiting." Desi didn't look at Justin as she got up and walked to the kitchen.

The breakfast had an air of false pleasantness to it. They all knew what was at stake, but no one talked about it. Desi felt a little awkward as she filled the spot that should have been Ava's. After breakfast there was the normal chaos as everyone tried to get out of the door to start their day. Desi noticed that Mr. and Mrs. Anderson hugged Justin a little longer than normal, though they didn't say a word. She wondered if his sisters knew that he wasn't planning on coming back that night as they high fived him on their way out the door.

"Were you and Ava able to translate Wolf's message?" Now that they were alone, it was time to get down to business. They still had a few things to take care of before the hearing.

Justin turned back to the living room where she had retaken her seat on the couch. Wiped a tear from his eye as he pulled out the note Wolf had given them and handed it to her. Ava had written the translation neatly below Wolf's crayon written message. "I was able to get ahold of Jax last night and tell him what we needed."

"Good." Desi read through the message one more time to make sure she had it memorized before grabbing a lighter off the mantel and burning it. They couldn't risk the wrong person finding it. Like her mom. "We should head over there."

"We still have a little time if you want to get your things and say goodbye to your mom." She knew what Justin was implying, but, despite everything, she still wanted to stay on Earth.

"I don't want to talk to her." Desi got up and walked to the other side of the room. She needed to put some distance between her and Justin's soft supportive presence.

"Desi, will you please tell me what happened last night?"

"She turned them in." The words fell out of Desi's mouth.

"What are you talking about?" Justin walked over and placed a hand on her shoulder.

"My mom. She turned Wolf, Price, and Grady in to the cops after we left. She's the reason they're sitting in a jail cell right now."

Justin slowly turned Desi around so she was facing him. "The chances of all of us making it to the embassy last night were so slim," he reminded her. "Even if your mom hadn't made that call, we would probably be in the same place we are now."

She knew Justin was trying to comfort her, but it wasn't working. "Except that she wouldn't have betrayed me and people I care about. She's changed Justin. I don't know who she is anymore, but she's not the same women that raised me."

"I'm sure she thought she's was protecting you."

Desi appreciated that the forgiving understanding Justin was back, but that's not what needed right now. She needed the Justin from last night that would take out anyone who kept him from Wolf, even if that person was her mother. They had been out of sync since they came back to Earth. Maybe it was for the best. They'd never make it through the last day of the hearing if they had both lost control of their emotions. "None of that matters right now. The only thing that matters is getting to the embassy and making sure our people have a way off this planet." She turned and walked out of the apartment before Justin could try to comfort her again. She was angry, but angry was an emotion she could work with. It would keep her going.

Crystal had only gotten an hour or two of sleep. Her mind was too anxious. She had gone over the plan from every angle she could think of, but there were still too many unknowns. If the timing was off, they would put Justin and Flint at risk. If the cops didn't respond the way she thought, they wouldn't make it out of the cell. If Jax hadn't been able to get them a shuttle home, they would be fugitives on the run with nowhere to go. Hunted by everyone around them. If Ryan didn't do his part, then she would likely be killed.

The door outside the holding cell opened, and an officer walked in carrying a tray. It was a different cop than who they had dealt with the night before. Crystal wasn't surprised, but it just added another unknown to the equation. She tried to look into the main station before the door shut to see how many other cops were out there, but it was hard to tell. She had to assume that there would be more people to get through than the lone officer guarding them last night. Maybe it would have been better to try to break out then? The officer pushed the tray of food through the gap on the cell door and walked away without saying a word.

Grady got up and retrieved the tray. "Not much of a breakfast," he said handing it to her. There were three pieces of toast, half a glass of juice, and two circles of what Crystal assumed was some kind of meat product. It was barely enough to feed one person, let alone all five of them. They would need every ounce of energy they had to make it to safety.

"Melody," Crystal said giving the girl a slight shake. "It's time to wake up." Melody shot up at once. Her breathing was heavy, and her eyes darted around the cell. "Hey, it's ok. I'm here." Crystal pulled the girl into her lap. She held Melody against her chest and stroked her hair until the girl's breathing returned to normal.

"I need you to eat something." Crystal shifted Melody so that she was back on the bed.

Melody nodded and grabbed a piece of toast from the tray. Crystal handed her the juice to go with it. She needed to keep her strength up. They were going to ask a lot of her today.

Crystal grabbed a piece of toast from the tray and handed it back to Grady. He took it over to Price. She walked over to Ryan, still sitting alone on the opposite side of the cell. She handed him the toast without saying a word.

"Thanks." He ripped the bread in half and handed part of it back to her. "You need to eat too."

Crystal nodded and took a small bite. It was stale, but he was right, she needed to eat something.

"Do you remember our final exam for survival class?" Ryan smirked as he played with his piece of toast.

"I haven't thought of that in ages," she said, a laugh escaping as she sat down next to him. "Everyone was so mad at us by the end of it." They had been dropped off in the woods alone with nothing but a knife, a compass, a piece of rope, and a communicator to call for an evacuation when they had had enough. Their only direction was to use their resources to survive for as long as they could. Crystal and Ryan had gone in with a plan. It had taken them about six hours to find each other. From there it was easy. Crystal built and maintained their shelter, Ryan hunted. They needed to last three days to pass the exam. The longest anyone had ever gone was ten days. It was day eighteen when their instructor found them living happily in the small shack Crystal had made. Ryan had offered him some of the dinner he had just finished cooking. Their instruction was equal parts impressed and furious that they had found a loophole in what was meant to be the toughest exam at the Academy.

"I'm pretty sure they changed the rules for the exam after that," Crystal said.

"It's not our fault that no one else thought to team up." Ryan chuckled and took a bite of toast.

"How long do you think we would have lasted if they hadn't come to get us?"

"We would probably still be there right now." The intensity in his eyes surprised her. Was that what he wanted? For a moment she allowed herself to imagine it. A life with Ryan before he had changed, when he had loved her more than anything in the world. It was a lot easier to go back there than Crystal would have liked.

"I'm not sure about that. If I remember correctly, your cooking left a lot to be desired." Crystal couldn't keep the smile off her face.

"Yeah, well, your shelter leaked." He gently nudged her with his shoulder.

"I would have fixed that eventually."

"We always did make a great team," Ryan said with a longing in his voice.

Crystal stood, not willing to let him take her there with him. "In a couple of hours, we'll get to see if we still do."

Desi prepared to encounter the same chaos they'd experienced last night as she exited the apartment building, but the streets were eerily quiet. They made their way to the embassy without seeing another soul. The whole thing put Desi on edge. She almost preferred the mobs of the night before. Right now, the planet really did feel dead.

They arrived at the embassy without any issues. At the very least Desi expected to see a crowd out front, but again, there was nothing. Two security guards approached the gate, checked their IDs, quickly opened the gate, and locked it behind them. Once they entered the embassy, things were drastically different. The entire first floor was filled with people. Men, women, and children were camped out all over the house, looking scared and tried, but at least they were safe. Desi couldn't even begin to count how many were there. It put the party attendance to shame.

It took Desi a few minutes to spot Natasha among the crowd. She was in the living room, carrying a tray loaded down with food. She looked like she had been up all night. Desi tapped Justin on the arm and started to make her way across the room. "It's quite the operation you have going here," she said once she got to Natasha.

"Yeah," Natasha looked around the room as if she was just as amazed to see if full of people as they had been. "Once we got a handle on things last night, thanks to you guys, we were able to take in every Neophian that showed up. It was a long night." Natasha kept moving, handing out food as they worked their way through the crowd.

"Let me handle that dear," an older woman said and took the tray of food from Natasha.

"Did you have anyone show up that wasn't

Neophian?" Justin asked.

"Actually, no. Everyone's been really helpful. We even had a few former LAWON military members show up and offer to manage the security detail at the gate."

"We noticed, they're doing a great job," Desi said trying to reassure the ambassador's daughter.

Natasha rubbed her hands along her back. It was like she wasn't sure what to do with them now that they were empty. "My dad's upstairs in his office. I'll take you to him."

"Why don't you go get some rest? We remember where the office is," Justin said.

"I think I will." Natasha turned and walked up the stairs. It was like she was floating. The poor woman had been through a lot in the last eighteen hours. Desi wasn't sure how she was still functioning.

Justin led the way to the ambassador's office and knocked. Desi was glad he remembered where it was, because she hadn't been paying attention the night before. She would have wasted precious time roaming around the embassy's upper floors until she finally found the right door.

"Come in," Jax's voice carried through the door to them.

Desi didn't think it was possible, but Jax looked even more worn down than his daughter. He waved them over to a folding table set up in the middle of the office. It was filled with computers and phones that didn't seem to stop ringing. "I'm glad you're here."

"Is there any word on Marcell yet?" Justin asked. Of course he would think to ask that first. He should be the one to lead this mission. He had the best people skills out of any of them.

"He's in a coma," Jax answered, his voice heavy. "We

aren't sure if he's going to make it or not. He was in surgery when the gas was released, and they were able to seal off the room before too much made it inside." The ambassador hesitated for a moment, reigning in his emotions before he continued. "We should know more about how bad his exposure was if he wakes up."

"He'll wake up. Have faith," Justin said.

"I don't want to seem like I don't care, but we're under a bit of a time crunch," Desi reminded them. "Were you able to get a shuttle lined up?" Desi looked down at her watch. The hearing was supposed to start in an hour, and they still had to make it to the Pentagon.

"Two actually. Unfortunately, they are launching from opposite sides of town, so once you commit to one, that's it. There won't be time to make it to the other if something goes wrong."

"We can work with that," Desi said.

"We're going to start moving the people here to the shuttles shortly. We'll hold them for you as long as we can."

"Were you able to find anything out about Melody Lambert?"

"I'm afraid it isn't good news. Her parents were killed by rioters last night like Commander Wolf suspected. Her aunt has been looking for her all night. The police never bothered to notify anyone when she was brought in." Jax's lips tightened in disapproval, and for a moment, he was more father than ambassador. "I've requested a list of all Neophians that have been detained, but I haven't received anything yet."

"So she does have family here?" Desi asked. "That's good news."

"Yes. Her mother's younger sister," Jax confirmed. "We sent someone to go get her early this morning. She will be on the shuttle waiting for you."

"Thank you for everything," Desi said. The exit plan was set; now all they had to do was get through the hearing

Chapter 19

Crystal wasn't sure if the clock outside the cell was a blessing or a curse. She couldn't stop herself from looking at it and counting down each minute until it was time to enact her plan. She was so distracted that she hadn't realized the cop that had brought them that pathetic excuse of a breakfast had left the door leading to the main part of the station cracked until she heard voices coming from it.

"What do you mean they were questioned last night? We're the only team assigned to interrogate detained Neophians in this area, and I can assure you we weren't here last night," someone yelled. Crystal's stomach dropped to the floor. This couldn't be happening.

"I don't know what to tell you. My records show that two of the five detainees were questioned by the military police last night." The second voice was calmer, but matched the first in volume.

"I want to see your security footage."

This was really bad. If they recognized Flint, it would be all over. Crystal looked back up at the clock. It was too soon. The hearing wasn't set to start for another forty-five minutes. If they broke out now, it would still be possible to tie Justin and Flint to the jail break. On the other hand, if the military police figured out what was going on, they would all be in trouble. There was no good answer. She wiped the sweat off her palms and started to pace. For the first time, she realized how small the cell really was. How was she supposed to think without more space? She felt her breath starting to get shallower as her heart began to race. She glanced to the bed where Melody was watching her intently. Crystal couldn't let herself slip away now. Everyone was counting on her.

Grady came over and put his hands on her shoulders. She felt her breathing slow instantly. He was her anchor. She could get through this with him by her side. "You got this," he said, searching her eyes. She wasn't sure if it was a question or an affirmation. She decided to take it as the latter. She nodded, but put her hands on top of his to stop him from removing them. She needed his strength a little longer.

"I don't really care what you say. We're going in there and talking to those people. They could be the ones we're looking for," the first voice said.

"What do you want to do?" Grady asked, maintaining eye contact with her.

She removed Grady's hands. The risk of slipping away had passed. "We move now." She nodded to Tyler, who was sitting on the bunk next to Melody.

Tyler turned to Melody. "Go over there with Crystal." The girl nodded and ran over to her.

Tyler pulled the bottom mattress off the bunk and

tossed it across the cell, while Grady went to work prying the wooden bench off its braces. They needed to make it look like they had trashed the cell while escaping. It was the best chance they had of the cops unlocking the cell door. Crystal was a little surprised to see Ryan helping Tyler. She had expected him to stand back and let them do the majority of the work, only stepping in when he absolutely had to. Between the two of them, they rocked the bunk bed back and forth until the rusted screws securing it to the floor pulled free and the bunk crashed down in the middle of the cell. The cops in the other room were certain to hear that. They didn't have much time.

Crystal knelt so that she was looking Melody in the eye. "I need you to stay with Jim and Tyler until we get to the surface, ok?"

"I want to stay with you." Melody wrapped her arms around Crystal's neck.

It broke her heart to remove the girl's arms from around her. "I know, and I wish you could, but you will be safer with them. I promise, once we're through this first part, I'll be by your side the rest of the time." Crystal nodded to Grady, who took Melody's hand. Grady placed his other hand on Tyler's shoulder, and a second later, they vanished from sight.

"Are you ready?" Ryan was standing next to her.

"As ready as I'll ever be." Crystal only flinched slightly when he put his hands on her. She didn't feel any different, but she knew she was no longer visible. Having a Sertex extend their ability to another person was tough and drained their energy much faster than if they were just camouflaging themselves. They couldn't maintain this for long.

They stationed themselves next to the cell door to

make it easy to slip out once it was opened. This part of the plan caused Crystal the most anxiety. She could only hope they had done enough damage to the cell to draw the cops inside to investigate. The voices in the station got louder, and footsteps signaled that the cops were heading back to the holding cell. It was time.

"What the hell happened in here?" one of the military officers demanded at the sight of the trashed and apparently empty cell. It was a risk to assume the officers hadn't been trained to spot Sertex while camouflaged, but it was probably the safest risk they would take that day. "Get this cell open."

The cop stumbled forward. "They were here a few minutes ago." He jammed his fingers against the keypad, and the door to the cell flew opened. This was going better than Crystal had imagined.

The cop and military officer rushed in the cell, leaving the door wide open behind them. Why bother to shut it when their prisoners had already escaped? Crystal watched the barely visible outline of Grady, Tyler, and Melody leave the cell and head for the back door of the police station. She was about to follow when she felt Ryan pulling her in the other direction. He was going after the cop. Crystal pulled him back. They couldn't break contact, or she would be seen, and any chance she had of getting out would be lost. She used all her strength to pull him back. "We can't," she whispered, hoping she wouldn't be heard by anyone except him. Ryan relaxed, and they were finally able to slip out of the cell undetected.

Grady, Tyler, and Melody were waiting for them behind the police station. They were all visible. Crystal wanted to scold them, but she knew how exhausting it was for Grady to maintain the camouflage for himself and Tyler. At least Melody could blend in on her own, but Crystal had no idea how long she was able to maintain it.

"We're two blocks from the river," she reminded Grady. "Can you make it?" Once they reached the water, they could get some distance between them and the police station.

"I'm good." Grady placed his hand on Tyler's shoulder again, making them invisible to the untrained eye. Melody took Grady's hand before disappearing from sight.

Crystal turned to Ryan. "Do you need minute?" It had been a long time since he had extended his ability to her. She wasn't sure how long he could hold it.

"Of course not," Ryan scoffed. "I'm not nearly as weak as him."

"Good. Then let's pick up the pace." They moved down the street as fast as they could given the awkward closeness between them.

Desi and Justin arrived at the hearing with minutes to spare. The feeling in the room was much more subdued than the day before. Desi looked over at the other table where Corwin sat alone. She wondered if the LAWON officers had been arrested, too. She doubted the military would offer them any kind of protection from the president's order. The whole situation made her sick.

Their table felt lonely as they sat with empty chairs between them. Justin had suggested they sit next to each other, but Desi thought the visual was more powerful this way. She would do everything she could to make the government see how wrong they were. The panel arrived and took their seats. There was no need to ask for silence.

General Sloan looked around the room before he began. "Lieutenant Flint, will the rest of your team be joining us today?" Desi couldn't read his face. Was he really not aware that they were locked up, or was he trying to emphasize a point?

"The rest of my team were arrested last night while trying to make their way to the LAWON embassy to provide some much-needed assistance to the hundreds of Neophians that showed up there, terrified from being hunted down in the streets." Desi didn't even try to keep the anger from her voice. These people needed to know what they had done.

"I'm sorry to hear that," Sloan said. "I'm sure once they've been questioned, they will be released."

"There's nothing to be sorry for," another member of the panel said. "These precautions are necessary to ensure national security until the Neophian Integration Alliance is caught."

"And what about the eight-year-old girl who was arrested after her parents were killed by an emboldened mob last night? Is she a threat to national security?" Justin slammed his palms down on the table. Desi looked at him in shock. It wasn't like him to speak so boldly. He could be putting his whole career at risk. Then Desi remembered, he wasn't staying. Even if they failed and the exchange program was canceled, he would find a way to stay on Neophia. He still needed to be careful, though; even if he was safe from the U.S. military's reach, Ava and his younger sisters still had to serve here. The military wasn't above making them pay for Justin's insubordination.

"We aren't here to discuss the detainment order. Though if I'm being honest, I'm sure you and I have similar opinions, Ensign Anderson," Sloan said, causing a wave of voices to cascade through the audience. Sloan ignored them. "We are here to discuss whether or not the officer exchange program with LAWON should continue. We have heard arguments from both sides. We will allow for one closing statement from each side before we make our final decision. Captain Corwin, would you like to start us off?"

Corwin rose to his feet. Desi was happy to see a small slit on his upper lip. A constant reminder that she had beaten him. He shot Desi a dirty look before turning his attention to the panel. "I think it is clear that the program needs to be canceled and all officers returned to their rightful planet. The officers from Neophia can't handle military service on Earth. They are a liability to the teams they are placed with and, if I can speak candidly, we don't want them here. The tragic events of last night only make that more apparent. The Neophians are not the same as us, and they don't belong here." He sat back down and folded his arms over his chest. He was clearly confident that he was on the winning side. Desi wished she could punch him again.

"Lieutenant Flint, is there anything you'd like to say?" Sloan asked.

Desi slowly rose to her feet. She needed to keep her anger in check if she wanted anyone to hear what she had to say. "Captain Corwin couldn't be more wrong about the exchange program. What he doesn't understand is that, if given the chance, the exchange program can be the very thing that heals the wounds of last night's tragedy. It's only from learning to understand the Neophians that we can achieve a real partnership between our two planets. The exchange program can be the start, but we need a much larger solution if we want to get to the heart of problem. We have so much to learn from Neophia if only we can get our egos in check and pull our heads out of our asses. We aren't the best or most powerful nation in the universe, and it's about time we recognize that. The biggest mistake you can make here today is to cancel the program. You'll only be hurting yourselves." Desi sat back down. If people weren't calling her a traitor before, she was certain they would now. Honestly, she didn't care. She believed every word she said.

"Thank you for your honesty Lieutenant Flint. We'll take a brief recess and return with our decision." Sloan got up and left the room through a side door. The rest of the panel followed behind him.

"Now we wait," Justin said to Desi as he moved closer to her. Neither of them was up for much small talk.

"Hopefully we don't have to wait too long." Desi lowered her voice so that no one would be able to overhear her. "Wolf should be putting her plan into action soon, and if we did our job, they'll be breaking out right when Sloan announces the continuation of the exchange program."

"Do you really think there's any chance that will happen?" Justin slumped down in his chair.

"I thought you were the eternal optimist. Where's your faith Justin?"

"I lost it when our team was arrested last night. There's no good left here." He turned around and surveyed the room with disgust.

Desi couldn't blame him, but she refused to let this be the thing that broke his spirit. "Don't say that. Just because things look bad right now doesn't mean all hope is gone. You heard Sloan; he agrees that the detainment order is wrong. He could convince the rest of the panel to see our side."

"Justin." Desi turned to see Olivia standing behind them. "Can I talk to you for a minute?"

"I thought I told you the other night to leave him alone," Desi said. She couldn't believe Olivia's nerve.

"It's all right, Desi." Justin stood up. "I'll be right back."

Desi rolled her eyes but didn't stop him. She had tried to save his relationship with Wolf once before. If he was determined not to take her advice, that was on him. She closed her eyes and leaned back. She needed to start mentally preparing for what they needed to do after the hearing. These few minutes to herself were all she was likely to get.

"You must think you're something pretty special don't you," Corwin said.

Desi took a deep breath before opening her eyes. Why did everyone feel the need to goad her? "Most of the time, yeah." She folded her arms so that he couldn't see her hands clenched in fists. He wasn't worth it, she told herself over and over again.

"You're pretty cocky for someone who claims to want to continue to serve here. Don't think this won't come back and bite you in the ass."

"I'm not worried. In time you'll see that I'm right, and you're just a racist asshole with more ego than sense."

"If you make it that long," he said through gritted teeth.

"How's your jaw?" Desi asked with a smirk.

"Is there a problem here?" Justin had returned and stood behind her chair.

"None at all." Corwin turned and left. Desi guessed he didn't have the guts to continue his threats now that he had a witness.

"I had that under control." Desi sat up straight and looked down at her watch. She wondered what was happening in the police station across town. Were they going to be ready to pull off their part when the time was right? The not knowing was driving Desi crazy.

"I'm sure you did." Justin retook his seat next to her.

"What did Olivia have to say?"

"She wanted to apologize again. She said the detainment order made her see how bad things had gotten and how she had let her prejudice take over."

"And?" There had to be more to it than that. She had apologized to Justin at the embassy party. If that was all she wanted, she could have said it in front of Desi.

"That she isn't giving up on us. Before you say anything, I told her about Crystal, but she believes that fate isn't done with us yet. That she and I are meant to be."

"You shot her down, right?" Justin was about to answer when the panel started to file back in. "Don't think we're done with this," Desi hissed as Justin got up and retook his assigned seat.

"If you all will please take your seats, we have reached a decision," Sloan said. "Given the state of affairs on Earth, we have decided that we need a better understanding of Neophia and its people. As such, it is our recommendation that the officer exchange program continue." The room erupted into chaos. The noise that reached Desi's ears was not supportive.

"Quiet, now!" Sloan ordered. The noise in the room slowly subsided. "There will be changes made to the program, however. New procedures will be put in place to help protect the Neophian officers severing here and to allow their voices to be heard. In addition, all units will receive cultural awareness training on Neophia."

Before Sloan could continue, the side door flung open and someone ran in carrying a tablet. "There's been a jail break," they yelled as they made their way to the front of the room. Desi looked at Justin in panic. It was too soon. They had expected to be able to make it to the rendezvous point before the press got ahold of the story. Something must have gone wrong.

"What are you talking about?" Sloan reached for the tablet.

"It's all over the news. A group of Neophians broke out of the local jail an hour ago. The press believes they are connected to the NIA and are extremely dangerous. It's Commander Wolf's team."

The noise in the room reached a level Desi wouldn't have believed possible. This was bad. She wasn't surprised the breakout would be reported, but to automatically link them to the terrorist group was dangerous. Their pictures would be plastered on every screen in the city. The chances of them making it to the shuttle unseen were nearly impossible now.

Justin looked at Desi for some kind of direction, but she didn't know what to do. This wasn't how things were supposed to happen. They should have had more time. Out of the corner of her eye, Desi caught General Sloan looking at them. He nodded to the side door where the panel had entered from a few minutes ago. Desi nodded back. She grabbed Justin and they slipped out of the door unseen among the chaos.

They were still two meters from the river when Crystal first heard the sirens. That hadn't taken long. She'd hoped that the confusion of their disappearance would buy them enough time to get to the water. At least they were still invisible. She was banking on the fact that most of the cops wouldn't even know that Neophians had abilities that humans didn't. It was something Flint had been unaware of when she first arrived on Neophia. Crystal hoped Grady and Ryan could hold on long enough to get everyone safely into the water.

Ryan pushed her against a building. "What you are doing?" Crystal hissed. "We have to keep moving?" She wouldn't let Ryan get them both thrown back in jail.

He pressed his body against hers. "Hang on a second."

That's when she heard the footsteps running down the sidewalk behind them. Several cops were combing the street looking for them. Crystal held her breath as they passed them. She knew the chances of the cops seeing them were almost zero, but they were solid. If one of them bumped into her or Ryan they would be discovered.

Once the cops had passed and the street was clear, Ryan removed his body from hers. "Ready to get moving again?" She could hear the smirk in his voice, even if she couldn't see it on his face.

"Think you can get us to the water before the next wave of cops comes?" Crystal looked down the street and saw the awkward outlines of Grady, Tyler, and Melody moving a few buildings up ahead. Crystal would feel so much safer once they were all in the water.

"Try not to slow me down." Ryan took off down the street with one hand wrapped around her wrist. They reached the river at the same time as the others. Crystal scanned the street quickly then nodded to Ryan. He released her, and she was once again visible. A second later Grady, Tyler, and Melody appeared in front of her.

She noticed Ryan didn't lower his invisibility.

Crystal knelt in front of Melody. "You did great." She searched the girl's face for signs of a breakdown, but she was holding up much better than Crystal expected. "Are you ready for the next part?"

Melody nodded. Crystal squeezed her hands and stood up. Grady and Tyler were looking over the ledge into the river below. It was a ten-foot drop, and the water was moving fast. It would be hard to keep everyone together.

"I'll go down first, and then you can lower Melody down to me." Grady climbed over the wall and lowered himself down as much as he could before releasing. He dropped the last few feet into the river. He disappeared below the surface. It was a few seconds before he emerged. The river was deep—good. They would need to stay as close to the bottom as possible to keep from being seen, though Crystal wasn't sure anyone could see anything through the murky green water.

Crystal picked Melody up and put her on the wall. "Take our hands. Grady will catch you."

Melody grasped Crystal and Tyler's hands. They lowered her as far as they could before they released her. Grady caught her easily. "Go down about five feet and wait for one of us to grab you," Crystal called down to her.

"Ok." Melody's voice sounded more confident now that she was in the water. Crystal knew how she felt. The water always gave her strength.

"We need to move!" Ryan yelled.

Crystal looked behind her to see several cop cars heading in their direction. "Shit." She hoisted herself over the wall. "Jim, grab Melody and get moving. We'll meet you at the rendezvous point."

Grady nodded and disappeared below the surface. Crystal looked to her right and saw Tyler lowering himself into the water. He was there one second and gone the next. He never came back up to the surface. Crystal had to trust that he had started swimming as soon as he hit the water.

Crystal looked over the wall one last time. The cop cars had stopped, and several officers raced toward her with their guns drawn. She was certain they weren't set to stun. One of the cops fired. It hit the wall a few inches to her left where Ryan should have been, but he was gone.

"Crystal come on! What are you waiting for?" Ryan yelled below her. He had already dropped into the river and was treading water. "I can't do this without you."

Crystal let go of the wall and plunged into the river. Her Aquinian skin cells tried to kick in as soon as she hit the water, but it was so polluted that it was hard for her to draw out the oxygen. How was she going to be able to get enough for both her and Ryan? She pushed herself harder until she was getting enough oxygen from the water. She wouldn't be able to sustain this for long.

Bullets entered the water around her. They needed to get out of there. She searched for Ryan. She could barely see more than a foot in front of her. She jerked around when she felt something grab her ankle. Ryan pulled himself toward her. She wasn't sure how long he had been holding his breath, but the look on his face told her that he would have to surface for air soon, where he would be met with a hailstorm of bullets if she didn't help him. Crystal cupped her hand and focused her skin to push all the extra oxygen there. A small pocket of air began to form. Ryan lunged at it. He grabbed her cupped hand and held it to his face. She gave him a second to catch his breath before motioning to him that they needed to get going. She didn't want to be here when the cops sent divers in after them.

Almost no light penetrated the water, making it hard for Crystal to see where she was going. She knew they needed to swim east for at least a mile. She was usually pretty good at gauging distance underwater, but nothing about this river felt right to her. She could feel her skin cells becoming saturated much faster than normal. It was like there wasn't enough oxygen in the water to go around.

They made decent time considering she had to swim with her hand over Ryan's mouth. From what Crystal could tell, they were about halfway to their exit point when a current pulled Ryan away from her. She searched for him frantically. It was tempting to leave him, but it was her duty to protect people, and no matter what he had done to her, she couldn't let him drown. The current didn't feel too strong; he couldn't have gotten far.

She swam along with the current, assuming he would try to follow it back to her. She crashed headfirst into him a few seconds later. Their bodies tumbled through the water. As the current slammed Ryan against her again, she felt something hard in his pants pocket. She pulled him close to her, pressing her whole body against his. She wanted him to feel like she was trying to regain control as the current pushed them further off course. She attempted to reform the air bubble in one hand while holding onto his waist with the other. As Ryan sucked in the oxygen she let her hand slip into his pocket and removed the slime metal case. She tucked it into her pocket before he realized what she had done.

They regained their balance, and Crystal put her hand

over Ryan's mouth again. He pressed it to his face as he gasped to catch his breath. She waited until she felt his breathing return to normal before trying to push forward. They were behind, and it would be a huge risk to make the others wait for them to catch up. She hoped that Grady would go without her and get the others to safety, but she knew he would wait for her as long as possible.

Ryan didn't move. He clung to her hand, taking in as much air as he could. Forming the bubble was hard enough without him going through it so fast. She wouldn't be able to maintain it if he didn't slow down. She tapped him on the shoulder and motioned forward. Ryan shook his head. He took one last breath, pulled back his fist, and punched her in the face. The force was enough to send her into the current. They were separated again.

Crystal had no idea what was going on. It made no sense for Ryan to try kill her now. He had a much better shot of doing it once they were on land. She waited for the next attack, but nothing came. Was he just trying to get away from her? He had to know he couldn't get out of this without her. If he showed up to the rendezvous point without her, the rest of her team would never help him.

Maybe he wasn't planning on going back with them, and this was all a set up to separate her from the rest of her team so he could take them out. They wouldn't suspect an attack until it was too late. She still had the advantage. Ryan couldn't breathe underwater without her.

She pushed forward, swimming as fast as she could to the exit point. It was a lot easier now that she wasn't breathing for two.

Chapter 20

Desi was confident General Sloan was the only one to see them leave. They walked through the halls of the Pentagon at an unnatural pace. It took everything ounce of restraint she had not to break into a run, but they didn't want to draw attention to themselves. Everyone here knew they were connected to Wolf, Grady, and Price.

"It's too soon," Justin said once they were on the street.

"Something must have gone wrong." The billboards around them were changing. One by one, their advertisements disappeared, and were replaced with pictures of Wolf, Grady, Tyler, Young, and Melody, each including the words "extremely dangerous," with a number to call to report any information. Desi wanted to laugh at the idea of an eight-year-old girl being considered extremely dangerous, and she might have if the sign weren't also a death sentence. Any idiot with a gun would see these and think they were doing the right thing by taking a shot.

"We can't be out in the open." Desi slowly spun to take in the full effect of the signs. She'd never realized how many billboards there were. There was no angle free from a wanted poster for one of her friends.

"What will they do if we aren't at the rendezvous point when they get there?" Justin was already moving. She noticed that he kept his head down. She wasn't sure if he was trying to not be recognized or avoiding looking at Wolf's face shining from the screens all around them.

Desi shook her head as she fell into step next to him. "I don't know. I hope we don't have to find out." Every muscle in her body urged her to run, but she knew they couldn't. They had to stay calm.

"You think they got out ok?" Justin's gaze flicked up to a billboard displaying Wolf's face.

"They must have. Why else would the government be going through all this to try to find them?"

They came to a deserted alley between two rows of stores. After one look at each other, they took off running. Every second counted now. They were ten blocks from where they were supposed to meet the rest of their team.

They paused when they reached the end of the alley. The streets were beginning to fill with people again. Desi suspected most of them were out looking for her friends. And thanks to the mandatory military service laws, they all had experience. They were up against a nation of trained killers.

Desi turned to Justin. "Let's split up. Keep going no matter what happens." Justin nodded and took off into the street. Desi waited a few minutes before going after him. She glanced up at the billboards as she moved through the crowd. How long would it be until their faces joined their teammates up there? Even though Wolf had gone to great lengths to protect them, too many people knew they were connected.

It took her another half hour to get to the abandoned warehouse. Justin was the only one there when she walked in. He was bouncing on the balls of his feet as he looked around the space, though Desi wasn't entirely sure what he was looking for. If the others had already come and gone, they would have left behind some sign, but there was nothing Desi could see.

"Jax was supposed to have someone hide some supplies here for us," she reminded him. "Try to find it. I don't want to waste time looking for it once the others arrive." Desi couldn't let Justin know that she was worried too. She looked down at her watch as she searched. Wolf's team had gotten a head start; they should be here by now.

"It's over here." Justin removed two large duffle bags from a drum labeled hazardous waste. He handed one of the bags to her. It was filled with dry civilian clothes. He placed the second bag, filled with weapons, on a wooden crate and opened it. He pulled out his sidearm and put it in the holster on his hip before tossing Desi her gun. She felt better the moment it was in her hand. "Everyone else's weapons are still in here," he confirmed. "I doubt they would have gone ahead without them."

"Then where the hell are they?" Desi peeked through the dirty glass in the window closest to her. She could barely see anything, let alone try to spot the outline of their camouflaged friends.

"We got held up." Grady materialized in front of them with Tyler and Melody. He looked exhausted. Desi wasn't sure he would have the strength to get to the shuttle. They were kidding themselves if they didn't think they would need to fight to get there. Desi reached into the bag, pulled out a handful of protein bars, and passed them to Grady and Price. She noticed Melody clinging to Grady's leg. She knelt and offered the girl a protein bar as well. Melody looked to Tyler for approval before she took it from Desi.

"Where are Crystal and Young?" Justin asked. He looked out the door, straining his neck to in an attempt to see farther.

"We got separated as we entered the water." Price took a bite of his protein bar. "The cops caught up with us. They shouldn't be too far behind."

"I hope not. The longer we wait, the more danger we're in." Desi noticed Melody clutched Grady's leg tighter. "You guys should change into dry clothes so we'll be ready to go as soon as they get here." Desi nodded behind her to where the bag of clothing was waiting. Running through town in wet clothing would draw too much attention, even if they weren't being hunted.

Desi checked her watch. Five minutes had passed since Grady and the others had appeared. Wolf should be here by now. She could tell the rest of the group was getting anxious. Grady spent an excessive amount of time buttoning up his shirt, while Price took his time retrieving his sidearm from the duffle bag. They all knew they needed to get moving, but no one wanted to leave without Wolf.

She walked over to Price, who had taken up a post at the door. "How long can we afford to wait?"

Price looked at her. "At least a few more minutes."

Desi wasn't sure if that was his answer, or if he was asking her. She didn't want to be the one to say it, but there was the possibility that Wolf and Young wouldn't make it. Without Wolf here, Desi was the commanding officer, and she had a responsibility to get the others to safety. She knew that was what Wolf would want her to do.

"All right guys," Desi called to the group. "We give them three minutes, and then we move out, with or without them."

Crystal made it to the exit point without any further trouble. Now that Ryan was gone, she was able to move through the water faster than she had before. She had a lot of ground to make up. Unfortunately, any time she made up in the water was lost the second she reached the shore. She knew they must have reported the breakout by now, but she wasn't prepared to see their faces shining down from every billboard in the area. If the people on the street didn't know who she was before, they would now. To make matters worse, she was soaking wet when everyone else on the street was bone dry. Why couldn't there be a rainstorm? It wouldn't have been a problem if Ryan hadn't bailed on her. With his help, they would have easily made it down the street unseen.

She peeked over the wall along the shoreline. She couldn't have picked a worse spot to surface. People were everywhere. There was no way she could enter the street unseen. She considered going back in the water and coming out somewhere else, but she didn't have that kind of time. She knew her team would wait for her longer than was safe. Every second she wasted was putting them at risk. She needed a diversion.

She looked around until she found the perfect rock. It

had to be large enough to cause some damage, but not too big, or she wouldn't be able to control it. Once she found what she was looking for, she peeked over the wall again. There were a few cars heading down the street. She waited until they were in range, then threw the rock at the closet one.

She ducked back behind the wall the second the rock was out of her hand. She held her breath and listened. Screeching tires, broken glass, and crunching metal made music to her ears. She didn't hesitate. As everyone was focused on the crash, she jumped over the wall and ran in the other direction. Every instinct in her body screamed to go to the scene of the accident and make sure everyone was ok, but she resisted. She allowed herself a quick glance over her shoulder to see the drivers getting out of their cars right before she disappeared down a side street.

It was far from a direct route, but she couldn't risk being seen. The problem was that it was taking her way too long to get to where she needed to be. Part of her hoped her team would have moved on without her by now. She hated putting them all at risk. She hated that she had allowed herself to trust Ryan again.

She was a block away when she ran out of places to hide. The only way to get to the warehouse was to cross one more major street. She took a deep breath and slipped out into the crowd. She tried to keep her head down to avoid making eye contact with anyone. She was halfway across the street when someone with their eyes glued to the tablet in their hands walked into her.

"Watch where you're going, asshole," they said as they looked up at her. Crystal watched in horror as their eyes went from annoyance, to recognition, to fear. "It's you!" They pointed at her. "You're one of the terrorists that broke out of jail this morning." The people nearest to them had stopped and were watching her.

Crystal didn't respond. She took off running. The best thing she could do right now was put as much distance between herself and the person who had IDed her. Behind her people were yelling and screaming, but she didn't slow down. It would take the crowd at least a few minutes to realize what was going on and get organized enough to start going after her. She didn't plan on being there when that happened.

She knew it was a risk running to the warehouse where the others were waiting, but she didn't have a choice. She needed to get off the street. Besides, her weapon would be waiting there for her, and she had a feeling she would need it soon. She turned down the alley beside the warehouse and slipped in the door. "I'm here," she said before anyone had even noticed she had entered. "Everyone, get down and stay quiet."

They all obeyed without question. Crystal peeked out a nearby window to see a crowd running down the street, looking for her. Soon the cops would get here and start to search for them, but they were safe for the moment.

"What happened? Where's Young?" Grady murmured.

"I was spotted," she answered quietly. Crystal got up and went over to bag of dry clothes and started to change. "Young bailed." She tucked her hair up into an old baseball cap and pulled the brim low.

"How will he get back to Neophia?" Tyler asked.

"That's not our problem. He managed to get here on his own; I assume he can get back as well. At least I didn't come away empty handed." Crystal pulled the case she had taken from Ryan's pocket out of her discarded pants and handed it to Tyler. "Tell me it's what we thought it was."

Tyler opened the case carefully. "It looks like it, though there's no way for me to know what's actually on them." He closed the case and handed it back to Crystal.

"There's only one thing it could be." Crystal put the case in the pocket of her fresh pants.

"What is it?" Justin walked over and handed her a gun. He wrapped his arm around her and pulled her close for a moment. It was something she normally wouldn't have allowed on a mission, but this wasn't a typical mission. Besides, she needed the strength his touch gave her.

"We'll tell you later, Justin," Grady answered. "We should get moving." Grady was looking out one of the windows. "Now that they know where we are it won't be long before they start sweeping the buildings in this area."

Crystal nodded. She had wasted enough time. She walked over to Melody and gently grabbed her hands. "You're doing so well. I'm proud of you. I just need you to hang in there a little while longer, and we'll all be safe, ok?"

"Ok." Melody squeezed Crystal's hands.

"I want you to stay by my side. I promise I'll keep you safe." Crystal turned to the rest of her team. "Stick together. Don't pull out your weapon unless it's absolutely necessary. Remembered, no matter what it seems like, these people aren't our enemies. They're scared and misinformed. Guns set to level three." Everyone nodded. Crystal hoped they wouldn't have to use their weapons. At least if they did, they wouldn't kill anyone this way. They had told the U.S. military that they valued the lives of their enemies. Now it was their chance to put that belief into practice. "All right, let's get to that shuttle and go home."

Chapter 21

Flint and Justin exited the warehouse first. Crystal figured they would be the safest. She felt confident that the cops hadn't connected them to the breakout yet. Crystal could feel every beat of her heart as she waited for their all-clear signal. She nearly jumped out of her skin when it finally came.

She walked into the street with Melody at her side. The others filled in around them, keeping Melody in the middle so that she was protected from every angle. It helped to give the mission a sense of normalcy. All they were doing was protecting a civilian, something they had done countless times before.

They moved as one to the end of the building. Crystal expected the street to be full of people, like it had been when she exited the river, but it was eerily quiet. Had the police managed to close this block already? Did they even have the power to do that? It would be nearly impossible to completely shut down a city block in

Kincaron's capital city. The lack of people was a bad sign. She grabbed Melody's hand and started to run. The cops had to be close. Crystal wouldn't let them take Melody again. She didn't care what it cost her; she was getting that girl home.

They ran for two blocks without seeing another soul. Crystal was impressed by how Melody kept up, though she knew they couldn't sustain it much longer. Her energy reserves were low; Crystal could only imagine how bad it must be for Melody. She looked to her side at Grady. He was breathing harder than normal as they ran and had fallen a few steps behind her. She had pushed him too hard. She wasn't sure he would have enough energy to even make it to the shuttle if they kept up this pace.

Flint and Justin stopped suddenly. Crystal put out her hand to keep from knocking Justin to the ground as she skidded to a halt behind him. The street in front of them was filled with cops. They were lined up along the road. There was no way to get past them. Crystal frantically scanned the area. There had to be another way through. There was an office building to her left. The bottom level was nothing but glass windows. Crystal could see a deserted street on the other side.

"Stay where you are and put your hands up," one of the cops yelled through a bullhorn as the line slowly moved in their direction. They were dressed in riot gear and had their weapons pointed at them.

Crystal bent down and picked Melody up as she did a quick head count. They were greatly outnumbered. Even on their best day, it would be tough to get through before they were over run. One look at Grady and Tyler and she knew there was no way they would be able to fight their way through given the condition they were in.

"What do we do?" Tyler reached for his gun, but didn't pull it out.

She turned to Justin. "Were you able to get everything I asked for?"

Justin nodded and started to rummage through the bag slung over his shoulder and pulled out a canister. "Just tell me when."

"They need to be a little closer." Crystal watched the police advancing, trying to calculate the perfect moment to release the gas so that it would cause the most chaos.

"How much closer?" Flint looked from Crystal to the cops and back again. Crystal could see the concern on her face.

"We're heading left, through the glass." She nodded toward the building she had spotted earlier. "I need you to hold your breath for as long as you can," she whispered to Melody. She shifted the girl to her other side so that she could pull out her gun. She powered it to level four then yelled, "Now!"

Justin threw the canister of tear gas at the cops. Crystal took off running the second it was in the air. The gas should give them a few minutes of cover. She fired two shots at the window in front of her, shattering the glass. She jumped through it with Melody still in her arms. She slid on the tile floor of the building's lobby and threw her hand out to keep them from falling, cutting it on the shards of glass on the floor. She picked up her gun and kept running, ignoring the glass now imbedded in her palm.

Justin had already shot out the window on the other side of the lobby. The others jumped through, but Justin waited for her. Behind her, Crystal could hear the cops regrouping. "How much farther?" she asked as she passed Melody to Tyler, who had already climbed through the window.

"Four blocks," Flint said.

Crystal climbed through and took Melody back from Tyler. She nodded and pointed to a side street two buildings down. "That way." They all took off running. Again, the street was deserted, but Crystal could hear noise up ahead. They had reached the end of the area the police had closed off. She pulled her team behind a dumpster. They needed to regroup. She had never seen her team so beaten down before. She set Melody down and motioned for Flint to follow her to the end of the street.

They stayed in the shadows as they watched people and cars moving up and down the street. If they went that way, they would be seen within seconds. She looked to Flint. "Any suggestions?"

"We have no other option. We can't go back. The cops won't hesitate to kill us after that." Flint pointed between the buildings. "The shuttle's there. We can make it." Crystal could just make out the tip of the space shuttle on the launch pad. It was the lighthouse calling them home.

"It's risky." Crystal watched a family passing by pushing a stroller. How many more lives would she endanger while she tried to get her people to safety?

"It's a risk we're going to have to take." Flint tapped her on the shoulder and started to head back to the others.

Crystal was about to follow when noticed the billboards starting to change. "Flint, hang on a second."

Flint was back by her side. "What is it?"

Crystal pointed to the billboard. It now showed a profile shots of each of them, including Justin and Flint. On the bottom of the screen it read cash reward for information or capture. "This complicates things."

"More than you realize," Flint said, her lips thin. "Everyone on that street has been trained by the military to seek out and acquire dangerous, valuable targets. Now that's us."

"We need to go. The longer we're out in the open, the more danger we're in." Crystal went back to collect Melody. One last push and they would be safe.

Wolf had them enter the street together. There was no good way to approach the situation. There was safety in numbers, but they were also more likely to be recognized. The street was filled with civilians out on their lunch break. Desi prayed they were too distracted to pay them any attention. She glanced up at the billboard as they moved. What would her mom think when she saw it? Desi pushed the thought from her mind. She needed to focus. They needed to make it down one block and across the street. From there they would be able to take alleys and side streets the rest of the way to the launch pad. She checked her watch. They still had over an hour before the shuttle was scheduled to depart. That was the only good thing about having to enact their plan earlier than expected.

They were about to cross the busy intersection when a flash of metal caught Desi's eye. A gun. Its owner was moving toward them fast, and he wasn't the only one. Several people worked their way through the crowd, their eyes fixed. They were all civilians. This was exactly what Desi feared. She was at war with her own people.

The man wasn't bothering to keep his gun concealed any more. He had it pointed straight at them. Desi reached for her weapon but didn't pull it out. If she fired at her own people, she really would be a traitor. She didn't think she could come back from that. It didn't matter, though, because when she looked back up the man with the gun was gone. She turned to see Wolf had her gun out pointing in the direction of the man coming after them. That's when Desi noticed that he was lying on the pavement.

Screams filled the street. Anyone who hadn't recognized them before certainly did now. People rushed toward them. Wolf took off running, still carrying Melody on one hip with her gun in her other hand. Desi started after her, but noticed that Grady had fallen behind, the day's exertions finally catching up with him. She hung back; none of them could afford to be alone right now.

Desi pulled out her gun as she pushed her way through the crowd. She would do what it took to protect her team, even if that meant destroying her military career on Earth. She fired at the people moving in on them, but there were too many to keep up with.

Out of the corner of her eye, she saw Grady hit the ground. There were three men on him. Desi spun around and fired at one. It was enough to allow Grady to fight his way back to his feet. He quickly took out the other two. Having been on the receiving end of his right hook while sparring, she felt a twinge of sympathy for one of his opponents—but not enough to stop her from fighting her way to Grady's side.

Between the two of them, they were able to take down the nearest people. It gave them enough of a break to start running again. They had lost sight of the others, but Desi was sure Justin would get them to the shuttle. She had only taken four steps when she heard Grady scream behind her. He was on the ground again, this time with a knife sticking out of his calf.

Grady's attacker was on the ground with him. Desi watched as Grady pulled the knife out of his leg and stabbed his attacker in the stomach. She rushed toward Grady and helped him to his feet. She slung his arm around her shoulder and started to drag him down the street. "I got you," she yelled. He was having a hard time putting any weight on his injured leg, and she had to pull him up more than once. At this rate, they were never going to make it to the shuttle.

People were closing in again. "Here," Grady groaned. He pulled a can of tear gas out of his pocket and handed it to her. This was exactly what they needed. Desi pulled the pin with her teeth and threw it into the crowd behind them. They were out of the street before the gas dissipated.

Panic spread through the street the moment Crystal fired. She knew it would, but she didn't have any choice. She wouldn't let them get to Melody. She used the chaos to her advantage and took off running down the street. The best-case scenario would be to get her team off the street before the civilian army hunting them could regroup. Too bad the best-case scenario was something she hadn't experienced since she landed on Earth.

She ran through the crowd, the arm holding Melody growing heavy, but she wouldn't put the girl down. Tyler and Justin were on either side of her. They both had their guns out and were firing on anyone who appeared to be a threat. Crystal strained her neck to look behind her. She expected to see Grady and Flint bringing up the rear, but they were nowhere in sight. She stopped and spun around. Guilt surged through her. She knew

Grady couldn't be at 100% after everything it took to get them out of jail. She had asked more of him than anyone. She should have eased up on him. Now he had fallen behind. At least Flint was with him. She would keep the crowd from overrunning him. Crystal's priority had to be Melody.

She turned back to start running again, only to find two large men standing there. One of them ripped Melody from her arms, while the other punched her in the face. Crystal was sure he expected his punch to take her down, but she barely flinched. Her rage tapped into an energy reserve deep inside of her. She grabbed her attacker and kneed him in the groin. This was not the time to fight fair. He doubled over in pain. Crystal shot him for good measure, sending him all the way to the ground. She couldn't have him coming after her again.

She turned her attention to the man now holding Melody. The girl was trying to break free, but he had a firm hold on her. The man took one look at Crystal and started running. "I'm coming Melody," she yelled. She ran after them, not caring who she bulldozed along the way. The path ahead of her started to clear. Tyler and Justin had seen what was happening and were shooting anyone who got close to her.

Without obstacles, Crystal was able to gain on the man carrying Melody. The girl screamed and reached for her, but Crystal was still too far away. She wished she could shoot him, but it was too big a risk. Instead she pushed herself to run faster.

Crystal reached out her hand and finally was able to grab Melody's wrist. She pulled, hoping it would be enough to free Melody from the man's hold, but it wasn't. It was only enough to get the man to stop and turn around. He tried to punch Crystal, but his aim was terrible, and she dodged easily. The man stumbled as his punch missed. Crystal used the opportunity to sweep his legs out from under him. He finally released his hold on Melody as he tried to use his arms to break his fall. Crystal dove for the girl. All three of them hit the ground, but Crystal made sure she took the brunt of the impact.

Crystal quickly jumped to her feet, swinging Melody onto her back. "Hold on tight." Crystal would need both hands.

The man was back on his feet, but Crystal was ready for him. With Melody clinging to her back, Crystal punched him twice in the face and then kicked him in the chest. He dropped down to one knee, winded. Crystal pulled her gun and aimed it right between his eyes. It would only stun him, but he didn't know that. "Big mistake," she said and pulled the trigger.

Justin and Tyler had caught up with her. "It's not much farther now," Justin said as he looked down at the man at Crystal's feet.

Crystal nodded and adjusted Melody so that she was holding her on her left hip again. They began to run through the crowd. Crystal made eye contact with a few people as they ran. No one dared to attack them now.

Finally, after two more side streets, the launch pad came into the view. The only thing standing in their way now was a fifteen-foot electric fence. After what they'd just been through, getting past the fence should be a piece of cake.

"Over here." Justin led them away from the main entrance. She could only imagine how tight security had gotten since the detainment order was announced.

They made their way around the fence line to a row of dumpsters. She breathed a sigh of relief when she saw

Grady leaning against one of them — until she noticed Flint bandaging his leg. "What happened?"

"It's nothing. I'll be fine," Grady grunted.

"He got stabbed. He'll need stiches, but this should hold for now." Flint finished securing the bandage and stood up. "Are you guys ok?"

"Yeah, we're fine." Crystal squeezed Melody a little tighter.

Justin was on the ground searching through the bag he had been carrying since they left the warehouse. He pulled out a pair of wire cutters, walked over to the fence, and pulled out his communicator. "We're here."

"Is anyone hurt?" Jax's voice asked through the communicator.

"Nothing life threatening." He glanced back at Grady. "There's no way to tell if we were followed. We need to get inside fast."

Silence filled the line. The seconds passed by slowly. Had something gone wrong? Was it just a bad signal or had the authorities managed to stop Jax? Crystal's heart skipped a beat when Jax's voice came back on the line. "The power's off. You have ninety seconds."

Justin didn't hesitate. He used the wire cutters to quickly cut a large hole in the fence. Crystal had never been more attracted to him. Justin pulled back the fencing. "After you."

Crystal placed Melody through the fence first. She felt so much better the second the girl was on the other side. Normally, Crystal would have let the rest of her team go through to safety before her, but one look at Melody and she knew she couldn't leave the girl alone for even a second. She ducked through the opening and picked Melody back up. Crystal felt the girl's body sag against hers. Melody had held on as long as she could.

Crystal stood back as the rest of her team quickly passed through the fence before the electricity hummed back to life. "Where to now?" She looked over her team. They were all worn down with visible bruises on their arms and faces. Grady had his arm slung over Flint's shoulder to help keep his weight off his bad leg. This was not how they should look at the end of a diplomatic mission.

"This way." Justin took the lead.

It was nice to walk for a change. They rounded a couple of buildings and the launch pad came into view. The shuttle appeared to be close to take off. Steam billowed around the engine, exhaust and the smell of fuel hung in the air. Crystal saw Jax at the bottom of the stairs, heading into the shuttle with a women Crystal didn't recognize. The second the woman saw them, she ran to them.

"Melody! Is she all right? She's not hurt, is she?" The woman reached for the girl. Crystal took a step back. She didn't know this woman. How could they be sure she wouldn't try to hurt Melody? It was Crystal's job to get her home safely.

Justin put a hand on her shoulder and whispered in her ear, "Crys, that's her aunt. You did you job. You can let her go."

Crystal reluctantly handed Melody to her aunt. "She's fine, just tired. She was so brave today." Crystal stroked the girl's hair.

"I thought I lost her when I lost my sister. You'll never know how grateful I am that you saved her." Melody's aunt kissed the top of the girl's head.

"You should go get settled in the shuttle." Crystal smiled as she watched the pair go without another word.

The team made their way over to the ambassador.

"We're leaving you with quite the mess to clean up." Grady shook Jax's hand, wobbling slightly.

"I'll mange. I'm glad I could help." Jax's eyes were missing the joy that Crystal had come to expect there.

"Maybe this will make things a little easier." Crystal pulled the case she had taken from Ryan out of her pocket and handed it to Jax.

He opened it and looked back at her confused. "What is this?"

"Microchips that we think contain information on the location of the Neophian Integration Alliance."

"Make sure you sterilize them first. You don't want to know where they've been." Grady tried to laugh at his joke, but it came out as a painful groan.

Crystal rolled her eyes. "Get in the shuttle and get the weight off your leg." Justin took Grady and helped him up the stairs.

"Thank you. This will change everything." Jax stared at the case in his hand in amazement.

"I hope so," Crystal said.

"Um, I have your bags here. We packed everything we could find of yours at the embassy."

Tyler went over to his bag and pulled something out. "Here," he said handing the device to Jax. "This should let you access the information on the chip. It's programed to decrypt things automatically. I'm sorry we can't stay and help more."

"You've done more than enough. Now go. The shuttle will take off shortly. I need to get back and get the next group to the other shuttle." Jax turned and walked over to the car waiting to take him back to the embassy.

Crystal turned to Flint. There was still one lose end to take care of. "So what's it going to be Flint? It's now or never."

Flint was quiet for a moment as the shuttle's engines revved behind them. They must be going through their preflight checks. "What the hell?" Flint finally said. "Let's go home."

"That's the best decision you've made all day," Grady called from the top of the stairs.

They quickly climbed the stairs and made their way into the shuttle. It was packed. They spilt up to find seats among the refugees. They were going home.

Chapter 22

Desi fidgeted in the front row of the space shuttle. She was sandwiched between the wall and Price. As soon as they got on, Grady had been escorted to the back of the shuttle, where a doctor patched up his leg. The shuttle had barely been comfortable when they were the only ones on it; now that it was packed with people and their belongings, she knew it was hopeless.

"What's wrong?" Price shifted in his seat so he could see her face.

"I can't get comfortable." Desi kicked his shin for probably the tenth time in the last five minutes.

"It's more than that," Price said quietly. "I'm your friend Desi, talk to me."

"Maybe I'm having second thoughts." She meant to make up some excuse, but the words escaped on their own accord. Now that they were out, she knew she couldn't take them back.

"Second thoughts about what? Coming back to

Neophia with us?"

"Yeah." She was having a hard time coming to terms
with her decision to leave Earth, probably forever. It had
seemed like the logical choice at the time with her team
all around her, having just survived half the city hunting
them. But now that they were about to take off, she
wasn't sure. Earth was her home; that was where she
belonged. Even if she was sure they wouldn't welcome
her back. She didn't even have any of her things. She
was leaving Earth empty handed, without saying
goodbye to the one person who wanted her to stay.

"If you had stayed, you probably would have been
arrested by now. I can't imagine what the punishment is
for treason."

"It's the death penalty." A roaring filled the shuttle.
She turned to the window to get one last look at her
home as they launched. The buildings faded away until
there was nothing but darkness outside. She turned back
to Price. "It's my mom. She's expecting me to be there
when she gets home from work tonight. She's going to
make herself sick with worry."

Price reached down and pulled out his tablet. "We
haven't entered the portal yet. You can still send her a
message. Otherwise you'll have to wait till we land on
Neophia."

Desi took the tablet from him but didn't turn it on.
"It's not just that she'll worry. We had a fight last night,
and I walked out on her. That might be the last time I see
her. I shouldn't have left things like that. I should have
made a point to go talk to her this morning."

Tyler gently took the tablet from her, turned it on, and
handed it back. "Send the message. You'll beat yourself
up until you do."

Desi nodded. What could she say that would fix

things? She took a deep breath and started to type.

Mom, I've decided to return to Neophia. It really was the only option after everything I've done. I know you don't approve, but I hope you'll understand. I love you. ~Desi

It was short and simple, but Desi couldn't think of anything else to say. At least nothing she could put into words. What she really needed was to give her mom a hug. To feel her heart beating against her own. She had to have faith that she would get that chance one day.

Crystal was more relaxed during takeoff this time. She was just happy to be getting off Earth in one piece. Now that she had gotten everyone to safety and returned Melody to her family, she could allow herself to rest. She leaned her head on Justin's shoulder and breathed in his scent. She didn't know what she would do without him, and she was happy she wouldn't have to find out.

"You never told me how the hearing went this morning," Crystal said without picking her head up off his shoulder.

"We were a little busy," Justin said with a small laugh. "They agreed to continue the program and to put procedures in place to protect the LAWON soldiers serving on Earth."

"That's good, though I'm not sure why anyone would volunteer to go there." She didn't want to insult him, but she had to be honest. She knew she would tell anyone she knew who might be interested in the program to think long and hard before signing up.

"I don't know why either, honestly." Justin leaned over and kissed her forehead.

"Do you know what you're going to do with your

leave now that you'll be spending it on Neophia?"

"I have no idea."

"You can come stay with me if you want," she said as nonchalantly as she could.

Justin nudged his shoulder slightly so that she was forced to sit up and look at him. "Are you serious?"

"I am. I want to spend the six weeks, just the two of us. Try out this normal life thing you're always talking about." Crystal took his hands in her.

"I would love to, it's just—" He removed his hands from hers and looked away.

"Look if you don't want to that's fine. I don't want you to do anything that makes you uncomfortable." Crystal could feel her heart closing as she pasted a fake smile on her face. She wouldn't let him see how this rejection hurt her.

"It's not that."

"Then tell me," Crystal said. She gently grabbed his chin and turned his face back toward hers.

"I wasn't completely honest with you on Earth. That woman you saw me dancing with at the embassy, that was my ex-girlfriend Olivia."

"Oh," was all Crystal could think to say. "Was that the only time you saw her?"

"No." Justin looked down at his hands. "She was at the hearing too. She told me that she still has feelings for me and that she wants me back."

Crystal felt like all the air had been sucked from her lungs. Was Justin breaking up with her? "I need you to be completely honest with me Justin. I love you, but if you still love this woman and want to be with her, you need to tell me."

A sly smile crossed Justin's lip. Crystal had no idea what to make of it. "That's the first time you ever said you loved me."

Crystal's stomach twisted in knots. "I do love you, but I still need you to answer the question."

"I don't want to be with Olivia. Chances are I'll never see her again."

"All right then." Crystal shifted in her seat so that she was facing forward. She wished she could get away and sort through her feelings in private, but she was trapped.

"And Crystal?" Justin grabbed her hand. She turned to look at him. He was still wearing that grin that made her heart skip a beat. "I love you too."

Desi was the first one off the shuttle when they landed back on Neophia. She stood at the bottom of the stairs and helped the refugees as they descended. It was a much different feeling than the first time she had landed here. This time, it felt comforting seeing the lush vegetation and clear blue skies. Perhaps Neophia could be her home.

Once everyone was off the shuttle and the landing pad had cleared, Desi saw Captain Reed standing off to the side. She made her way over to him with the rest of her team. Somehow Grady had acquired crutches on the flight and could move without any help.

"Welcome home," Reed said. "I heard you had an eventful trip."

"That's one way to put it," Desi said under her breath.

"I'm especially glad to see you, Lieutenant Flint. Can I take this to mean that you have decided to join *Journey* for her second tour?"

"If you'll still have me, though I understand if you have already filled my position. I know I've missed the deadline."

"I had a feeling you might be coming back, so I set your position aside. It's yours." Reed held out his hand and Desi shook it with a huge grin.

"Thank you, sir." This meant more to her than being offered her own SEAL team back on Earth.

"Before I give you all your leave orders, I thought you'd like to see this." Reed handed the tablet he was holding to Desi. The others crowded around as she hit play on the video Reed had queued up. It was a news report from Earth.

"The members of the Neophian Integration Alliance have been captured thanks to information provided to the government by the LAWON Ambassador, Jax Donnelly. The information was recovered by two U.S. soldiers who were working alongside visiting military officers from LAWON."

"They had no problem calling us out by name when they were accusing us of being part of the NIA, but couldn't be bothered now," Grady grumbled.

"The terrorists were residents of New You City and, as far as authorities are able to tell, they have no connection to Neophia," the news report went on.

"I win. You owe me two months of quality checks," Wolf said "And don't think that's going to get you out of it." She pointed to Grady's crutches.

"Information obtained from computers at their base of operations suggests their motive was to try to turn Earth again Neophia in order to have the portal connecting the two planets shut down." The video ended and Desi handed the tablet back to Reed.

"I've also received word from ambassador Donnelly that all of your criminal records on Earth have been expunged. You are free to return to Earth without fear of prosecution if you desire."

"I think we've had enough of Earth for a lifetime," Gardy said

Desi, on the other hand, was glad to hear that there was the possibility of seeing her home again, though she wasn't sure she would ever be welcomed back. She had been called a traitor for speaking against the U.S. military; what would they accuse her of now that she had helped to break five Neophians out of jail?

"Now that's out of the way, here are your leave orders." Reed tapped his tablet. "I look forward to seeing you all in six weeks."

"Thank you, sir," they all said and started to disperse. Desi noticed Justin heading off with Wolf. She wasn't sure why she was surprised. Of course they would want to spend their leave together. That did mean that Desi now had no idea what she was going to do for the next six weeks. At the very least, she had thought she would have Justin to keep her company. For half a second she thought about going after them, but she couldn't intrude on them like that. Besides she wasn't sure she had the stomach to witness all their lovey-dovey nonsense for six weeks.

Instead she went after Reed. "Sir, I don't have anywhere to go."

"I have just the thing in mind for you Lieutenant," Reed said with a smile that made Desi nervous.

"You do?"

"I want you to come to the Academy with me and teach."

Reed had to be joking. She wasn't exactly the best role model. "You want me to teach the next class of LAWON military officers?"

"I do. I have an advanced combat class I would like you to take over."

Desi hesitated. "I'm not sure I'm cut out to be a teacher."

"I think you might surprise yourself. I heard you were the biggest advocate for increased understanding between humans and Neophians. What better way to do that than to expose our students to the ways of Earth? Come on, let's go get you settled in." Reed started to walk away. Desi quickly followed. She wasn't sure about this assignment, but it would certainly be a new challenge, and she was looking forward to a little break from people shooting at her.

Acknowledgements

As always, I need to start off by thanking my husband Mike. Without him, I would never be able to finish any of these books. His unwavering support gives me the confidence to keep writing and his amazing skills as a father gives me the time I need in order to actually sit down and get the words on the page. He is my knight in shining armor, best friends, and the best partner I could ask for in life.

I also need to thank my parents, especially my mom for again reading several drafts of the books and helping me pinpoint errors in the plot and with the writing. She will always be my first reader and I love her for that.

To my writing family, R. Dugan, S. W. Raine, M. K. Marteens, Joy E. Fetters, Chief, Atty, Jerusha Renee, and everyone else in my writing groups, I would be lost without you. Your love of these stories and characters is what keeps me going when I feel like giving up. You push me every day to be a better writer and I can never thank you enough for that.

To Maja Kipunovic, you swooped in and the saved the day when I was beyond stressed trying to figure out what to do with the cover for the book. Not only did you design absolutely stunning covers for the whole series, but I feel like a new friendship was formed at the same time. Your energy is infectious and I'm so happy we started working together.

A big thank you to my incredible editor Alana Joli Abbott for coming into this book with so much excitement and passion. Your feedback is invaluable and your comments throughout the draft always bring a smile to my face. This series would not be what it is today without your talent and support.

Thank you to all my early readers, especially Laura Bratby, R. Dugan, and Jerusha Renee for your encouragement and support. And finally a huge thank you to all of my readers for loving these characters and Neophia as much as I do.